PENGUIN BOOKS
BLOOD ATONEMENT

Dan Waddell is a journalist and author who lives in west London with his son. He writes about the media and popular culture, and has published ten non-fiction books, including the bestselling *Who Do You Think You Are?*, which tied in with the BBC TV series. His first novel, *The Blood Detective*, is also published by Penguin.

Blood Atonement

DAN WADDELL

PENGUIN BOOKS

PENGUIN BOOKS

Published by the Penguin Group
Penguin Books Ltd, 80 Strand, London WC2R ORL, England
Penguin Group (USA) Inc., 375 Hudson Street, New York, New York 10014, USA
Penguin Group (Canada), 90 Eglinton Avenue East, Suite 700, Toronto, Ontario, Canada M4P 2Y3
(a division of Pearson Penguin Canada Inc.)
Penguin Ireland, 25 St Stephen's Green, Dublin 2, Ireland (a division of Penguin Books Ltd)
Penguin Group (Australia), 250 Camberwell Road, Camberwell, Victoria 3124, Australia
(a division of Pearson Australia Group Pty Ltd)
Penguin Books India Pvt Ltd, 11 Community Centre, Panchsheel Park, New Delhi – 110 017, India
Penguin Group (NZ), 67 Apollo Drive, Rosedale, North Shore 0632, New Zealand
(a division of Pearson New Zealand Ltd)
Penguin Books (South Africa) (Pty) Ltd, 24 Sturdee Avenue, Rosebank,
Johannesburg 2196, South Africa

Penguin Books Ltd, Registered Offices: 80 Strand, London WC2R ORL, England

www.penguin.com

First published 2009

1

Set in Monotype Garamond
Typeset by Ellipsis Books Limited, Glasgow
Printed in England by Clays Ltd, St Ives plc

ISBN: 978-0-141-02566-7

www.greenpenguin.co.uk

Mixed Sources
Product group from well-managed
forests and other controlled sources
www.fsc.org Cert no. SA-COC-1592
© 1996 Forest Stewardship Council

Penguin Books is committed to a sustainable future
for our business, our readers and our planet.
The book in your hands is made from paper
certified by the Forest Stewardship Council.

This one's for 'Sunshine'.
Thanks for helping me through.

Acknowledgements

For answering what were a lot of stupid questions about police, genealogical and genetic genealogical procedure, my humble thanks go to Neville Blackwood, Nick Barratt, Megan Smolenyak Smolenyak and Jim Wilson. Donald R. Snow at the Hyde Park Family History Centre helped point me in the right direction in finding some information about early records of the LDS. Carole Reeves did likewise when it came to trying to find out more about the treatments and conditions in mental hospitals of the 1940s and 1950s. Any mistakes are entirely my own.

For reading and editing the manuscript in its early stages – and much, much more besides – I would like to thank my agent, Araminta Whitley, and Lucy Cowie. Thereafter, Stefanie Bierwerth, Daniela Rapp and Shân Morley Jones all made sure the finished entity was as good as it could possibly be. Thanks to you all.

The candle on the ledge guttered as it neared its end, shadows dancing on the wall. Beside her Sarah sensed the rhythmic rise and fall of her sisters' chests. Henrietta's and Emma's ability to fall asleep as soon as their heads lay on the pillow infuriated her, while she tossed and turned seeking sleep that took an age to arrive.

Not tonight, though. She lay rigid, pinned down beneath layers of blankets, not wanting to move and so drown out the muffled voices from the adjoining room.

Her future, her whole life was being discussed in there.

She could hear her mother, softly pleading, occasionally sobbing. Her father's sonorous voice in response, calm and unyielding.

'I do not mean to disobey you,' she heard her mother say. 'But he is in his sixty-seventh year. Does that not seem wrong to you?'

The low rumble of his words was more difficult to decipher. Sarah eased herself from under the weight of her covers and crept silently to the door, the breath from her nostrils frosting in the crisp night air. She shuddered. The September night was clear and cold but the undergarments beneath her nightclothes warded off the worst of the chill. She eased the door open and slipped into the dark hall. The words were more audible out there.

'Sarah is only fourteen!'

'You were only fourteen, Annaleah, when your father, or the man who acted as your father, pledged you to me.' Sarah sensed her father's impatience. Her boldness had reaped its harvest many times.

Her mother choked back a sob. 'May the Lord forgive me, I must protest –'

'Enough!' Silence.

Lord, no. Not Hesker? Sarah thought of his enormous stomach, bulging eyes, sagging, bewhiskered jowls and flabby wet lips, habitually moistened with a flicking pink tongue. There was a metallic taste in her mouth now, testament to her rising bile. She felt sick.

'The matter is agreed. I will hear of it no more.'

'But Orson . . .'

'Annaleah!' The voice was resolute, commanding.

She knew then that her mother's protest was at an end. A hot tear ran silently and slowly down her cheek. She retreated quickly back to her room before her father left for his. It had been a long time since he had favoured her mother's room as his place of rest.

At her bedside, she fell to her knees and buried her salt-wet face in her hands. The Lord was her only chance of reprieve.

'Our dear Heavenly Father, I thank thee for the blessings bestowed on my family and me. The food on the table, the bounty in the fields, the health of our livestock. The manner in which Joseph junior was spared when plague-ridden in the summer and it seemed all hope was vanquished. I thank thee for those and many other blessings. I beg here for thy mercy. If it be according to thy will that I be wed to Hesker Pettibone, then I beseech thee to think again. I apologize for my insolence, but I request with all reverence and humility that I not be married to that disgusting fat old hog – I seek thy forgiveness for that ungodly description. Should thou ignore my plea, so help me, Heavenly Father, I will not answer for the actions I henceforth take. Amen.'

As Sarah climbed back into bed, her ice-block feet seeking a *source of heat, she heard the soft whimpers of her mother in the room next door. Strangely it gave her strength.*

I would rather be cast into the fiery pit than live a life of quiet desperation and suffering, she thought.

I

Detective Chief Inspector Grant Foster emitted a weary sigh as he crouched over the woman's corpse, arc lights in the garden bathing them both in bright light, anticipating the first light of dawn. During his convalescence, human nature had not taken a turn for the better. He rose to standing, wincing slightly at the bolt of pain searing up his leg from the metal plate holding his right shin together, then shuddered as he felt a cold cough of wind on the back of his neck. He'd not worn a coat, assuming when he was called and told of a woman's murder at her house she would be found inside, and not outside on a small, slightly overgrown lawn.

The throat had been cut. The body was framed by a wide slick of blood. He looked around the garden. The fences at all three sides were high, giving a degree of privacy, though the upstairs windows of the properties on both sides would have had a partial view. Young professional couples lived either side and got home after dark. Neither of them had seen the body. Still, to Foster it seemed the killer had taken a strange risk.

He returned to the house. The sitting room was neat and ordered, no signs of a struggle. Foster rubbed his face with his right hand. It was his first week back, early November. He'd insisted on being on call. The call had come that Tuesday morning at 4 a.m., four hours after the body had been discovered. He climbed into his old suit, realizing only then that he could fit his thumbs into the gap between his gut and the waistband, forcing him to dig out a belt and pull it to the tightest notch. It had been just over six months since he'd been tortured and beaten and saved only seconds from death. The thought of getting back on the job had kept him going during some long dark nights of the soul. During some nights, when the dreams were at their worst, Karl Hogg's hot breath still in his nostrils, the excruciating pain as both tibia and fibula snapped under the weight of Hogg's mallet, he'd thought this moment might never arrive.

But here he was; his first case back.

He had anticipated a gang killing, probably some hapless kid stabbed in the street in Shepherd's Bush or Kensal Rise. Instead he'd got this – a woman lying dead in a garden, in a lavishly furnished Victorian terrace, on a quiet affluent street in Queen's Park, a middle-class ghetto between Kensal Green and Kilburn.

Detective Inspector Heather Jenkins walked into the sitting room with a scene of crime photographer at her shoulder. 'Mind if I . . .' he said, motioning towards the garden nervously.

'Fill your boots,' Foster said.

He turned to Heather. Her hair was scraped and tied back off her face and she looked pale and worn. Bad news, he thought.

'The victim's name is Katie Drake,' she said. 'Thirty-seven years old. An actress. The neighbours two doors down found her. They had a set of keys. They were alerted by a friend of Katie's after she and her daughter failed to turn up at an ice-skating rink to celebrate the daughter's fourteenth birthday.'

Foster felt a shudder of apprehension. 'And where's the daughter?'

'We don't know. She's missing.'

Everything and everyone was gathered. The Met's murder squad and all its resources out en masse. Dogs, helicopters, hundreds of officers preparing to knock on doors, ready to shake down every paedophile and pervert in West London and beyond. All waiting for the onset of daylight before they got started. A cursory check of Katie Drake's body estimated she had been dead since the previous afternoon, perhaps as early as 2 p.m. Her daughter, Naomi, was last seen leaving school at 3.15 p.m. Her schoolbag was downstairs. She'd made it home. But then what? The signs weren't good. Find them in the first six hours or you're looking for a dead body. That was the mantra when it came to a missing child. Unless . . .

They could not discount the idea she had done this. Killed her own mother and run.

Foster stood in the victim's sitting room, holding and staring at a school photograph of her daughter as if it would yield him a secret. He replaced it on the mantelpiece, her face etched on his mind. The long, straight blonde hair; the pale blue eyes; the hopeful, uncertain smile of a girl on the edge of womanhood. He wondered with a sense of dread about what state she would be in when they eventually found her.

He glanced around the room. It was immaculate, barely a spot of dust anywhere, books and magazines straightened into neat piles on the coffee table, cushions plumped and cornered neatly at each end of the sofa. Perhaps Katie Drake was one of those people who couldn't abide mess. He wandered through to the kitchen, situated at the back of the sitting room, off what was presumably once a dining room until it was knocked through.

Again, nothing out of place. Two glasses sat on the draining board. They had been washed. The kettle was unplugged and the coffee-maker pristine. Foster pressed the lid of the metal bin with his foot and it swung open. Nothing much to report in there. The fridge was well stocked. Looked like Katie and her daughter liked to eat healthily going by the amount of soups and salad materials.

Foster called a member of the forensic team over to remind them to examine the two glasses beside the sink. He checked the windows and doors all over the house. No sign of forced entry. The killer had been allowed in. The girl? He glanced one more time at the photograph on the mantelpiece. Slit her mother's throat? He doubted it. But he could be wrong.

Foster returned to the garden where Katie Drake's body still lay, housed in a tent. Edward Carlisle, the pathologist, was going about his duty with grim efficiency. The body might not be moved for a while, until the whole scene was processed.

Carlisle spotted Foster enter, the serious frown he adopted for his work lifting briefly.

'Good to see you again, Grant,' he said, his usually rich public school voice ravaged by the effects of a cold. 'On the mend?'

'Never better,' Foster replied breezily, not wanting to dwell on it. 'What have you found?'

He turned his face up. 'I'll need to have a closer look in a post mortem. The throat was slit out here, though.'

Heather slipped into the tent beside him. He could tell from her face she had more news.

'What?'

'We've found Naomi's father,' she said. 'Stephen Buckingham.'

'Let's pay him a visit.'

Stephen Buckingham looked like a man standing on the edge of a precipice from which he would soon be pitched. He sat in the blue-upholstered armchair in the living room of his house in Esher, eyes wide. Foster sat across from him, nursing a cup of tea provided by Buckingham's second wife, a shy, conservatively dressed woman, who padded around them softly, casting nervous, anxious glances at her husband. It was shortly after nine o'clock and the couple's two children had left for school.

Foster had broken the news about his ex-wife's death and his daughter's disappearance. He'd asked whether Buckingham had had any contact with either of them the day before.

'I was in Leeds on business,' he said softly, looking down at his fingers, which picked and played with each other. 'It was Naomi's birthday so I called her mobile at lunchtime. The call was very quick because she was out getting something to eat with friends and it was difficult to hear over the traffic, the sirens . . .'

Foster nodded, he knew the feeling. The sound of the city.

'She seemed pretty excited about going skating with her mum and her friends and then a meal. I said I'd see her Saturday . . .'

His voice tailed away. Foster didn't interrupt.

'We were going shopping in town. My treat. Her mother wasn't fond of it, thought I was spoiling her. But there was little I did with Naomi that her mother approved of.'

Foster asked when he had arrived back from Leeds.

'I flew back. My plane arrived at Heathrow just before ten o'clock at night. I was tired so I got a cab back here. It was shortly after eleven when I got here, isn't that right, Sheila?'

Sheila bit her lip and nodded. 'About that time, yes,' she agreed softly.

'Sorry, can you excuse me?' Heather said, standing by the door. 'I just need to make a call.' She slipped out.

'When did you and your first wife separate?' Foster asked.

'Eleven years ago, when Naomi was three. It just wasn't working. It was pretty volatile for a while afterwards, but while Katie was hot-headed, she also loved Naomi with everything she had, and knew she couldn't keep me away. We soon fell into a routine. My work takes me away, but I always make time to see her and spend time with her. I've remarried since, had two more kids, but it never affected my relationship with Naomi.'

Had Katie remarried?

Buckingham shook his head. 'No. There had been other men, that much I know from Naomi. But she wasn't a tittle-tattle and, to be honest, I wasn't really that interested. I don't think she was seeing anyone at the moment. In fact, from what I'd gleaned from Naomi, I sensed Katie had been having a hard time of it.

'In what way?'

'Not entirely sure. She was an actress. When I first met her, she was a real beauty. She got lots of work, some TV, adverts, mainly stage work, which was her real love. In recent years it had all gone a bit quiet. I think that got her down. Naomi made a few oblique references to her mother drinking. She never touched a drop when we first met, which was why it jarred with me a bit. She liked to smoke reefers back then.'

'What about Naomi? Did she have any boyfriends?'

Buckingham smiled for the first time. 'You've seen her picture. What do you reckon? From what she said, she seemed to be beating them off with a stick at school.'

The smile vanished. The vacant stare returned.

Had she mentioned anyone in particular?

Buckingham looked up at Foster, as if noticing him for the first time. 'Sorry,' he muttered. 'Miles away.'

'Did Naomi mention any boy in particular, one that might have been pursuing her perhaps?'

'No. She did mention one boy she fancied who was a bit older. He was in a band. The name escapes me. The reason I remember is that he was quite a bit older, seventeen or something, and I thought that was a bit too old and said so. She said she was at the back of the queue anyway.'

There was another silence as Buckingham scratched at his wrist and Foster wondered whether, if his own life had

11

taken a different turn, or his personality had, he might have been playing an active part in a fourteen-year-old's life. And, not for the first time, given the pain and suffering this man was experiencing, whether it was all worth it. Was living your life with only one person to worry about the easiest option?

'What do you think has happened to her, detective?' Buckingham's weary voice betrayed his hopeful expression.

Foster shrugged. 'I hope we find out soon,' he said. 'Rest assured we're putting every resource we can muster into finding Naomi.'

He paused before his next question.

'Are you a wealthy man, Mr Buckingham?'

The man's eyes narrowed. Then he realized what Foster was alluding to. 'I'm comfortably off, no more. I publish three magazines, none of them that successful. You think I'll get a ransom demand?'

Foster could see a glint of hope in his manner and expression. That would at least mean Naomi was still alive. He also knew Buckingham was downplaying his wealth. This house, Foster estimated, was worth at least a million. A black Mercedes convertible was parked on the drive. He had spoken about the money he liked to spend on his daughter. They could not rule out a financial motive.

'Keep your phone switched on,' he said. He cleared his throat. 'If we don't find Naomi, you might want to consider making a public appeal.'

'Whatever it takes.'

Heather slipped back into the room, smiled apologetically at Buckingham. She caught Foster's eye and nodded.

She'd made a few calls. Buckingham's story stood up. He'd been on that plane.

'Did you know much about your ex-wife's daily life, her routine?'

Buckingham shook his head. 'Next to nothing. She was quite often at home during the day, I know that. We really had very minimal contact outside the odd conversation about Naomi.'

'Did she have friends?'

'I'm sure she did. Her best friend was always Sally Darlinghurst, another actress. They met in repertory shortly before she met me. They were inseparable back then. I think they were still in touch, but don't quote me on it.'

Foster scribbled the name down. 'One last question, Mr Buckingham. What was the relationship like between your daughter and Katie?'

He gave it some thought. 'OK. I think they were very close. Too close, perhaps.'

'What do you mean?'

'Well, her mother was very possessive of her. I got the feeling that as she moved away – grew up, met boys – her mother would feel left out. Naomi was Katie's entire world in many respects. I actually feared for Katie when the time came to cut the apron strings. Naomi was already feeling a bit smothered by her, so she said.'

'Did they fight?'

'I think so. You know how it can be, mothers and daughters.' His face dropped. 'You don't think . . .'

Foster shrugged. 'We need to look at all eventualities. You mentioned to me that your ex-wife was a good-looking woman. Given the fact she'd been in the public eye, did she ever receive the attentions of any unwanted admirers?'

'What? Like a stalker?'

'Yes, like a stalker.'

He shook his head slowly. 'Not that I'm aware of. She did get a few letters when I knew her, blokes who'd seen her in a play or on television. She once did a nude scene in a TV play that attracted a slew of cards and letters, some rather ribald in nature. The odd photo, too. I wasn't particularly enamoured with all that but she brushed it off, made me feel a bit of a prude. But no one physically followed her or pursued her – not that I knew of, anyway.'

Foster nodded. They were already in touch with her agent. She might know more.

'How about family? Before we take steps like making a television appeal and using the media, we need to track down her next of kin. Make sure they're all aware of her death. Can you tell us where to start?'

Buckingham rubbed his chin ruefully. 'I'm afraid I can't.'

'Why not?'

'I knew Katie for more than five years, intimately. She never once mentioned any family, and never spoke about it.'

'Never?'

'Never. I asked. I probed. But she closed down any discussion about it. She acted like she had no family. She went to school, came to London and went to drama school, and supported herself by waitressing in her spare time, which is how I met her. That's all she ever told me.'

He must have noted Foster's incredulity; he sniffed derisively, as if sharing the detective's disbelief. 'I know – madness, isn't it? But I just grew to accept that it was a closed book. I did find out that Drake was a stage name. You'll understand why she changed it when I tell you that her real surname was Pratt.'

'But surely Naomi must have asked, wanted to know who her grandparents were?'

'She did. But her mother always changed the subject. She told me that one day she would do a bit of research into the family history, find out more, but she wouldn't do that behind her mother's back.'

Foster found himself looking at Jenkins.

Her eyes told him she was thinking the same.

2

Nigel Barnes stopped walking and brought his hands out from behind his back, holding the skull. He did it too quickly. The skull wobbled in his right hand, which was itself shaking, and almost fell to the floor. He looked at it, silently counted to three, then composed himself and looked forward.

'He has remained silent too long,' he said. *One – two – three.* 'Now it's time to hear his story.'

The cameraman brought his equipment down from his shoulder. 'Good,' he said impatiently. 'Only problem with that one was I clearly saw you mouthing "one – two – three" before you delivered the last line.'

'And I nearly dropped the skull.'

'And you nearly dropped the skull. Also, when you were walking to camera, I could see your eyes glancing down at the mark.'

Nigel cast his eyes to the floor. Three feet in front of him was an 'X', scratched into the cemetery path by the cameraman's trainer. He'd been looking at the shape for most of the twenty paces rather than at the camera, yet had still ended up missing it. He sighed.

'You also look very ill at ease.'

Because I am, thought Nigel. What sort of person could walk and talk to a camera with a fake plastic skull in his hand and feel comfortable? Probably someone who had spent their life practising for such a moment in front of a mirror. The only thing Nigel had done in a mirror when he was younger was squeeze spots.

'Mind if I have a ciggie before we go again?'

The cameraman nodded. 'I need to make a call or two anyway.' He looked ruefully around at the graves on either side of them. 'Think I'll go and make them on the street,' he added. 'Seems a bit disrespectful to do it here.' He put the camera down at Nigel's feet and loped off, giving his sagging jeans an upward tug as he left.

Disrespectful, Nigel thought, sitting back on an anonymous gravestone. Unlike smoking a cigarette. He produced his fixings from his pocket and rolled a smoke. He lit it, exhaled loudly and studied the clichéd, stilted script they had given him to memorize.

The call had come in a week ago. In the summer, encouraged by Scotland Yard's press office, he'd given an interview to a Sunday newspaper about his role in the Karl Hogg case. 'The Gene Genius' it had proclaimed. 'The Family Historian who helped make a savage killer history.' Nigel had groaned when he read it, embarrassed by the way his role had been exaggerated, worried by what the officers who worked on the case would think of it. Would think of *him*. Then the phone started ringing. Radio, television, the odd magazine; he was too polite to say no. Not when he learned he could make some money from it. He downplayed his role, praised the police. 'Every bit the modest hero, aren't we?' a DJ from Radio Shropshire had told him, winking as if he knew what Nigel was doing. Come to think of it, what was he doing?

One of the calls had come from a TV company. They

were making a pilot for a series investigating burial sites unearthed during building development. The idea was to take the remains and find out who they belonged to, how the people died, dig out their stories. Lysette, the producer, called and said she'd seen the piece and that Nigel seemed ideal. They had met in a coffee shop off Oxford Street and over lattes she ran through the idea and asked if he'd be interested in taking a screen test. Why not? he thought. A chance to get away from rooting around in other people's pasts. Or, at least, doing it for more money and getting recognized in the street. He felt flattered. Particularly when she said they were looking for a photogenic young historian with what she called 'phwoar factor'.

So here he was, in the middle of Kensal Green cemetery on a drab morning in November, performing the televisual equivalent of patting his head and rubbing his stomach, and proving terrible at it. Guy the cameraman, now stepping back through the cemetery, hands plunged deep into a green combat jacket, had been very patient, but Nigel knew that all four attempts had been amateurish at best.

Guy hoisted the camera back on to his shoulder. 'Let's go again,' he said.

Nigel flicked his fag on to the grass and twisted his heel on it, shivering against the cold. He should have worn more than his tweed jacket, but felt it was the 'look' they wanted. He made his way back to the grave of Alfred Rossiter, 1829–1892, which marked the start of his walk. He flexed his shoulders, drew in a breath and turned around. *One – two – three.*

'The dead are always with us,' he said, and started to walk. 'Sometimes closer than . . .'

'Cut!' shouted Guy.

'What now?' Nigel asked, perplexed.

'You've forgotten the skull.'

Shortly before lunch, Nigel was back in the more familiar surroundings of The National Archives. The Family Records Centre, previous home for birth, marriage and death indexes, was no more: he would not miss it. The indexes were now housed at TNA, which at least put an end to his daily pinball ride between leafy Kew and the urban grime of Islington.

A pile of undone work was growing – a stack of birth, marriage and death certificates to track down and scour for his private clients.

He was skimming the April quarter of birth certificates for 1894 when he heard her voice call his name. He spun round and there she was. Heather Jenkins.

'Hi, Nigel,' she said, her smile wary.

'Detective Sergeant Jenkins,' he replied, a lurch in his stomach.

'Detective Inspector now,' she said.

'Congratulations.'

'Thanks,' she said, smiling. 'How are things?'

'OK. And you?'

'Tired. I've been up all night. Murder and abduction in Queen's Park. Mother killed, fourteen-year-old daughter missing.'

'God,' Nigel said. 'How awful.'

'Any chance we can get a coffee, somewhere private?'

Nigel checked his watch. Midday had just passed. 'I'm very busy, but there might be a corner of the canteen we can find.'

They walked down there in silence. Nigel didn't know what to think. Four months ago she'd broken his heart. They'd had a few dates, when her work allowed, and it seemed to be going well. Then she disappeared. Not a word. Stopped returning phone calls or e-mails. He'd even sent a text message, a first for him. Then he wrote a letter wondering what was going on. Either something had happened or he was simply terrible in bed.

She finally sent him an e-mail. Something had happened. Her mother had died, a sudden heart seizure; she needed time and space etcetera. He understood. Gave her some room.

A few weeks later he heard she was seeing an ex-boyfriend. Confused didn't even begin to describe how he felt. It was only in the past few weeks he'd managed to stop himself thinking about it. Now here she was to remind him all over again. She seemed to sense his unease.

'You must be wondering what the hell I'm here for?' Heather said, sitting down, a fake laugh in her voice.

'Well, I am actually,' he said.

'Foster and I . . .'

'Foster? How is he?' he interrupted.

'Back at work this week. He seems the same as usual; or rather, he's acting the same as usual. Anyway, we're trying to find out as much as we can about the murder victim, hope it sheds some light on her murder and where her daughter might be. We also need to track down family and next of kin so they all know before we get word out to the press. But there's a problem.'

'What?'

'She was very secretive about her past. Even her ex claims to know nothing. We were wondering if you could wave your magic wand and find out a bit more about her, parents, siblings, that sort of thing. Of course we'll pay.'

'I'm on it,' Nigel said, eager to help. Heather gave him Katie Drake's details, her real surname, Pratt, which he scratched into his notebook. 'Shall I phone it through? Are you still, er, on the same number?'

'I was hoping I could stick with you as you do it, and then I'll phone it through. There's a girl missing – it's extremely urgent.' She pulled a face. 'You don't want me around, do you?'

He wasn't sure. 'I don't mind,' he lied.

She leaned forward and put her hand on his arm. 'Nigel, one day I'll explain to you what happened. I just can't do it now. Not at a time like this.'

Nigel sipped his tea. He didn't know what to think.

But one thing he did know. A woman had been killed and a young girl was missing. He would help if he could. This was no time to act wounded. 'We'd better get cracking then,' he said.

It took Nigel an hour scouring the indexes of births, marriages and deaths to discover that Katie Drake née Pratt was born Catherine Mary, the only child of Robert and Vera Pratt of Shoeburyness in Kent. When she was four, her father died of pneumonia. A year later her mother followed him to the grave, claimed by a heart condition.

Heather's face creased. 'Poor thing. Maybe the mother died of a broken heart.'

'Perhaps,' Nigel said. 'Presumably she was adopted.'

'Can we find out who adopted her?'

'As long as you know the adoptive name you can find the child in the adoption index. But unfortunately we don't know it. Let's check anyway, and see if there's anything we can find.

He flicked through to the year of Katie Drake's birth.

'You're adopted, aren't you?' Heather asked.

He nodded.

'Is Barnes your birth or adoptive name?'

'Adoptive. My birth name is Wilkinson.'

'Why haven't you reverted to that?'

He shrugged. 'I've always been known by my adoptive name. There never seemed any particular reason to change it back.' Nigel felt the first signs of discomfort prickle his neck. The day he found out exactly who his parents were and the reason they abandoned him would be the day he took their name. He wasn't even sure Wilkinson was his real name.

There was no mention of Catherine Pratt or Drake in the adoption index.

'What happened to her then?'

Nigel shrugged. 'She could have been adopted by a relative without any need for paperwork, an aunt or grandparent. If you want, I can trace the other members of the family. Aunts, uncles . . .'

Heather thought for a few seconds. 'We need to know if there's any close family we should inform about her death before it becomes public knowledge. I think it's fair to say that if she didn't speak about her upbringing, then there was nobody close to her so it doesn't really matter. I see no real point for now. Thanks for your help.'

Nigel felt the need to say something. 'I hope you find the missing girl,' was the best he could manage, as Heather shouldered her bag and turned to leave. She smiled back.

'So do I,' she said, but Nigel could sense resignation in her tone. 'Send your invoice . . .'

He held up his hand. 'That was nothing,' he said. 'It's on the house.'

'You sure?'

He nodded

'OK. Very kind of you. I'd better get off,' she said, gesturing with her hand towards the door. 'Thanks again.'

'Good luck with the case. And everything else,' he said.

She smiled, fondly he thought. Then she adjusted her bag on her shoulder, and turned away.

Yet again Nigel watched her walk away from him.

3

The net had been cast across London. Foster stood at the window of Naomi Buckingham's bedroom, a converted attic, and looked out over the roofs and chimneys and trees that stretched westwards against a pale clouded sky, wondering where in the grey benighted city she might be. Were they still looking for a living person? He checked his watch. Almost twenty-four hours since she left school, the last time she had been seen. If she had been abducted, all his experience told him she would be dead within days. But while her body remained undiscovered there was hope.

He turned back to face the room, watched by the blue eyes of an effeminate young English film star whose name he couldn't recall. Apart from a few books, pictures and a red plastic cup filled with pens, the desk where Naomi's gleaming new personal computer once stood was now bare, the machine removed for its contents to be searched and checked. Everything else remained in place. Her unmade bed, a few items of clothing that spilled from a giant cupboard on to the floor, a stereo and a rack of CDs, and a dressing table whose top was scattered with make-up and toiletries.

Foster stopped at a small chest of drawers. The top drawer was filled with underwear. He closed it quickly. Clothes were crammed hugger-mugger in the second and third drawers. He was about to close the third when his eyes caught sight of the corner of a thick black exercise book beneath a T-shirt. He pulled it out carefully with the thumb and forefinger of his gloved hand – the scene was still being processed – and immediately felt his heart beat a little faster. He opened the front page. It was her diary for the second half of that year, from late July onwards, all written in legible clear-blue pen. He pulled the chair out from beneath her desk and sat down.

The late summer entries were filled with the usual mundanities and worries of a teenage girl's mind. Feuds with friends, thoughts about boys, fears about her appearance; there was little to suggest that Naomi Buckingham's preoccupations were any different from other girls of her age. Various phrases, acronyms and abbreviations puzzled him but he was able to keep up with the main gist. He skipped a month or so and started reading the entries for the weeks preceding the murder of her mother and her own disappearance. One extract, exactly two weeks before the murder, caught his eye.

Mum continues to be t. pissed every time I come back. Gets embarrassing. Espec when got back from night out with T and L and they saw her. OMG, she was so gone could hardly speak, slurring + everything. This morning no mention before I went school but she looked like shit. When I got back she said she was going to order pizza and making lotsa fuss, like she knew she totally o.o.order. Still didn't stop her putting away best part of a bottle afterwards, though . . .

Two days later and her mother was the subject of another entry.

> Really worried by Mum. She seems so unhappy.
> Last night I swore I heard crying after she'd
> gone to bed. Was going to go in and ask what
> wrong. Didn't. This morning I asked if
> everything was OK and she gave me a big smile
> and 'Yeah. Why shouldn't it be?' But it must
> have registered cos when I got back from L's,
> and a couple of glasses of red had loosened her
> up, she said 'Don't worry about me, love.' Then
> said she was fine really but that life was a bit
> tough, no work, feeling a bit sorry for herself
> but she'd come out of it. We put a date in for
> lunch on Saturday at Tate Modern which'll be
> nice because she never seems to get out. Used
> to have lots of friends, but she never sees them
> now. I worry about her even though she says
> not to because sometimes she looks v. sad.

A week on, four days before the murder, and there seemed to have been an improvement.

> Mum defo seems better, glad to say. Not seen
> her drink all week. Not even seen any booze in
> house, which is a first. And how about this? I
> offered to make her coffee and she says 'No, I'm
> off it.' Wanted peppermint tea instead!! OMG!
> This from Mrs Caffeine. Has someone beamed down
> replacement Mum from planet Zog? Seems

brighter and smilier though a bit distant. Can't have met a man cos she not been out in years. Maybe the chance of some work? I hope so. Prefer this clean-living, body-is-a-temple Mum to pissed-slurring-can't-get-out-of-bed version.

The last entry, the night before her disappearance, looked forward to her birthday – Foster could not prevent himself smiling at the words '*OMG! 14! Feel so old!*' – and the skating trip to celebrate it. Nothing else.

He closed the diary, rendered doleful by reading the words of a vivacious teenage girl, her whole life before her, who now probably lay dead in a ditch, the mother she appeared to care for so much murdered.

'Life sucks,' he muttered to himself.

'Tell me something I don't know.'

He looked up. Heather. She'd sneaked in unnoticed. She was staring at the exercise book.

'The missing girl's diary,' he explained.

'Anything of interest?'

He shrugged. 'Don't know. Seems like Katie Drake was a bit of a lush, but at some time in the last few weeks of her life had a Damascene conversion and went teetotal.'

'Think it's relevant?'

'Could be, I suppose. In her diary, Naomi speculates it might be work-related. Have we spoken to her agent?'

'Andy Drinkwater's done it, yeah. Said apart from one voice-over she hasn't had any work for the best part of a year, and none pending.'

'So much for that theory.'

'A bloke?'

'Naomi's diary appears to rule that out, too. Said she hadn't been out in years. I'm assuming she's employing teenage hyperbole.'

It was Heather's turn to shrug. 'It could be that she simply decided to clean up her act.'

'You may be right. Have they tracked down the next of kin?'

'She was adopted. Unofficially, probably by family or friends, Barnes thinks.'

Barnes? he thought. She'd always referred to him as Nigel. He'd been aware that the pair of them had something going on, not that he cared. There had been enough things for him to worry about – like walking without agony – without worrying whether the two of them were going to swap body fluids. They clearly hadn't. Or not for long, at least. Foster had heard she'd shacked up with an old flame, a copper from Murder South. Might explain why she seemed a bit different since he'd returned to work. More passive, less feisty.

'How was he?' he asked

'OK.' A smile played on her lips. 'He's doing the pilot for some TV show. About digging up the dead.'

'Who's interested in watching that?' he sneered.

'You really don't watch TV much these days, do you, sir?' Heather said.

He shrugged and turned back to the window. The street below was closed, silent and empty. They had knocked on almost every door within a mile radius. So far, they had one lead, a white van seen entering the street around four o'clock the previous afternoon by two independent witnesses, who both watched it pull up somewhere near the Drake house. Neither had seen it go and so far they had no other witnesses who saw it leave. A team was spooling through hours of CCTV coverage to see if there was any sight of it. But the clock was ticking and each second that passed reduced the chance of Naomi Buckingham being found alive.

The smell in the morgue had not changed, Foster thought, as he and Heather made their way to the post mortem suite that evening. The stench of death always won through the masking scent of deodorizer and disinfectant. He'd not missed this place: the tiled floor that echoed every footstep; the sterile, gleaming stainless-steel equipment; the unnerving quiet; and the cold that eventually seeped into your soul. But it was here he hoped the hunt for Katie Drake's killer and her daughter's abductor might begin in earnest.

Inside, a technician was preparing to stitch Katie Drake's corpse back together. Edward Carlisle signalled for him to hold on as he took the two detectives through what he'd discovered.

'The cause of death was asphyxiation,' the pathologist told them.

'She was strangled first?' Foster replied, unable to hide his surprise.

Carlisle nodded gravely. 'Without doubt,' he said. He gestured towards the woman's neck. 'In situ, the wound and blood from it hid a light ligature mark on her neck, but you can clearly see it above the cut.'

Foster leaned in and noticed a faint red weal above the gaping wound across the neck.

'The hyoid bone is broken and there is severe damage to the thyroid and cricoid cartilage. The assailant was very strong, almost certainly a man.'

At the very least that ruled out any notion that Naomi Buckingham had been physically responsible for her mother's murder, Foster thought.

'The ligature wound, as I mentioned earlier, is not too severe, so I would guess it was made of soft material, perhaps a towel or scarf.'

Foster guessed the killer might have removed the evidence, but made a note to tell forensics to examine every item of clothing and material in the house.

'What about the wound to the throat?' he asked.

'Committed post mortem,' Carlisle responded. 'The carotid artery and jugular vein remain intact so the cut is not actually all that deep. More of a token gesture. Your killer is right-handed by the way. There are also signs of bruising and lividity on the back. I'm not yet one hundred per cent certain, but it seems likely she was killed inside the house, then dragged outside where her throat was slit.'

That made no sense to Foster. Most killers took care to hide a body. This one had done the opposite, bundling the body from the privacy of a house out into a garden where it might be seen.

'There was no blood in the house,' Foster said. 'But there was plenty in the garden.'

Carlisle nodded slowly. 'The lividity on the back is congruent with being dragged outside, which is why I made an educated guess that he killed her inside, then hauled her into the garden where he made the wound on her throat.'

This really isn't adding up, Foster thought. 'Any sign of sexual activity?' he asked.

Katie Drake had let her murderer into her house. Had she allowed him into the bedroom or had he followed? Was she surprised by his attack or quiescent? They could not rule out some sort of sex game, even though she was fully clothed.

Carlisle shook his head. 'None whatsoever.'

A few scenarios ran through his mind. Had Naomi Buckingham arrived home and interrupted the killer? Is that why she had been abducted? But he had the tools at his disposal to kill her there and then. Why risk being seen taking her away?

'Any idea of the time of death?'

'Difficult to be absolutely precise, but I'd say with some certainty that it was around mid-afternoon yesterday.'

Naomi could have disturbed the killer. Yet there had been no sign of a struggle anywhere in the house. Which indicated that Naomi might also have known her abductor and gone with him willingly, unaware that her mother lay outside murdered.

'I've sent samples of blood to toxicology,' Carlisle continued. 'The liver was quite fatty, in the first, very early stages of liver disease, which indicates the victim was a heavy drinker. Other than that she was in reasonably good physical condition. She hadn't eaten for a few hours, not since breakfast.'

'Any idea when the nail varnish was applied to her fingers and toes?' Heather interjected.

Carlisle shrugged.

Heather wandered over and took a look. 'I'd say very

recently. And with some care, too. She was wearing quite a lot of make-up when we found her. Mascara, foundation, lippy, the works . . . What have you done with her clothing?' she asked Carlisle, urgency in her voice.

'They're about to go forensics. They're in a bag somewhere . . .' He turned to one of his technicians for confirmation. A few moments later the bag was produced. Heather put on a pair of gloves and took it to an empty dissecting table, where she poured out the contents, Foster at her shoulder. She ignored the blood-soaked shirt and skirt, and went straight for a black, diamanté-studded bra, which she picked up between thumb and forefinger.

'*Ta da!*' she said, turning to show it to Foster, making him flinch. 'Push-up bra. Not the sort of thing you wear around the house on a Monday afternoon. As I thought: she was on a promise.'

Naomi Buckingham was wrong. Her mother did have a man.

They managed to track Sally Darlinghurst, Katie's best friend, down to a small terraced house in Kentish Town. Darlinghurst had been out all day, but returned at some point during the evening. She'd already been told the news of Katie Drake's death and her proud, handsome face, which looked familiar to Foster, presumably from one of her TV appearances, was still blanched by shock. She let Heather and Foster into her sitting room, adorned with ethnic artefacts, grotesque carved masks, a few wooden statues and colourful batiks hanging from the wall. The air smelled of incense and smoke. Once inside and seated on the sofa she lit the first of a chain of cigarettes.

Foster made their apologies and offered the usual condolences. Darlinghurst drew deeply on her cigarette, pushing away a blonde curl of hair that constantly fell over her right eye.

'Awful,' she said in a crisp, well-enunciated voice. 'Just fucking awful. Any news about Naomi?'

Foster shook his head sadly. Heather explained the reason for the visit – to build up as detailed a picture as they could of Katie Drake's life, in the hope it might lead them to her killer.

'What do you want to know?'

'What sort of person was she?' Foster asked.

'Wow,' she said. 'What a place to start. What sort of person was she?' Katie's friend looked away for a short period of time, lost in thought. 'She was honest. She was loyal. She was a fabulous mother, a good friend and a fucking good actress.'

'How long had you known her?' Foster asked.

'Sixteen years. She was twenty-one and I was a year older. We were in rep, doing a version of *Salad Days*. Bloody awful play. But we had a scream doing it. We came back to London and stayed friends. Through marriages, divorces, childbirth, for her at least, and all manner of job crises. She was always there for me, as I was for her.'

Foster nodded. 'How had she been recently?'

She tapped another cigarette from the pack and lit it. 'How had she been?' she said, repeating his question once more and glancing away. After another drag she answered. 'I haven't seen her for two months, though we spoke on the phone a couple of weeks ago. She was . . . OK. I mean, work was causing her a bit of angst, or rather the total bloody lack of it. I'd just landed a little part in a TV drama. Load of bloody shit it is, too, but it's work. Usually we took great pleasure in each other keeping the bastards at bay and finding work, but I did sense she was a bit deflated. I think it must have been a year since she did anything and I'd not been doing too badly in comparison . . .'

'What do you mean by "keeping the bastards at bay"?' Heather said, the beginnings of a smile on her face.

'Oh, that? Well, when you're an actress approaching forty the work tends to thin out, either that or the roles you get are pretty shitty ones. The men, of course, just keep getting more work. But that's the way it is. You can either plug away and keep the bastards at bay, or you can give up and walk away and . . . well, God knows what you'd do. Teach, or something.' She pulled a face.

'So if work had dried up, do you know how Katie spent her days?' Foster asked.

'She read. She wrote. I know she was trying to write a novel of some sort. Two days a week she helped out in a charity shop near her home.'

'Which one?'

'Cancer Research. Other than that, I know she had other friends, ones she'd made through Naomi, other single mums.'

'What did she do for money?'

'A bit of voice-over work every now and then. Crappy but it pays good money. She had a lovely, clear voice. And whatever contribution she received from her ex-husband, though most of that was towards Naomi's upkeep.'

'Was there a man in her life?'

She let out a derisive snort. 'Men? We'd given up on those

shower of bastards a long time ago,' she said and laughed. 'Sorry, detective,' she added, looking at Foster. 'And no, she wasn't a lesbian if that's what you're thinking. Bloody hell, no. What I meant is that neither of us enjoyed much luck with men. Both had a failed marriage. A couple of aborted relationships since. It was a major topic between us – that and the whole work thing. I think it must have been at least a year since her last relationship. Maybe even longer.'

Heather went through the details with her; the names of other men she'd seen in the past. Darlinghurst's memory was not too good with the details, and the ex-lovers would take some tracking down.

'But there was no one recently?'

'Not that I'm aware of. Why, do you think someone she knew did this?' Her voice betrayed her disbelief.

Foster nodded. 'We do. Can you think of anyone, absolutely anyone who would wish Katie or her daughter harm?'

'No one whatsoever,' she said without thinking. 'She was a very passionate woman, quick to anger and quite tempestuous, but she was also kind, decent and loyal. Everyone who knew her absolutely adored her. I can't think of anyone who would do something like this.' She picked up an empty wine glass and walked towards the kitchen. 'Can I interest either of you, or is all that stuff about being on duty true?'

'I'm afraid it is,' Foster replied.

'Tea? Coffee? Water?'

Heather asked for water, Foster said he was OK.

A few seconds later their hostess re-emerged with a brimming glass of white wine and a tumbler of water.

'You'd known Katie for some time,' Foster continued. 'Did she ever speak to you about her past, her upbringing maybe?'

'Never,' she said emphatically. 'She was adopted, I know that. She once mentioned both her parents died. But she made it very clear it was a part of her life that she wanted to forget. You find a lot of people in this business are trying to escape their backgrounds – or transcend them, at least – and she was one.'

'Did you get an indication that it was the result of some event or incident in her past?' Foster asked.

'You mean abuse?'

Foster was somewhat startled by her frankness. 'I suppose I do, yes.'

Again, the scramble for a cigarette and a pause while she gave it some thought.

'No. And I don't think it was anything like that. I'm not basing it on fact, but simply because I truly think she would have told me. I just got the sense that she and whoever it was who brought her up didn't get on. She was quite wild; at least, she was back then. I sensed they, whoever they were, were quite conservative.'

'Do you know who "they" were?'

'They lived in Kent somewhere, some shithole seaside town. The bloody name escapes me. But she hated it.'

'Kent?' Heather said. 'Not Shoeburyness in Essex?'

'No, she definitely said Kent. I think it might have been Deal.'

Heather scribbled a few more notes. 'She never mentioned who the people were that raised her?'

Darlinghurst drew on her cigarette and looked away.

Then she shook her head. 'Not specifically, no. I always thought it was an aunt or something, but I don't remember her actually saying that.'

'So presumably they weren't invited to her wedding to Stephen Buckingham?'

'God, no. Few people were. Just a small group of friends at a registry office in Chelsea then a gigantic piss-up afterwards. His parents were not amused at being frozen out. Don't think they ever forgave him.'

'What sort of relationship did she and Stephen have?'

'Quite a good one until he started shagging everything that moved. Egregious little shit. He broke her heart. I'm not sure she ever really got over it. After he left she turned down several jobs because of Naomi. She had friends who would take her – and I did a few times, too, when she was a bit older – but Naomi remained the priority. Stephen did more than just break Katie's heart. He screwed up her career. Yet despite all that, she tolerated him for Naomi's sake. Actually, for the past few years her attitude towards him had softened somewhat. I remember her telling me it was difficult to stay angry for all that time. She still hated the miserable little prick, though, and with good reason.'

Foster thanked her and handed her his card in case anything else came to mind. As she showed them to the door, she remembered something.

'Last time we met Katie, two months ago, said she'd lost her belief.'

'Her belief in what?' Foster asked.

'That's what I asked her. She didn't really answer, so I assumed she meant in her ability.'

'What exactly did she say?'

'She said, "There's just an empty hole where my belief used to be." That's all. Then she switched the subject.'

As she closed the door behind them, Foster saw the tears well in Sally Darlinghurst's eyes.

It was almost midnight when Foster returned to his terraced home in Acton, swallowed two painkillers and washed them down with a hearty slug of red wine. It was at least a day or two past its best and no way to treat a bottle of Haut-Brion so prized by his father, but the old man wasn't around to berate him for it and the nearest off-licence had long since closed. He refused to drink water except in times of extreme thirst. Grown men and women walking around clutching little bottles of water like a child with its milk because they were told it was good for them. When did people start asking to be treated like big babies?

He sat at the kitchen table where his laptop sat idle, and took the weight off his aching leg by pulling out another chair to rest it on. It was a familiar position. Much of the last six months had been spent in the same seat, staring at the same screen, drinking from the same glass, often until dawn seeped through the window. He avoided bed and the dread that accompanied the silence and the dark. On the nights he did try to sleep, he would wake up sweating after reliving those hours of agonizing torture at the hands of Karl Hogg: his 'payment' for the sins of his ancestor, a Victorian detective who helped speed an innocent man to the gallows, thus allowing a demented serial killer free to butcher his family, and leaving a stain on the bloodline that Hogg sought to expunge. Foster's jaw, his collarbone, wrist and shin bones had all been shattered, and his life would have been taken had it not been for Nigel Barnes's intervention. The wounds would always be with him but his spirit remained intact. Just about.

He fired the machine up and as it rumbled into life he took another gulp of wine. After visiting Darlinghurst, he and Heather had gathered together the team working on Katie Drake's murder at their Kensington headquarters to sift through what information they had, while the team scouring London for her daughter continued their search. Each hour was vital. Leave was cancelled, overtime a necessity, accepted without question. The likelihood that she had been meeting a lover, or prospective lover, at her home had given them a renewed sense of purpose. They were in touch with every dating agency they could find to see if Katie Drake was on their books. Foster kept coming back to the entry in her daughter's diary: '*Can't have met a man cos she not been out in years . . .*'

The computer was ready. He joined the Internet, a home from home for the six months of his recovery. But he bypassed the motoring sites, the poker sites and the message boards where he debated the modern world with anonymous Internet warriors, and headed straight for the Internet Movie Database. There he entered Katie Drake's name into the search field. In return he was met with her entire TV output and a picture, showing dark hair that fell alluringly over hooded eyes, full lips and a look of youth that bore little similarity to the mutilated corpse he had seen earlier that day. She had been, as her ex-husband said, a real beauty.

There was a short biog that mentioned her training at

RADA. Foster made a note to check their records in the morning. Her CV appeared to list every popular TV show of the last two decades of British television, among them a long-running police drama so inauthentic that simply the sound of the theme tune raised Foster's hackles. She appeared in two different bit parts more than a decade apart, the makers presumably assuming their viewers had short memories.

He leaned back in his chair and rubbed his eyes. He was aiming to get back to work for 6 a.m. the next morning, well before the search for Naomi resumed at first light. In his mind he reviewed all that he knew about Katie Drake. An actress who took the first opportunity to leave her small-town upbringing and head for London, where she quickly got work. The dream appeared to be going well, regular theatre and television work, until she had her daughter. But even then, she was soon back at work, though when her husband left her it dried up. From that point it had never recovered. Her daughter had become her life but at the back of her mind her missed opportunity must have gnawed away at her. She started to drink, heavily it seemed, and retreated from the world. Foster glanced at his glass of wine. He wondered what a fourteen-year-old's diary might make of his habits.

She would be fourteen now. Perhaps fifteen. The date of her birth was vague, probably because he hadn't been present. By then Linda had long gone, bored of his absences. He tried to explain that being a detective wasn't a vocation, it was a curse. She'd ignored him and said she'd rather raise a child on her own than with him, words that still cut to the quick. Not that he blamed her. He'd treated her terribly, particularly when he learned she was pregnant and determined to keep the baby, no matter how much he tried to dissuade her. Last Foster had heard they were in Edinburgh, living near her family. But that was more than ten years ago. Who knew where they were now? Happy, he hoped. He drained the glass of its remnants. Fuck the past, he thought. As Katie Drake's story showed, there was nothing but vanquished hope and regret. Reasons to be cheerless.

He put those memories out of his mind and returned to the case. After a few moments in thought he was overcome with a dull ache behind his eyes. I'm tired, he thought, even though it's not long after midnight. He flicked off the kitchen light and trudged up the stairs to his bedroom.

For the first time in months he slept without seeing Karl Hogg's face in his dreams.

4

A beautiful, wholesome blonde teenager from a respectable home had gone missing. Attractive mother, an actress, which meant lots of pictures on file, brutally murdered. All in the sanctuary of their £850,000 home. Innocence despoiled. A community united in shock and terror. It was all guaranteed to have the most placid newspaper editor salivating. The British press had not disappointed. The picture Foster had seen on the Internet the previous day now stared out from the front pages of every tabloid and broadsheet, while rolling news channels cleared their schedules, star reporters put on the lipgloss, fretted over whether to do their piece to camera hair up or hair down, and decamped to the end of the road within sight of the scene.

Faced with the media's feasting, Detective Superintendent Brian Harris had taken overall charge of the investigation. Foster had been summoned to a meeting with him, DCI Williams, DCI Chilton and a few other senior detectives. He entered with a heavy heart, and fended off the inquiries into his health and well-being with as much good humour as he could muster. Harris looked pale and drawn but grimly determined. *What wonderful strategy does he have in store for us?* Foster wondered.

His spirits rose when Susie Danson, former forensic psychologist turned professor of applied psychology, entered the room, trailing a strong scent that instantly afforded him a remembrance of investigations past. It had been four or five years since he'd last seen her, but time had treated her well. Same dyed-blonde bobbed hair, same pale-blue eyes lit by a fierce intelligence, same flame-red lipstick. She was wearing a tight blue suit, white low-cut top underneath her jacket. He thought she'd given up criminal profiling in favour of writing books, giving lectures and making money.

Harris introduced her to those who hadn't had the pleasure, as if she was the Queen and they were a football team, putting a slightly creepy hand on her back as he ushered her round them. She nodded politely, almost brusquely. He came to Foster last.

'DCI Grant . . .'

'We know each other pretty well,' she interrupted, and flashed him an immaculate smile. 'How've you been, Grant?'

'Aren't you a sight for sore eyes?' he said, shaking her hand. 'I've been better.'

'Yes, I heard,' the smile faded, replaced by a look of concern. Foster wasn't sure if it was clinical.

'I've asked Susie to get involved because she's the best there is,' Harris explained to the group. 'She's had a look at the files, the autopsy report and the scene. She's going to help us narrow the search.

Good, Foster thought. Before he'd met and worked with Susie Danson, he'd dismissed profiling as a bit of well-meaning mumbo-jumbo. She had taught him other-wise.

Harris gestured that the floor was hers.

'Gentlemen,' she said, surveying the room, her file in front of her. 'Of course, all that I'm about to say is based on only a glancing acquaintance with the facts. These are some impressions I've formed that you're free to do with as you wish. I'm going to try and come up with a more considered opinion but you know as well as I do how time in these cases is utterly crucial.'

She paused, looked down at her notes, clasped her hands in front of her.

'This killer was organized,' she said. 'There was no frenzy – he was cool, calm, collected and methodical. This was planned, not opportunistic. There was no sexual molestation of Katie Drake. He did not masturbate near the body, strip her or interfere with her in any way, pre or post mortem. There is an absence of any sexual desire in her killing. However, given what she was wearing, the fact she allowed him entry, all suggests he has charm. She wanted him. I'd suggest this is a man in his late thirties at the youngest, but probably in his forties and still in pretty good shape. I'm also convinced his intended target was Naomi and that his interest in her *is* sexual and predatory. He reasoned the way to abduct her was to befriend her mother, whom he knew to be vulnerable.'

No one said anything. Foster knew Susie didn't like these briefings to be a soliloquy. That she liked her opinions to be challenged. 'But why did he kill Katie?' he said. 'Why not just abduct the daughter? Most paedophiles don't kill other people to get to their targets.'

'Good point,' she said, nodding. 'I've given that a lot of thought because, as you point out, it doesn't fit the usual pattern. But we know that paedophiles can be very enterprising and very determined. Maybe he deduced that the only way he could abduct Naomi was by getting inside her house to do it. Fourteen-year-old girls are not easy prey, not so easy to pluck off the street, unless he knew her very, very well. I guess he decided his best method was to charm and seduce her mother and be inside the house when she came home. And that to abduct Naomi without her mother preventing him he needed her silenced.'

'What sort of bloke do you think we're dealing with?' Harris asked.

'I think this man has dated women. I think he's probably of above-average intelligence. His real interest is young girls, early teenagers, on the verge of womanhood, between the ages of eleven and fifteen. You need to look at men who might have been charged with sexual offences with women of that age group, and men who have been charged with offences against their girlfriends' daughters, or even their own daughters. Start with the local area and move out. I'd also add that your killer obviously drives. He is also reasonably fit and strong. I think I can come up with some more given time.'

'Thanks, Susie,' Harris said. 'That's all very helpful.' A murmur of assent passed around the gathering. She flashed a quick smile but her look swiftly became sombre once more.

'What about a media appeal?' Foster said. 'I spoke to Naomi's dad. He's willing to do one.'

'Your call,' she said. 'Some paedophiles get their kicks from watching the family of their victims suffer. That may well be playing right into his hands.'

'I agree,' Harris said. 'Let's make him sweat.' The others nodded their heads.

'I don't,' Foster said. 'A girl is out there, perhaps still alive. We need the public as our eyes and ears if we're going to find her quickly.'

Harris went silent for a while. 'We'll revisit this later, but for now we hold the appeal back for another day.'

'Fair enough,' Susie said. 'But I can only echo Grant's point about finding her quickly. You know the rule in these cases – find them sooner rather than later, or they're dead. These cases very rarely have happy endings. He will almost certainly kill Naomi once she's served her purpose. If she's not dead already, you have three or four days maximum or you're looking for a corpse.'

After the meeting broke up, Harris asked Foster to stay behind.

'I owe you a coffee,' Foster said to Susie as she left.

'I'll hold you to it,' she replied.

Harris closed the door behind her. 'Grant, how does it feel to be back?'

'Good. I suppose there have been gentler reintroductions, though.'

'Yes. Nasty business. But it's good to have you back when something like this breaks.'

He's flattering me. This is definitely not good news, Foster thought. 'Well, it's nice to know I'm appreciated.'

'Do you remember the evaluations and tests you underwent prior to your return to work?'

Remember? How could Foster forget? After three months' convalescence he'd decided to explore the idea

46

of going back to work. It soon became clear that it might be easier to retrain as a brain surgeon. First he met with the force's medical officer, a schoolmarmish woman in her late fifties with a double-barrelled name and a fearsome bedside manner. Then he met her again. Then he met with Harris and other members of the management team. Alongside the physiotherapist he was already seeing as part of his recuperation, he was sent to see a young doctor who took it upon himself not only to check Foster's pulse and tap his chest but for some other unfathomable reason stick a gloved finger up his arse. He also underwent something called psychological evaluation with a young blonde woman in her thirties. He was then referred to a counsellor, whom he was still seeing monthly. That, actually, had been the thing that proved beneficial.

Once his evaluation was complete he went back to see the Medical Officer, who took off her glasses and sucked one of the arms before asking what was his rush, wouldn't he rather spend time at the police convalescence home in Harrogate? Foster said he would spend time in a home when he was eighty and unable to wipe his own backside, at which point she accused him of being hostile. He was referred back to another psychologist for a second opinion because his outburst was apparently in keeping with the first signs of post-traumatic stress disorder, and then sent to see Harris who tut-tutted at his attitude and told him if he wanted to return to work then being aggressive towards the person whose job it was to allow him back might not be the most politic thing to do. The second opinion agreed with the first: Foster was fit to return, though with a few caveats. He then spent countless hours

47

in meetings with a dreary woman from Human Resources to discuss a 'return to work plan'. When he pointed out in his most patient voice that he wanted that plan to be 'return to work', she'd shaken her head slowly as if he was a drooling vegetable. By this stage he'd switched off and just agreed and nodded and agreed and nodded, anything to stop the tests and the meetings and the action plans and get back to doing what he believed he did best. The upshot was that he was now back at work, with a letter at home explaining the terms of his return, but beyond noting his first date back he'd not taken any of it in.

'Vaguely.'

Harris didn't detect the rueful irony in his voice. 'One of the conditions of you returning so soon was a restriction on your working hours. For the first six months, we agreed that you should work no more than forty-five hours a week.'

He knew that bit. 'Yes, no more than nine hours a day.'

'And how many hours did you work yesterday?'

Foster furrowed his brow. Was he being serious? 'What do you mean?'

'It's hardly a difficult question, Grant. How many hours did you work yesterday?'

He was up at four, home at midnight. Take an hour or so off for getting dressed and driving to and from home. 'About nineteen,' he said to Harris.

'Ten more than you should've done.'

Foster tried to speak but the words wouldn't come. Instead his jaw flapped open like a fish. Did Harris really just say that? He ran the words through his mind again. Yes, he had said it.

'Brian, are you being serious? A woman was murdered, her daughter kidnapped. I was on duty – I was at the scene. Do you expect me to clock off and go home just because it's teatime?'

'You have an action plan . . .'

'Action plan? I'm a detective. I solve crimes. I put people in prison. A fourteen-year-old girl is missing, maybe murdered. You honestly expect me to ignore all that and go along with some spurious timetable created by bureaucratic, time-serving pen-pushers with no idea of what actual police work entails?'

'I helped draw up that timetable,' Harris snapped back.

Foster put his hands on his hips, shook his head. What can I do in the face of such lunacy? he thought.

Harris took a breath and continued. 'It's my job to do what's best for this department, this police force and the people of London. And for you.'

'What about what's best for Naomi Buckingham?'

Harris's face darkened once more. 'Don't flatter yourself, Grant. There are two other DCIs working full time on this case. I'm in charge. If she's alive, we'll find her. You will help us do that, but within the bounds of your return to work action plan.'

If I hear the words 'action plan' once more then I'm going to run to the window and hurl myself into the street below, Foster thought. He ran his hand down his face.

'And you've also missed your last two counselling sessions. You must keep going – when's your next one?'

'Tomorrow, 5 p.m.'

'Then you'll go. We can cope. We need you fit and well and able to give of your best.'

Foster shook his head. It was beginning to ache. No one had been this concerned about him since his gran passed away when he was seven. His mental health appeared to be of more concern to his DS than the safety of a missing girl. The world has gone bloody mad, he thought.

'So what's happening today?' he asked, eager to switch the subject back to the investigation, even if he was to have only a peripheral role in it.

'We're going speak to every paedo and pervert in a fifteen-mile radius. I will save you that particular pleasure, however, in favour of some victimology. I want you to get out there and have a word with Katie Drake's colleagues at the charity shop. Find out as much about her as you can. There's some news from forensics. Good news. A hair was found on Katie Drake's clothing. Apparently, because of its length, first impressions are that it belongs to a male. I need you to try and find out who the men were in her life. The hair's being tested as we speak. Should be something new on the details later today. I'll make sure forensics give you a shout.'

'Make sure it's not too late,' Foster said. 'My action plan says bedsocks and cocoa by nine.'

Heather was waiting for him in her car outside the charity shop on Chamberlayne Road, a drab traffic-choked street that bisected Kensal Rise, a suburb that still carried a crackle of danger despite gentrification.

He parked up and walked to her new Saab, battling great gusts of wind that transformed the fine rain into blasting hoses of cold water. He got in the passenger seat and looked around. 'Very nice,' he said, inhaling the heady scent of a new car. 'Came with the promotion, did it?'

She smiled. 'Felt like treating myself.'

'Yeah, I heard about your mum's death. Why didn't you tell me?'

'You were off work, recovering. I didn't want to bother you with personal stuff.'

'Well, you should have. Anyway, I was sorry to hear about it. How've you been?'

'I won't pretend it's been easy,' she said.

He paused, looked out of the window and watched the rain spatter against it in the breeze. 'I happen to think the death of your mum is the one that feels the most profound. The body that carried you, brought you into the world, reduced to dust. You never get over that one – you just learn to live with it.' He turned back to face her.

She nodded. 'I know what you mean.'

Her face was pale, severe even. The eyes, usually lined with kohl and dancing with energy, anger, humour were hollow and lined with stress.

'Is everything OK?' he asked.

She smiled again but he could see there was little genuine about it. 'Just not feeling great. Loads of stress, loads of grief, loads of stuff to mull over. I didn't think it would hit me this hard. I seem to have lost a bit of faith in my judgements and myself. I'm all over the place, to be honest with you.'

He looked at her for a while. It had been his plan to moan about Harris and being sidelined on this case, rant about the absurd amount of cotton wool he was being wrapped in. In light of Heather's woes, it didn't seem that important any more. Her life was a mess and she was working through it. He'd been doing that for years. Look where he was. Part of him felt he should try to persuade her to get herself signed off sick, go somewhere warm where she could get away from it and recharge. 'Look at me,' he might say, 'this is what happens when you close yourself down.' But there would be little point. The job had pulled her in and then tightened its tentacles. It was like that. You tried to make the world a safer place; you poured your life into your work, even if it meant your own went to the wall.

'What happened between you and Barnes? Didn't that work out?' he asked.

She shook her head. 'Not really. No fault of his. When my mum died, I didn't fancy the idea of a new relationship. An ex got in touch to express his condolences and, you know, the familiar, the devil I knew, seemed preferable to . . .'

Her voice trailed away.

Foster sensed some regret, as if she wasn't convinced. 'Wish I hadn't sent you along to see him yesterday. Must have been awkward.'

'Not really,' she said. 'I'm glad you did. It was nice seeing him. I wasn't very fair but I think he understands.' She paused, looked out of the window. 'He's a nice bloke.'

That's enough Agony Aunt crap, Foster thought. 'Come on,' he said. 'Let's get cracking.'

They climbed out and hurried the short distance to the shop. As Foster pushed the door, a bell rang inside. The place was empty of customers but teeming with bric-a-brac: books, CDs, a few toys and racks of unwanted clothes. At the counter two women, one elderly, the other in her thirties, stood talking in hushed voices. One of them glanced irritably at Foster and Heather as they entered, before adopting a helpful smile. Foster flashed his ID.

'Morning, ladies,' he said, before making his introductions. The elderly one was named Yvonne, the younger lady Maureen. 'We're here about Katie Drake.'

'We were wondering when you might come,' Yvonne said, eyes wide with what Foster presumed was shock. 'It's just terrible. Horrible. We're devastated. We thought about closing the shop for the day, but then we thought that Katie would have wanted us to open.'

'Was she supposed to be working today?'

Maureen, a brassy redhead wearing a thick layer of make-up, nodded vigorously. 'She did Mondays and Wednesdays. She should have been in today. We have three on normally. Two out front serving customers and one at the back sorting the carry-in, usually helped by Trevor. It was her turn to be out back. We've not had time to ask anyone else to come in.'

Her voice quavered. She was about to burst into tears. Yvonne threw an arm around her.

'Is there a kettle?' Heather asked. 'Why don't you put the closed sign up for a few minutes and I'll make us all a brew?'

The women nodded.

'There's a kitchen through the back,' the elderly one said.

The younger one turned the sign on the back of the door and flicked the bolt.

'So did Katie work this Monday?' Foster asked.

Yvonne nodded. 'She did, yes. Only the morning. She wanted the afternoon off to shop for Naomi's present and a cake. I was on, Maureen wasn't. Katie was in the shop with me. Steph – she does a couple of days a week, too – came in to fill in as Trevor was off.'

'How did she seem?'

'Her usual self really.'

'And what was "her usual self"?'

'Friendly, good with the customers, helpful, polite. Her acting career wasn't going too well – "stalled" was the word she used – and I think she liked getting out of the house and doing some work, meeting people.'

'She used to joke about it,' Maureen replied, with a smile. 'She used to say, "I'm paying my debt. I do the voice for all these adverts for horrible companies that treat people like dirt and sell useless things. Working here is my penance."'

Foster watched as Heather returned with a tray bearing four mugs of tea. She put them down beside the till on the counter.

He continued. 'So you got no sense there was anything different in her life? No new events, incidents or anything like that?'

The women looked at each other for a few moments.

'No,' the elderly one said.

'Not at all,' Maureen echoed.

'She didn't mention the fact she was seeing someone?'

They raised their eyebrows so high it looked as if they might leap from their heads.

'*Was she?*'

Again, the pair glanced at each other.

'Did you know that, Maureen?'

'I didn't know that, no,' Maureen replied. 'I'm surprised. Katie used to joke about it. She used to say, "I've had it with men. They're nothing but trouble. A woman needs a man like a fish needs batter and chips."'

The two of them laughed.

'Oh, we'll miss her,' Maureen said. Her eyes began to moisten.

Foster let them drink some of their tea. There was a loud rap on the door behind him. He turned to see a large man with unkempt hair and burgeoning beer gut, wearing an anorak over a navy V-neck jumper and white shirt and a pair of grey slacks. Foster guessed he was in his late thirties. He looked agitated.

'It's Trevor,' Maureen announced, and went over to unlock the door to let him in.

The man stepped in, wiping his feet furiously on the floor despite the fact it wasn't raining outside and there was no mat to wipe them on.

'Hi, Yvonne,' he said to the elderly woman, eyeing Heather and Foster warily before looking away. 'Are they here about Katie?'

'Hi, Trevor love,' Yvonne replied. 'Yes, they are. They're investigating her death.'

Trevor gazed directly at Foster. 'I wish I could get my hands on the bastard who did it,' he said in a flat monotone that belied the ferocity of his statement, though his face had reddened. 'What sort of animal could do that? And take a young girl, too.'

Foster introduced himself and Heather. 'Let me go and

hang my coat up and use the loo,' he muttered. 'I'll be right back.'

After he disappeared, Yvonne leaned in towards the two detectives. 'Trevor works here full time, though like the rest of us he isn't paid. He's not really up to taking a proper job. He's had a few problems, you see. We're a bit worried how he's going to take all this because he was very close to Katie.'

'What sort of problems?' Foster whispered.

'Well, he had a job in an office somewhere and had a nervous breakdown after his mother died. They were very close. So he had to give the job up and he's never been back. He gets incapacity benefit and spends his time with us.'

'Does he work here all week?'

'Every day apart from Tuesday. He takes that off in lieu of Saturday.'

Trevor re-emerged from the shadows at the back. 'Sorry about that,' he said, sighing deeply. 'And sorry I'm late. Bloody buses.'

'Don't worry about it, love,' Maureen said. 'They were just asking us about how Katie was when she was here on Monday. Did you notice anything different about her the last time you saw her?'

'No. Not in the slightest. She seemed as bright as ever. It was Naomi's birthday coming up, and she was looking forward to spending time together at last.'

'At last?' Foster said. 'Had she been away?'

'No, no. You know what fourteen-year-old girls are like, always out, always with friends, never at home.'

Foster nodded.

'That's right,' Yvonne said. 'I remember now. She left at lunch to catch a bus to Portobello Road and get Naomi a present.'

'Do you know what it was?' Heather asked.

'Some clothes. A brand I'd never heard of. And some make-up, I think.' She gave the name of the shops.

Heather made a note. They would get CCTV camera footage from each of the shops, see if there was any sign of her being followed.

'Can you cast your minds back and remember if there were any customers in the shop who took an unusual interest in her? Or any times you can think of when you remember Katie having a dispute with a customer?' Foster asked.

The three went silent.

'You don't have to tell me now,' Foster said. 'But if anything comes to mind, anything at all, no matter how trivial or inconsequential it may seem, then let us know.' He took a card out of his wallet and put it on the counter. 'If it's OK, we'll take your full names and contact details in case we need to get hold of you when you aren't at work?'

They agreed. Heather jotted the details down before Foster bade them farewell.

As they made their way to their car, Heather spoke. 'What do you reckon to Trevor Vickers?' she asked, looking at the name in her notebook.

Foster didn't hear, his eye caught by two men loitering at the curbside near the shop. One was tall, hair slicked back, walking around in circles while talking into a mobile phone. The other was squat and sullen, slouched with a camera over his shoulder, smoking. The press. The tall one caught Foster's eye and put his phone down. Foster recognized him, but then all hacks looked the same to him. The reporter narrowed his eyes, obviously pondering over why a senior detective was at the charity shop. Routine, or something more? Let him stew, Foster thought.

'What was that?' he asked Heather.

Heather repeated her question.

'He fits the profile,' Foster said.

'There's a profile?'

'Yes, they've asked Susie Danson to do one.'

'Who's she?'

'She's good. Knows her stuff, rarely wrong. She thinks it's a man in his late thirties or early forties, who knew Katie, knew the area, who might have previous, particularly relating to teenage girls. Though she did say he had charm; Vickers seems to have precious little. Let's feed his name into the computer and see if we can get any hits. Get in my car and phone in from there.'

They climbed in. Heather dialled the incident room on her mobile. Foster checked the latest with Harris. They had managed to get hold of Katie Drake's application details for RADA. Her address was a London one, not Kent. They'd made a few inquiries that led them to a studio flat on Iffley Road in Hammersmith. A secondary school in Deal was listed. The school's policy was to destroy pupil records ten years after leaving; her details were long gone.

The harder they looked the more elusive her past became. Was it even relevant? What was becoming clear was how vulnerable Katie Drake appeared before her death, as if she was undergoing some sort of mini midlife crisis.

Heather ended her phone call, green eyes galvanized by excitement.

'What is it?'

'Trevor Vickers is on the Sex Offenders Register,' she replied. 'He accepted a caution for possessing indecent images of children on his computer in early 2006.'

'Just a caution?'

'The children were clothed apparently – or at least, they were wearing some clothes. But the poses were indecent.'

Foster snorted. He'd bang up anyone who had that filth on their PCs for five years minimum. Clothed or not, those kids were still being abused and exploited. 'It's a leap from having sordid pictures of kids on your PC to abduction and murder,' he said. 'But it's a leap we've seen before.'

'That's not all,' Heather added. 'Because it was recent, under the guidelines he was asked to give a DNA sample.'

God bless Big Brother, Foster thought. 'We need to find out what she was wearing on Monday at work,' he said. 'If it was the same outfit then his hair could have got on to her while they were lifting dead people's clothes around. If it was different, well, it's unlikely she would put on an unwashed top for her big date, isn't it?'

'I'll go ask,' Heather said, getting out of the car.

Foster watched her walk back towards the shop. The reporter and photographer were about to enter but backed off when they saw Heather approaching. She looked them up and down before going inside. Foster thought about Vickers. They knew he'd taken the day off on Monday, which implicated him further. Something at the back of his mind urged caution, but he was the only possible suspect they had.

Heather re-emerged. 'Different. She was wearing a black top and jeans on Monday. There're also two reporters hanging . . .'

'I know. I've seen them,' Foster interjected.

'What do you want to do about Vickers?' she asked.

'It's not my decision. Harris is calling the shots. We'll let him know and see if he wants him bringing in. If that DNA sample matches the hair on Katie Drake's clothes, then we've got our man.'

5

The nation's press and broadcasters laid siege to the charity shop. The two that Foster and Heather had witnessed loitering on the street had been the vanguard. Reinforcements arrived en masse as word spread that Katie Drake had worked voluntarily for Cancer Research, a morsel the press weren't going to pass up. Her deification was under way. Maureen, Yvonne and Trevor spoke of her as some modern-day saint. Trevor Vickers in particular was especially effusive, breaking down in tears at the end of one interview. The rolling news channel Foster caught back at the office showed his collapse in an endless loop. They ran the picture of Naomi, a uniform standing sentry outside the house, tributes from old friends and colleagues, garnished with footage of Trevor dissolving into tears. Calls and information poured into the incident room, all of it dutifully logged. But none of it brought them closer to Naomi Buckingham or her mother's killer. The teenager was out there, somewhere, and the possibility of finding her alive was bleeding away.

At the same time as they were filming him weeping about his colleague's death, the papers were alerted to Vickers's brief criminal past and began scrambling around for more info. The phones of Scotland Yard's press bureau rang hot with reporters wondering whether Trevor Vickers was a suspect, would he be brought in for questioning, would he be charged? One public-spirited reporter called in to tell them that a neighbour insinuated the relationship between Vickers and his mother wasn't normal, without quite saying why. 'They're making him out to be Norman Bates,' Foster said to Heather.

He was in the incident room when Heather called.

'The results of the DNA test on the hair found on Katie Drake's clothing are in,' she said.

'Do they match with Trevor Vickers?'

'No. How much do you know about DNA profiling from hair specimens?'

'That it's not straightforward. That's about it.'

'I've been speaking to the lab. All they had was a hair shaft and a dead follicle. This hair fell out – it wasn't pulled out. If they'd had a fresh follicle then they might have been able to obtain a full DNA profile, but in this case they've no chance.'

'So it's no use?'

'No. Not exactly. They weren't able to provide a match against the database. All they've been able to do is extract some mitochondrial DNA.'

Foster was no expert in either forensic science or genetics. But he did know that mitochondrial DNA was passed down by the mother and there was no database to check it against; it was useless unless there was a sample it might be compared to.

'They extracted it in case it became relevant in the hunt for Naomi. And they're going to see if they can get a sample of Vickers's hair to see if it matches. But there's one fact which interested me.'

'Go on.'

'The DNA sample matches the victim's.'

'What do you mean?'

'The victim and the person whose hair we found on her clothing share the same mitochondrial DNA.'

'It's the daughter's?'

'No, that's what I thought, too. They're certain it's not the daughter's. It's a short hair, congruent with that of a male, and it's black. The mother and daughter had brown and blonde hair. They're going to carry out some more analysis on it but we're certain this sample belonged to a male.'

'So it's a relative?' he replied. As far as they knew, she had no male relatives.

'How much do you know about mtDNA haplotypes?'

'About as much as I know about Belgian rock music.'

'Well, mitochondrial DNA barely changes over time – the pattern can last for thousands of years.'

'I'm still lost in the land of ignorance here, Heather.'

'OK, what I'm trying to say is that we know that the victim and whoever left this hair share a common maternal ancestor. Unfortunately, the problem is that we don't know *when* they shared her. It could be one generation ago. Or it could be a hundred generations ago.'

'So this ancestor could be their mum or it could be Cro-Magnon woman?'

'Exactly. There are some mtDNA haplotypes that many people share. But there are less-common haplotypes, too. This is one of them, but it's still shared by around one per cent of the population.'

'Then narrowing it down to one person, or even a small group of people, will be impossible.'

'Virtually. Harris and his cronies think that it's no use

unless we find a perfect match for it. Ideally, for them – and for us all, obviously – that would have been Trevor Vickers. They're going to get a strand of his hair and compare it to this, but as far as they're concerned the DNA sample is useless because it tells them nothing.'

Foster could sympathize. The clock was ticking, a girl was missing; it would be easy to dismiss it because it appeared to offer no solutions. Concentrate instead on the present, the leads you already have, sketchy though they may be. But twenty years of detective work had taught him that police investigations often ran aground because of a failure of imagination. Forensics told you this, a criminal profile told you that, blood spatter patterns indicated this. He was no Luddite, far from it, but that only went so far. Sometimes you had to take a risk and listen to your gut. Which is exactly what Heather was doing and why she had called him. While unsaid, both of them realized this was not a usual, routine case and it required more than a usual, routine solution.

He went over what Heather had just told him, seeking to hold it up to the light to see if it really was of no use. Katie Drake and the person who left that hair shared some DNA and therefore an ancestor. Given that she appeared to have no past – or at least, one that was unclear – was there any relevance to that? Yes, the maternal ancestor they shared might have been a knuckle-dragger who cooked sabre-toothed tiger for Sunday lunch, but there was also a chance that it might have been someone during the past hundred years or so. The probable killer and the victim and the missing girl shared DNA.

They shared the past.

'Get Nigel and meet me at The National Archives asap.'

She heard the noise. Not for the first night she had to stifle her giggles to avoid waking her two sleeping sisters. Her youngest brother, Thomas, had crept in, too — wedged in amongst them all, scared to sleep on his own with his elder brothers away.

There it was again. She must tell him to change it. It sounded like no owl on God's earth. She slipped from the covers and padded across the frozen floor, thankful for her thick woollen socks, slipping on her buckled shoes. Under her nightgown she was fully clothed; once she was outside in the woods she knew he would take off his coat and wrap it around her shoulders as always. Her heart beat quicker at the prospect of seeing him. It had been weeks since their last meeting.

She went to the window and eased it gently upwards, wincing at the gasp of cold air that blew into her midriff. She squeezed through the narrow opening and on to the wooden balcony that extended along the front of this wing of the farmhouse, closing the window behind her. Glancing upwards, she caught sight of the clear night sky, thousands of pinprick stars in the heavens. She crept slowly to the corner of the balcony, hitched her nightgown up and swung her leg over the rail. When both her legs were over the rail, her back to the house and her face towards the fields, she edged sideways along until she reached the central pillar, then holding on to the rails she lowered herself until her legs could grasp the pole. As they slipped down, so did her hands until she was low enough to jump without her landing making too much noise. Once on the floor she stopped. No sound from within that wing of the house. She turned. No sign of life in any other part either. She took a deep breath and from her right hand plucked a small splinter of wood that had become embedded on her descent. Then she cast her eyes over to the barn, behind which he was hiding.

The ground was firm, the edges of the grass tufts starting to crisp as the temperature plummeted. She hurried towards the barn. At the far end she turned the corner and there he was, on his haunches, back against the wall. He saw her and rose to stand. They embraced without a word, his arms wrapping around her, the smell of air and soil and the elements in his hair. Without a sound he took off his coat and put it around her, then took her hand in his and they half ran across the bare grazing field, to the shrouded sanctuary of the woods.

Once secluded in the dark he grabbed her waist and kissed her hard. After a few seconds, despite enjoying his warmth, she pushed him away. There was too much she wanted to say. The look in his dark-ringed eyes as she pulled apart was one of hunger. She bit her lip. What she wanted to say could wait a few more seconds . . .

He found a place where they could sit, him leaning back against the rough bark of a pine tree, her against his chest, his hand stroking her hair. She recounted her mother and father's discussion of a few nights before, feeling his body stiffen when she mentioned Hesker Pettibone's name. When she finished, he said nothing.

He remained silent for what seemed an age. 'They are trying to force me to leave,' he said eventually.

She sat up and looked at him. 'What? Who is?'

'My father. My elder brothers. My uncles. Their friends.'

'But whatever for? You do so much good work for them.'

'I know. It is not just me. The other day, Isaac Canfield was set upon and beaten. By his own kin. He's no longer welcome in his own home.'

66

'I don't understand.'

'Because we are young, Sarah. And they are old. And there are few young, women like you. They suppose you would prefer me as a husband – or Isaac Canfield – rather than Hesker Pettibone, for example.'

'And they would be correct.'

She shuddered, laid her head on his chest once more. 'I would rather die than become a breeding mare for that fat pig.'

'Then when I leave, I will take you with me,' he said plainly and with absolute certainty.

They lay there with only the sounds of the secluded wood and their thoughts. She thought of her sisters and brothers. How much she loved them and how much they would miss her when she was gone. How much she would miss them. The thought broke her heart.

Yet she knew there and she knew then that she would follow Horton to the ends of the earth.

6

Nigel hurried past the fountains and pond in front of The National Archives, bag banging against his hip as he moved. Outside the main door he could see Heather and Foster waiting, the latter pacing back and forth, clouds of breath billowing from his nostrils in the late autumn chill, like an impatient bull. Heather saw him approaching, nudged Foster and pointed. He immediately placed both hands on his hips in a familiar pose that, despite its inherent irascibility, caused Nigel to smile. Injury had not withered him.

'Sorry I'm late,' Nigel gasped.

'Well, you're here now,' Foster said.

'How are you, by the way?' Nigel asked. The last time he'd seen him was in a wheelchair at Karl Hogg's funeral.

'I'd be a lot better if people stopped asking me how I am,' he replied. Then he smiled and gave Nigel a wink.

'It's called small talk, sir,' Heather interjected.

'Yeah. Small talk, big waste of time,' Foster said, smile vanishing. 'Come on, let's get inside and I'll tell you what's what.'

On first impressions, Nigel thought, Foster didn't seem transformed by his ordeal. He followed them to a table in the canteen.

'I need to be somewhere else in ten minutes . . . actually, make that five now,' Foster said, looking at his watch once more. He was due to interview Trevor Vickers. 'I'll get straight to the point. I know you've delved a bit into Katie Drake's background. We'd like you to delve a bit more.'

'What do you mean by "a bit more"?'

'Into her maternal line.'

Nigel furrowed his brow. A few months ago, Foster had had nothing but disdain for genealogy, now he was talking about researching the 'maternal line'.

'Can I ask why?'

'Let's just say there's a chance, an outside chance, that the person who killed her and abducted her daughter is some sort of distant relation. So if possible, we need to know anyone who might be alive today who shared a common maternal ancestor.'

Heather spoke. 'We found a hair at the crime scene. There are any number of explanations for how it might have ended up on the victim's clothing. But one is that the killer left it – and, even if it wasn't, then the person who it belongs to is someone we'd like to speak to. Our problem is that we can't get a full DNA profile from it. All we could get out of it was some mitochondrial DNA . . .'

'Which proved they shared a common maternal ancestor. Fascinating,' Nigel said.

'You know about DNA?'

'I'm no scientist,' Nigel explained, 'to say the very least. However, you can't be a genealogist these days and not be aware of the use of DNA.'

'You've lost me,' Foster said. 'How the hell does DNA have anything to do with genealogy?'

'Well, there you're entering into a major debate. There

are some who think it should have nothing to do with traditional genealogy, that we should all trace our ancestry the old-fashioned way, by following the paper trail. I have some sympathy for that view. But then there are those, an increasing number, who think DNA testing has a massive part to play, that it's the future of genealogy.'

Foster didn't seem interested in pursuing the debate. 'How long will the research take?'

'If you want the entire maternal line, then it might take longer than usual, simply because unlike the paternal line you're dealing with a number of name changes, given that most of the women will have married. But pretty quickly if you give me the support you did last time and get the General Register Office to pull the certificates I find and read out the information over the phone.'

'No problem,' Foster said. 'Heather will help you. She's used to giving you a hand.'

Nigel felt his stomach turn. 'Great,' he said, squeezing out a smile. Her smile was as forced as his. He guessed it wasn't her idea.

Foster left. They watched him go.

'He's lost weight,' Nigel said, seeking to fill any awkward silence. Here he was, alone with Heather again. Someone up there was taunting him.

'Six months sipping soup and red wine through a straw while his jaw healed,' she replied. 'He could market it as a miracle diet.'

'He seems OK, though.'

'He's back at work. I spoke to him a few times and he feigned enjoyment at doing nothing, but he fooled nobody. It's quite sad. Other than his job, he has nothing.'

Nigel wracked his brain for something that defined his existence other than work. His quest failed.

Back upstairs the centre was filling up slowly, just as Nigel liked it. 'Is it still as busy as ever down here?' Heather asked as they walked.

'Oh, yes. It's a riot,' Nigel replied, earning a laugh, the throaty traffic-stopping one he loved. He'd do all he could to hear it regularly. He'd forgotten how much he enjoyed just being with her. Recently he'd been telling himself to live more in the moment, not easy for one who spent his life working in the past. Here was a chance to try his new approach.

'One day I'll explain,' she'd told him. Nigel wanted to postpone that moment. Any hope he still clinged to that she'd realized what a mistake she'd made might be snuffed out.

He aimed to trace Katie Drake's ancestry back as far as possible, before coming forward through the maternal line to identify as many living cousins as possible. With the help of the hotline to the GRO, the work was easy and without obstacle until 1891. In that year Horton and Sarah Rowley married four months before the birth of their daughter, Emma; he aged twenty-one, she just eighteen. His occupation was given as carpenter. Neither gave the name of their fathers.

Nigel discovered the couple had two more children, Isaac and Elizabeth. In 1909, Horton – a Christian name Nigel had rarely encountered before – died in an accident, run over by an omnibus. Isaac was killed in the First World War. In 1913 Sarah died of pneumonia and pleurisy. Yet he could find no evidence of the couple's births among the indexes or on census returns for 1871 and 1881. He located them on the 1891 and 1901 censuses. On both occasions under 'Where Born' were the letters 'NK'. He showed the results to Heather.

'What does that mean?'

'Not known.'

'I suppose that means their parents were itinerant.'

'Hmm,' Nigel said, pulling at his bottom lip in thought. Something wasn't right. He could sense it. Of course, he'd come across similar entries in the past. But rarely when both husband *and* wife were unaware of their birthplace.

'You're not convinced?' Heather asked.

'Well, there are many explanations. There's every chance they really didn't know where they were born. It's just odd for that to apply to both of them. And it gets even odder when you factor in their marriage certificate – no names for either of their fathers. Of course, they could both be illegitimate; they are adopted, taken in by others, and they don't know their original place of birth.'

'You can't say they had nothing in common.'

'No, exactly. They could have met in the workhouse, or some other place, discovered they shared a similar upbringing and that brought them together.'

'Actually sounds quite sweet. Love against the odds and all that.' She flipped a fallen curl of dark hair out of her right eye and surveyed him. 'But I see you don't agree.'

'It'd be the first time I've come across something like it, but that's not to say it didn't happen. And yet . . . you'd think one of them would declare the village, town or city they were eventually raised in, even if they weren't aware of where they were born. Or that one of them might enter the name of their adoptive father, if there was one. Both of them having similar gaps in their memory just, well, it strikes me as a bit suspicious, to be honest.'

'You think they deliberately left out those details?'

'The census was deeply unpopular among some people; the Victorian equivalent of Middle England thought it was a gross intrusion into their private lives. People gave away as little as possible because they were scared how the information might be used. That's one explanation. But there's also another, slightly less principled one.'

'What?'

'They were running away and didn't want to be found. Four months after they were married their child was born. Sarah was only eighteen. Of course we can only speculate, but it's not too much of a leap to imagine that one set of parents might not have been too happy with the prospect, tried to get in the way, and that Horton and Sarah eloped to a new place and tried to cover their tracks. Lied about their names and deliberately obscured their birthplaces.'

'That's even sweeter,' Heather added, tongue wedged firmly in her cheek. 'It has a Montague/Capulet thing going on. Perhaps Horton was from the wrong side of the tracks. She was the eldest daughter of a rich pompous landowner, he the horny-handed son of toil . . .'

'There's a future for you in romantic novels.'

'I'd hope I'm better at it in fiction than I am in real life,' she added.

There was a silence. She stared at him with a look he couldn't fathom. Wistfulness? Regret? He didn't know. Was he supposed to say something here? He couldn't find the words. After a few agonizing seconds in which unsaid words and feelings hung between them like a veil, Heather switched back to the topic at hand.

'But if these two have disappeared pre-1891, what can we do?'

'There's any number of things I can do, but they might all take some time,' he said, glad to be on steadier ground. 'In the meantime, we can take Sarah Rowley as the starting point and trace as many descendants of hers as possible to give you something to start working on.'

Heather agreed. The rest of the day was taken up with that task. By the close, Nigel was able to hand her a small list of maternal cousins. One, a Gillian Stamey, died three years ago (a suicide aged thirty-six), while another elderly woman, Edith Chapman, died five years ago. The living females were Naomi Buckingham, Leonie Stamey, Rachel Stamey, Lucy Robinson and Louise Robinson. The latter, mother and daughter, appeared to have emigrated to New Zealand along with Zach Robinson, a baby son, and his father, Brian. The male descendents were Martin Stamey, David Stamey, Gary Stamey – son of the recently deceased Gillian – Brad Stamey, who was the son of Martin and brother of Rachel, and Anthony Chapman. Christopher, another male, died three and a half years ago.

Heather looked at the list. 'So, there are four branches – the Chapmans, the Stameys, the Robinsons and the Pratt/Drake/Buckinghams?'

'Yes,' Nigel replied.

'It's not that big a list,' she said.

'It's all the direct descendants of Sarah, those who share her mitochondrial DNA. The bloodline isn't the strongest anyway. Many have died, very few kids born to replace them. The Chapman branch and Naomi's have almost died out. The Stameys are the biggest clan left. Seems the Robinson branch split off and set up in New Zealand. The whole family tree isn't much bigger, just one or two others. What will you do with it?'

'Track these people down, the males in particular, and speak to them. It's a punt, but one that's worth it.'

'Well, I'll look into why the line disappears pre-1891, explore some of the options. I can stay here until late, browse through some passenger lists for ships in case they came in from abroad, or have a glance at the change of name indexes to see if they shed any light on it. If I find out what happened and it leads to more ancestors and more cousins then I'll get in touch with you.'

Heather smiled. 'Sounds like a plan.'

7

Trevor Vickers picked anxiously at his fingers, occasionally putting one in his mouth to chew. At his side was a lawyer, a short man in an ill-fitting suit with an ill-advised comb-over. Neither spoke. While they were sitting here – with the press, who had been tipped off that he was number one suspect, camped outside – the Metropolitan police were inside his house. They'd covered every inch but found no trace of Naomi. It was late on Wednesday afternoon. Time had been magnified, each minute carried more significance than usual: every hour that passed without a lead was as fatal as any wound.

Foster stood watching from behind a two-way mirror. Harris had asked him to conduct the interview. If he was being cynical, he'd think it was to appease the pack of reporters that were trailing Vickers, to make it appear as if the hunt for Naomi Buckingham was gaining momentum. They didn't need it. Not for the first time, they were ahead of the investigation. They'd intercepted a phone call Vickers had made to his estranged father that lunchtime, warning him of the shitstorm that was about to break. It had already broken. His father told him that a reporter had already been round to the house to offer him money for an exclusive interview about Trevor, and was prepared to put him up in a hotel to 'protect' him from other reporters. When he refused, maintaining his son was innocent, despite them having barely spoken in years, the reporter had gone even further, offering the resources of his newspaper to help his father find Trevor the best legal representation available. This from a newspaper that peddled a flog 'em and hang 'em line. Foster knew that was a lie – the help would never materialize. To his credit, in Foster's opinion, the father still refused, not even backing down when the reporter became aggressive and threatened to drag his name through the slurry along with Trevor's.

He fitted the profile. Loner. Loser. Mummy issues. Perv with previous, particularly relating to young girls, to paraphrase what Susie Danson had said in her report.

Foster entered the room. Vickers shifted uncomfortably in his seat. He looked on the verge of tears.

'Afternoon, Trevor,' Foster said brightly. 'Thanks for coming in. Nothing formal, just a chat.'

Trevor Vickers nodded imperceptibly, then glanced anxiously at his brief who cleared his throat and spoke waveringly. 'I have to say my client wants to express his extreme displeasure at the press attention he's receiving. He feels certain that someone in your team must have leaked the details –'

He stopped abruptly. Foster had thrown the file he was holding down on to the table in front of him. The brief stopped talking. Foster didn't even look at him.

'I know you didn't do this, Trevor. But I'm probably in a minority of one at the moment.'

A mixture of hope and bewilderment spread across Vickers's large, pale face.

Foster picked up the file, which contained the details of his previous. 'You took your PC in for repair. You see, right there, very stupid. You can't hide four pictures of under-age girls, so I don't know how we expect you to actually hide a living, breathing fourteen-year-old girl.'

Anger flashed across Vickers's face. 'I thought they were grown women dressed as schoolgirls,' he said slowly.

'Course you did. You deleted them immediately when you found out they were under age.' He scanned the file again. 'Or, two hours afterwards anyway. The fact is there were only four pictures; there was no evidence you'd done anything like this before so you escaped with a caution. End of story.' He threw the file back on the table. 'But let's get the formalities out of the way before we get on to what I think you can help us with. What were you doing on Monday?'

'I was at home most of the day. I took the day off. Did some shopping.'

Foster raised an eyebrow.

'Online,' he explained. 'A few add-ons for my computer.'

Sure you did, Foster thought. 'Receipts for those would be nice,' he said, though he knew they would confirm little. 'You do anything else? Go anywhere? Speak to anyone?'

Vickers went silent for a few seconds, then his face lit up. 'I returned a library book in the afternoon. Shepherd's Bush library. About three thirty.'

The time Naomi Buckingham probably went missing.

'The book?'

Vickers's face reddened slightly. 'Is that necessary?' he asked.

'Well, you don't think we're going to take your word for it, do you? They have records. We want to check it out. Prove that you were there and you're eliminated from the investigation.'

He looked down at his feet. '*Escaping Obsession*.'

'Thriller?'

'No. A self-help manual.'

'Come again?'

Vickers looked up, face scarlet but jaw held defiantly firm. 'The full title is *Escaping Obsession: Dealing With the One You Want Who Doesn't Want to Know.*'

Foster nodded, bit his lip, made a note. 'Were you obsessed with Katie Drake?'

'You don't have to answer that,' his lawyer mumbled. Vickers waved an impatient hand in response.

'It's all right,' he said. His eyes had become moist. 'I loved her. I never told her that because I knew there wasn't a cat in hell's chance she'd be interested in me. I took a few steps to deal with my unrequited love. But I had nothing to do with her death. Now my life's just . . . *fucking* ruined.' He emphasized the profanity with absolute conviction and anger.

'We'll corroborate the library thing, Trevor. We'll let the press know you're no longer part of our investigation. Can I just ask a few questions, about Katie?'

He'd composed himself. Nodded slowly.

'Was she seeing anyone else, to your knowledge?'

'No.'

'Did you notice anyone in the shop hanging around when she worked?'

'No.'

'She have a disagreement with anyone in the shop?'

'No.'

This is going nowhere, he thought. Time to leave the bloke to the tender mercies of the press pack outside – and the attempt to rebuild his life. Just another bit of collateral damage in the media frenzy that engulfs some cases.

Last question. 'Did you notice anything different about Katie recently, anything strange, or odd in her behaviour?'

There was a pause instead of an instant negative. He looked at Foster directly, but the detective could see he was lost in thought. Eventually he spoke.

'There was one thing,' he said. 'It struck me as a bit odd. Last Monday, not the one just gone, the one before that, a woman came in with a great pile of stuff belonging to someone who died. She was from an old people's home round the corner. Apparently the dead woman had lost contact with all her family and they'd been unable to track down any relatives so they were giving away all her things. Very sad, but not uncommon. Which is why I was surprised that Katie got so upset. Don't get me wrong, she wasn't in hysterics or anything like that, but she was definitely moved. She said to me how sad it was that you could die and no one would know or care.'

'Did you respond?'

He nodded his head. 'I agreed with her. It is sad.' His voice was low, as if considering what Foster was at that moment thinking: how that desolate observation was applicable to him. 'Then she said, "But I don't have to worry about that any more."'

'What did she mean by that?'

'I don't know. Naomi presumably.'

'But she said "any more". As if dying and no one caring had been the case before.'

'I know. Someone came in and interrupted us. I'd forgotten about it. Until now.'

*

80

Foster stared intently at the list Heather handed him, as if the answer to the whole case lay buried in those names. It was late in the evening and yet another day had crawled by without an event of significance. Trevor Vickers's alibi checked out, as he knew it would. There had been two reported sightings of girls matching Naomi's description but neither turned out to be correct. Instead of sloping off home at five, he'd hung on until Heather returned with the names, the lights off and the door shut to make it appear he was out. When she arrived, he asked her to keep the door shut and her voice down.

'I expected more names than this,' he snapped, breaking his own rule.

'Nigel could only trace the maternal line forward from 1890 or so. Before that is a mystery. This is probably only about half the names we could've found.'

Foster rubbed his hand up the back of his shaven head, then tapped the space bar of his desktop PC. It crackled into life from its slumber. 'I suppose it makes our job easier. Let's feed these into the national computer first, and see if anything comes up,' he said to Heather. 'Then we'll seek out those we can.'

He started with the males. He entered each name, cross-referencing with their date of birth when more than one person appeared on the database under that moniker. He received three hits, all from the same branch of the family. Martin Stamey and his brother David, the former convicted of drink-driving and aggravated assault, the latter of handling stolen goods, driving without insurance and grievous bodily harm, for which he was currently spending three years at Her Majesty's pleasure.

'Nice family,' murmured Heather behind his shoulder, making a note of Martin Stamey's address. 'Should be worth having a chat with him.'

The third hit was Christopher Stamey, who'd served two sentences for serious drug offences and was found murdered three and a half years ago. No one was arrested for the crime.

'Coincidence?' Heather said. 'This lot certainly sound like the black sheep of the family.'

'There're a few dark woolly creatures who might sue you for that,' Foster replied. 'They sound like scumbags.' Logic told Foster it was all unrelated. But experience told him not to always trust logic. 'It's worth checking out.'

For the sake of completeness, Foster punched in the names of the seven women. The first six provided no matches.

'Here's the last one,' Foster said, typing in the name of Leonie Stamey, niece of the brothers grim. 'She'll be only seventeen, and even allowing for the criminality in her family that should –'

He stopped abruptly.

Heather was on her way out of his office to find out more about the Stamey clan. 'What is it?' she said.

'Fucking hell.'

'What is it?' she repeated.

'Leonie Stamey is missing.' He swivelled on his chair to face her. 'She disappeared on her fourteenth birthday.' He stood up and grabbed his jacket from the back of his chair. 'I don't think that's coincidence.'

8

Martin Stamey's home was a new build on an upmarket housing estate for the aspiring criminal classes on the outskirts of Purfleet in Essex. Each house appeared identical, surrounded by large well-manicured lawns and adorned with more mock Tudor fixings than a medieval banquet. As they tried to find the right house in a warren of homogeneous streets, Foster couldn't resist a sneer. It was the sort of place where the residents put up so many lights at Christmas you could probably see them from space.

The silhouette of a flag, presumably a Union Jack, flapped in the wind on top of the house. The earlier rain had stopped but the air was still damp. Heather knocked on the door, inducing some manic barking from a dog inside the house.

'Shut the fack up!' a gruff voice barked back. The light in the hall went on and through the frosted glass a large figure in a white T-shirt approached, unlocked several bolts and opened the door on a safety chain. The face that peered through was unshaven, handsome and sullen, the features carved and lean. There was no pretence at friendliness. He knew them instantly as police.

'What?' The voice oozed contempt.

'Martin Stamey?'

'Who wants to know?'

Foster flashed his ID, then introduced himself and Heather. The dog barked riotously as if on cue. A female voice told it to shut up and a door slammed, muffling the dog's excitement.

'The Met? What you doing out here?' Stamey said.

Harris would ask the same, Foster thought. Sod the action plan. 'It's in relation to a current investigation,' he replied. 'We'd like a word. Any chance we can come in?'

The man smiled bitterly. 'Yeah, cos I'm always inviting police into my house, aren't I? Tell me what it's all about and then we'll talk about whether you can come inside.'

'It's about Leonie,' Heather said.

The man's face froze. 'You found her, have you?' He sounded eager, expectant.

'No, but we have a case that shares some similarities with hers,' Foster explained. He felt a few spots of rain. 'Look, we've told you what it's about. Can we come in?'

Stamey looked at them for a few seconds impassively, then drew back and unhooked the chain. 'Come on,' he said, walking off in front of them. He was wearing blue jeans and an incongruous pair of navy-blue carpet slippers.

Foster and Heather followed him down a long hall.

'Nice place,' he lied.

'Yeah, well, it's home,' Stamey said, failing to conceal his pride.

'What's your game again?' Foster asked as they arrived at a large sitting room. Everything in it was cream – the leather sofas, the walls, the thick shagpile carpet and the rug by the cream fireplace, even the lampshade. With the overhead light, the cumulative effect was so bright Foster almost felt his retinas detach.

The only colour emanated from a huge wall-mounted plasma TV screen showing a loud action film. A boy and a girl, who Foster guessed to be around ten or eleven years old, sat entranced.

'Fuck off upstairs and watch this shit in your rooms,' Stamey said to them, picking up a remote control from the coffee table and turning it off.

The two kids trudged away.

'What was your question again?' he said to Foster, irritably.

Foster could see the contempt wasn't reserved for him. It was a default setting. 'I asked what you did for a living.'

'Carpenter,' Stamey answered, and sniffed. 'Some other stuff, too.'

I bet, Foster thought. Houses as big as this weren't bought on the wages of your average chippy.

A slim, attractive woman in her mid-thirties with blonde hair appeared in the doorway, waiting for the children to sidle past her before she spoke.

'Who are these two, Mart?' she asked, saving her most unsavoury look for Heather.

'Detectives,' he said, sitting on one of the sofas and spreading his legs and arms wide. 'They say they're here about Leonie.'

'Have they found her?' she asked, contempt giving way to agitation.

Heather shook her head. 'I'm afraid not.'

Foster sat down on the other sofa, trying to suppress a wince. More than an hour in his car had seized him up, and his leg and collarbone were beginning to ache, as they always did at the end of the day. He was a long way from his red wine and painkillers.

'Can I get you a tea or a coffee?' the woman asked.

Both Foster and Heather shook their heads.

'A glass of water would be nice, though,' Heather said. Foster marvelled at how much water she drank. Apart from wine, it was the only thing he saw her drink.

'Grab me a can of lager, sweetheart,' Stamey said, and the woman Foster presumed to be the mother of his children padded away. Stamey turned his saturnine face on them but said nothing. Foster had taken an instant dislike to him but reined it in. He sat forward.

'I'll be up front with you, Mr Stamey. We have nothing new about Leonie's whereabouts. But in the course of our investigation into the recent disappearance of a fourteen-year-old girl in London we noticed a few similarities.'

'Is this the one that's been in the news and plastered all over the papers?'

Foster nodded. 'It is, yes.'

A look of bewilderment spread across Stamey's face. 'Her mother was offed, wasn't she? Nasty bit of business. Some fucking nonce, I expect. You lot are too lenient on them. Let them out in the community and all that shit. Best thing to do is put them down like dogs. If you're gonna let 'em go, then you wanna cut the balls off 'em first.' He sniffed once more.

Foster didn't like being harangued on law and order by someone he suspected to be a small-time crook but he let it slide.

'I don't see the connection with Leonie,' Stamey added.

'Hang on, are you saying that Leonie's mum was murdered?'

'I was wondering if we could go through the details of your niece's disappearance one more time?' Foster asked.

'Details? I don't know what you mean. As far as we knew, her mother OD'd on smack. Stupid bitch. She'd had all sorts of problems with it. The place was a fucking dump. She was opening her legs to anything with a cock. She took a hit one night and that was it. Leonie saw the writing on the wall. Her and Gary were going to be taken into care. I was . . . away at the time, so I couldn't take her in. My brother Davey was working away and he don't have a clue anyway, so he'd have been no good. My other brother, Christopher, passed away a few years back so there was nowhere for the poor little mite to go. So she had it away on her toes and I don't blame her. Gary's gone into care and he's up to no good all the fucking time from what little we hear.'

'How old is Gary now?' Heather asked.

'He'd be about eleven. The same number of foster families he's been through probably.'

'You're sure Leonie ran away?'

'Well, I was until you showed up. And so were your colleagues when they looked into it. Which wasn't very much.'

'No one's heard anything from her?'

'Not a peep.'

'Any idea where she might've gone?'

'London, I presume. She was a bright girl – brighter than her dozy fucking muppet of a mother, at least. But I can't imagine what she's got herself involved with on the streets of London. Actually, I can, but I don't wanna.'

'There's no family there she could have gone to?'

'There's no real family beyond us, to be honest. You probably know that my brother's doing time, and I've told you the other one's dead. His wife has shacked up with a new feller. That's about it really. We're hardly the fucking Waltons.'

His wife came in with the beer. He leaned forward and sprung it open slowly before taking a hearty swig. 'These two are here because they reckon that Leonie's disappearance might've something to do with that girl who's gone missing, the one who's been all over the news.'

'The girl whose mum was done in?' his wife replied.

'Yeah. Can't see why. Gilly was a smack addict and she smacked herself up too much and died. Don't think someone topped her. Can't see who would want to, for a start.'

'We're looking for a girl who went missing on her fourteenth birthday, like Leonie,' Foster interrupted. 'Of course it might be, and probably is, just a coincidence, but we felt it was worth seeing if there were any more similarities. All we have on file are the bare facts of Leonie's case and we want to know more. Didn't she have a father?'

Stamey snorted derisively. 'Take your pick from half of Essex. Let's just say my sister was not exactly stingy with her favours.'

'Didn't Leonie and Gary share the same father?' Heather asked.

The snort turned to a whooping laugh. His wife joined in. 'Did you hear that, love?' he said, shaking his head.

'She asked if Gary and Leonie had the same dad?' The mirth continued for some time.

Foster looked at Heather, who was wearing a fixed grin.

Finally Stamey calmed down. He looked at Heather and raised a hand. 'Sorry, sweetheart. Really sorry. But you'll realize why that tickled me so much when I tell you that Gary is a half-caste. His dad's a nigger.'

Foster felt Heather stiffen at his side at the mention of the word. He decided to step in before she arrested him for discrimination.

'Martin,' he said, looking Stamey in the eye. 'We'd appreciate it if you watched what you said in front of us, please.'

'Whatever,' Stamey said. He took another slug from the can, watching Heather with amusement.

She was still rigid beside Foster. Time to start wrapping this up, he thought.

'Were Leonie and her mum close?'

'Beats me,' Stamey said.

'Not really,' his wife added. 'Like Mart said, Gillian had a lot of problems with the drugs and everything. She was off her brain half the time. Leonie was one of them girls who had to grow up quick. She had an old head on her, that girl. She basically brought Gary up herself. He was a little bit wild, even back then. Weren't his fault. He had no dad and his mum was a junkie. What chance did the poor little kid have? It always amazed me that Leonie turned out quite so well. And I don't blame her for running away, even if meant leaving Gary. Imagine finding your mum dead and thinking you might have to go into care.'

'She found her mother?'

'We think so,' Mrs Stamey said. 'She went missing the same day. She got back from school because her bag was at home. Her mum was dead in the bed. We reckon she just went downstairs, opened the door and ran.'

Foster and Heather shared a quick glance. He knew she was thinking the same as him.

'Where was Gary?' Heather asked.

'He was at some behavioural clinic or class or something. He was the one who got back and raised the alarm. Well, he got back and watched TV for about half an hour and then started screaming at his mum to get up and make his tea. He didn't understand. He went and got the neighbour and she called the police.'

Foster stood up. 'Well, thanks for your time. You've been a great help. If we find anything else relating to Leonie, we'll be sure to get in touch.'

Stamey nodded, a glassy look in his eye. Foster guessed the can of lager he was just emptying might not have been his first. His wife showed them to the door.

'Where's Gary now?' he asked as she opened the door.

'Last we heard he was in a Council care home,' she said. 'Good luck finding that girl,' she added, and went back inside.

They stepped into the pouring rain and headed for Foster's car. Once inside he could tell she was still seething.

'What do you think now? Black sheep or scumbag?' Foster said with a smile.

'What a wanker. I don't know how some women do it,' she said, echoing Foster's thoughts.

'What do you reckon?' he asked.

'Too many similarities. The mother dying on the same day as the daughter going missing. The fact it was her fourteenth birthday . . . It could still be coincidence, I suppose. And there's nothing else to link them, other than circumstance and a DNA sample that could be shared with another half a million people. Do you think our charming Mart had anything to do with it?'

'Who knows,' Foster said. 'We'll come back to him, though.' He started the engine. 'Let's poke around a bit more and see what comes up.' He put the car in gear and slowly pulled away. 'But first we need to find sweet little Gary.'

9

Horton and Sarah Rowley appeared to have been erased from the pages of history. At times when Nigel had lost the trail on other cases, he found sleeping on it helped; when he woke up, an idea of how to break the impasse was often there, fully formed. But that morning he remained stymied.

He was unsure what to do with his day. A heap of case-work was piling up, but it palled against the prospect of helping Foster and Heather. Then there was the matter of his nascent television career. Since his humiliation in Kensal Green cemetery earlier that week he had heard nothing. He could only think that the programme-makers had seen his screen test and, after they'd finished laughing, started tracking down a presenter with a modicum of aptitude. He should be pleased – after all, he rarely watched television himself, being more of a radio man. Yet part of him was thrilled at the prospect of appearing on television and where it may lead. He imagined himself being recognized in the street. Worse, he imagined himself enjoying being recognized in the street. He, Nigel Barnes, a man who struggled to get recognized in his own sitting room. He fired up his computer and checked his e-mails. Nothing from the producer.

He went to the kitchen, still in his striped dressing gown and pyjamas. A low pale early winter sun glancing through the window made him squint. He ate toast most mornings and saw no reason to change his routine. He carved the last slices from the brittle, stale sourdough loaf, made a mental note to get to the delicatessen to purchase another, and placed them in his eccentric old toaster. He flicked the kettle on and gazed out of the window, wondering when the house opposite, wreathed in scaffolding, would ever be finished. It had to be a year now and he was bored by the sound of poorly attached tarpaulin flapping in the autumn wind. What were they doing . . . ?

His thoughts were interrupted by the scent of burning. When he turned, he could see his toaster billowing plumes of black smoke, forcing him to lunge over and manually evict the contents. Being averse to any form of waste, he grabbed a knife and flipped open his bin, attempting to render the pieces edible by scraping off the bits that were burned beyond repair. It soon became clear they were beyond saving. Nigel cursed to himself. Must get a new toaster, he thought. Or get the grill in the oven fixed so he could make proper toast. Of course Agas made the best toast, but they were hardly compatible with cramped London kitchens. Whatever, there was no point spending his hard-earned cash on freshly baked bread while his toaster was so temperamental. The two blackened shards in his hand could have been two stale pieces of sliced white. Only the gourmet equivalent of a DNA test could have revealed their true identity. He laughed to himself. Then stopped.

Now there was an idea.

Ethnoancestry was based in Ealing, in a nondescript red-brick hutch down an anonymous side street.

Nigel announced himself to a security guard doubling as a receptionist and was told to wait. Five minutes later Dr Chris Westerberg, bearded and blue-eyed, greeted him with a vigorous handshake.

'Good to see you again, Nigel,' he said warmly in a soft southern Irish lilt.

'You too, Chris. How's tricks?'

'Mustn't grumble,' he mumbled. 'Find it OK? Come by car, did you?'

'I came by tube. I don't drive.'

A look of amusement spread across the scientist's friendly face. 'Yes, I forgot. The man with no car and no credit card. The last of the bohemians. Ideal – you can carry on drinking because you don't have to drive and someone else picks up the tab. Let no one say you're not a canny man, Nigel.'

He smiled. He'd forgotten how much he enjoyed the Irishman's company and good humour.

'It's been a while, hasn't it?'

'It certainly has,' Nigel replied. He guessed eighteen months, at a drab family history convention in a provincial northern town whose name Nigel couldn't even remember. Westerberg was there touting his company and their DNA tests and kits. For two nights they drank well into the night, arguing furiously and drunkenly over the role of DNA testing in family history, both of them enjoying every second of it. Westerberg had been among the vanguard of those arguing that a genetic approach could revolutionize genealogy and family history. Nigel was a sceptic.

Westerberg led him to a lift, up one floor and down a

sterile corridor to a small, cluttered office. 'I share this with a colleague, so apologies for the mess. He's from Scotland, that's all I can say. Coffee?' Nigel murmured his assent and Westerberg disappeared for a few minutes before returning with two steaming mugs. 'Instant not filter, I'm afraid,' he explained.

He sat down behind the desk and gave Nigel another friendly smile. 'So how's it going back at the coalface?'

Nigel pulled a face. 'It's improving.'

'You're joking me, aren't you?' he said, incredulously. 'I saw you all over the papers. Helping police catch a serial killer.' He let out a low whistle.

'Certainly was a break from the norm.'

'You're the master of understatement, Nigel. That wasn't a break from the norm; that was some fucked-up shit.'

'I suppose it was,' he said, inwardly rather pleased that his work and the publicity had been noticed. 'Listen, I was wondering: can you help me catch another killer?'

Westerberg's eyes widened. 'Jaysus, what now? You turned into Travis Bickle, cleaning the scum off the streets?'

'The police have asked for my help once more,' he explained, trying to remain modest.

'Who's been killed?' Westerbeg asked.

'That has to remain confidential, I'm afraid,' Nigel said. 'Part of the deal in the police allowing me to come here and explore this with you.'

'I suppose that makes sense. What's the deal?'

'Bear with me on this,' Nigel said. 'I'm a layman, after all. The police have a mtDNA sample that was found at

95

the scene of a murder – from a strand of hair, I believe. It turns out that it's the same type as the victim, except it came from a male while the victim was female. According to the police's forensic people, the victim and whoever left this hair – who may or may not be the killer – shared a common maternal ancestor.'

'Well, we could verify that for you,' Westerberg said.

'Thanks. But that's not why I'm here. The police are, in the original sense of the word, clueless. All they have at the moment is this hair and the mtDNA sample and the fact of the shared maternal ancestry. They've asked me to research the victim's family tree and find out all the people extant who share this mtDNA.'

Westerberg's face clouded over. He leaned forward across the desk. 'Nigel, you do realize that the maternal ancestor you speak of could have lived thousands of years ago? It may not be confined to five or six branches of the family. It may be confined to five or six per cent of the population.'

Nigel nodded. 'That's where you come in. Is it possible from the test you've devised to discover when this ancestor was shared?'

Westerberg shook his head. 'No.'

Damn, Nigel thought. I've wasted my time.

'Unless.'

'Unless what?'

Westerberg sat back. 'Do you have any details about the type extracted from the strand of hair?'

Nigel had. After employing all his powers of persuasion, Heather had agreed to ask Foster whether Nigel could have details of the type of mtDNA extracted from

the hair strand. The DCI had agreed, somewhat reluc-
tantly, and an hour later an e-mail containing an impenetrable sequence of numbers had arrived in Nigel's
in-box:

16111 16290 16319 16362

Second hypervariable segment 64 146 153

He produced the printout from his jacket pocket and
handed it to Westerberg. The scientist stared at it for several seconds. Put it down and stroked his beard.

'You might be in luck,' he said.

'Might I?'

'The group this sample belongs to is a relatively rare
one. Which means you won't have vast amounts of people
sharing it.'

'How many?'

'I can't answer that. But that's not the only reason you're
lucky. Let me check something out.' He tilted the screen
of his computer to face him and tapped in a few details.
Studied the screen carefully and then punched in some
more data. He started to nod. 'The person to whom this
belonged had a maternal ancestor that was Native American.'

'You can tell that from the piece of paper?'

'It gives the mtDNA haplotype, which means I can
assign it to a haplogroup, which means I can work out its
biogeographic ancestry.' Westerberg paused, taking a slurp
of lukewarm coffee. Nigel noticed the mug. It had a crude
drawing of a banana. Written inside were the words 'I
share half my DNA with a banana'. He wondered if it

was true, making a mental note to check it on the Internet when he got home. 'By examining a person's mtDNA and the mutations it carries, we can follow their ancestor's footprint and their lineage. The ancestor of whoever owned this DNA left a print in North America and it's one we know is shared by other people with Native American ancestry. Give me a day or two to check a few databases and I might even be able to tell you the tribe to which the maternal ancestor may have belonged.'

Nigel was amazed. 'You can tell me whether the victim's ancestor was a Cherokee or a Sioux or an Apache?'

Westerberg smiled. 'Not that specific. Most haplotypes are shared across tribes or are maybe restricted to a related group of tribes, but we could certainly narrow it down.' He could see Nigel was still impressed. 'I told you genetic genealogy was the future.'

While he found this revelation thrilling, Nigel knew the Native American population was not renowned for keeping records. There was no way he could use this information. Unless . . .

There was little evidence of any Native American blood in Katie Drake's features. The most obvious explanation was that this mysterious woman entered the Drake lineage hundreds of years ago on some great migratory route. However, another explanation occurred to him.

'Is there any chance of discovering a date or an approximate time when a Native American woman entered the bloodline?'

Westerberg ran his hand through his hair so that it stuck up as if caught by static. 'How would that help?' the Irishman asked, furrowing his brow.

'I'm not sure it would. The fact is, I've been trying to trace the maternal line of the victim as part of the investigation and the paper trail appears to end –'

'I knew it!' Westerberg slapped his hand down hard on the desk. 'I knew it! You need me. You've hit a wall and you need a hand to get over it. Hang on, what was it you said in the bar at that ball-aching convention?' He put his hand to his forehead. 'Hang on, I got it, it's coming. "The problem with genetic genealogy, old chap, is that it's a gimmick. A bloody lucrative one, but still a gimmick."'

Nigel winced as Westerberg, eyes sparkling with delight, slapped the desk a second time to underline his glee.

'So let me get this straight, Nigel. You want me to see if I can find out when the Native American mtDNA entered the bloodline so you can go back to the records and see if you can pick up the trail again?'

'In a nutshell, yes, that'd be very useful.'

'You can't do it.'

'Really?'

'Rather, you couldn't do it.'

'Your employment of the past tense seems to imply you now can.'

'Perhaps. I've developed a test, one that isn't even available to customers yet, which hopes to tell you that sort of information. It's simple maths. Testing how far back in the family tree the Native American ancestor came in translates genetically to what proportion of the person's ancestry and therefore genes are Native American. You would expect roughly one-eighth of the genes to be Native American with a great-grandparent, and one-sixteenth if it were a great-great-grandparent.'

'How do you know how much of a person's genes are Native American?'

'The test examines DNA changes which are more common in one continental group of people than another, for instance Africans, East Asians, Europeans or Native Americans. There are hundreds of these DNA changes that can be specific to a continent, but are more often found at a high frequency in one place, for example Native Americans, but at a much lower frequency in another place – they are markers of ancestry. Forensic identification normally uses about a hundred markers to compile a profile. Our test uses hundreds of markers across many genes, thus giving people an idea of their overall ancestry. We use a computer program which takes into account the number of each type of change you have and where these are found and how common they are, and calculates this as a percentage of the make-up of your ancestry – whether it's European, African or Native American. So by pinpointing the amount of Native American DNA in the sample we could work out when those genes entered the family tree.'

'Are you in a position to use this test?'

'No.'

'Oh?'

Westerberg picked up the printout Nigel had given him and dropped it slowly on the desk. 'Because I haven't got a sample to work with, just a piece of paper. If I had a DNA sample we might be in business.'

'I doubt they'll release the hair . . .'

'I don't need the hair. You said the person who owns the hair and the victim share a common maternal ancestor?'

'Yes,' Nigel replied hesitantly.

'Then testing her DNA should tell us when the mtDNA molecule entered the bloodline. You just need to get a sample from the body.'

Gary Stamey's arms were folded, face set hard. Apart from the molten hatred in his eyes, he looked angelic – flawless coffee-coloured skin, delicate features and dark tight-cropped hair. Yet the cute appearance disguised an eleven-year-old bearing the criminal record of an old lag. Just reading it made Foster's eyes water: fifty-four crimes since the age of eight years old. Mainly burglary or theft. On one occasion he stole a car, which he drove into a wall after ten yards. Foster found that last detail strangely comforting, evidence there was still a child in there. All these crimes had been committed across different parts of Essex because he'd been moved around so many times. Foster families, care homes, none of them had prevented him embarking on a crime spree within a few days of his arrival. Wherever he wound up the local crime figures spiked. Gary would then be arrested, sent to magistrates' court, and dispatched to another area to be someone else's problem. His latest hideout was a care home in Romford. A rare success. He'd not been arrested for a week.

Foster and Heather were sitting in a communal lounge. Gary sat on a sofa next to the home's duty manager, a large woman in a tent-sized dress who spent most of her time flicking worried glances at her charge. A ripped and frayed pool table stood at one end of the room, a TV surrounded by empty DVD cases at the other. Underneath the table in the middle, surrounded by sofas and chairs, were several battered board games. One of them was Monopoly. Foster laughed silently and mirthlessly at the thought of Gary Stamey playing that. His Get Out Of Jail card was his age. Soon he would be banged up in some young offenders' institution or other. Then his criminal education would be complete.

The duty manager launched into a stuttering introduction as Gary slumped deeper into the sofa, staring first at the blank television screen, then turning his sullen gaze on them, ignoring every word said. Heather said hello. He turned his stare to the window and wrapped his arms tighter around his chest, sinking even lower. Soon he'll be horizontal, Foster thought. He knew straight away the 'Watch-with-Mother' shit wouldn't work. This wasn't a time to be friendly. This wasn't an ordinary child. It was an animal. Foster didn't care about the 'circumstances' that explained Gary's behaviour. It wasn't his fault some people who weren't fit to raise hamsters had children. It was his job to deal with the consequences.

'We're here about your sister, Gary,' he said, once the niceties were over.

A flicker, no more. The boy turned his head to him slowly, glanced at him for a few seconds, and then returned his gaze to the window.

'Don't you care about what happened to Leonie, Gary?'

There was a pause. The hate-filled eyes on him again. This time the boy spoke. The first time. The voice unbroken yet sounding older than its owner.

'No.'

Back to the window. At least ten seconds of silence.

'You don't care whether she's alive or dead.'

This time the answer was immediate. 'Why fucking should I? Fucking bitch left me.'

The duty manager's face reddened. She put her hand on his arm. 'Gary, I really don't –'

'Get your fucking hand off me, you fat fucking cunt,' he screamed, flinging his arm to shake her off.

She sat back, hands up. Gary returned to his usual pose, eyes now ablaze. The duty manager looked at Foster.

'Can you give us a moment?' he asked.

She looked uncertain. 'I really shouldn't . . .'

'Five minutes. We'll be OK.' Foster noticed Gary's eyes were on him, though he avoided them.

The duty manager eventually nodded, got up. 'I'll be in my office,' she added, and left. She didn't seem too disappointed to be getting out of his way, even if it meant breaking procedure.

Foster stood up. He walked over to the pool table. He couldn't see any balls anywhere. Probably confiscated to stop the players putting them in a sock and knocking each other's brains out.

'I've got a problem, Gary,' he said, turning round to look at him. As soon as he did, Gary looked away. Got you, he thought. He put his hands in his pockets. 'Do you know what my problem is?' Nothing. 'Didn't think so. So I'll enlighten you. My problem is that I'm a murder detective. I go after nasty people that murder other people. I'm not used to dealing with kids that steal DVD players and PlayStations. Frankly I don't give two shits about kids who steal DVDs and PlayStations. But I do care about people who've been murdered. Most of all I care about their families and friends who have to live knowing that some scumbag killed their mum, or their dad, or brother or sister and to even begin to start dealing with that horrible thought they need to know that scumbag has been caught and punished. Of course, that's never enough, but it's often a start.'

'What's that got to do wiv my sistah?' he said. The accent was broad East London.

'That's what me and my colleague here are trying to find out, Gary.'

The boy looked confused.

'You see, I'm investigating a murder. Not only a murder. But a kidnap, too. Someone not so much older than you who's been taken. Now, there's a chance that what you know will help me find that person.'

'Know about what?' Impatience had replaced anger.

'About Leonie.'

'I don't know nuffing.' Anger was back.

'Gary, you're not listening to me. You don't know what I want to know. Let me ask you a few questions and – who knows? Maybe you'll tell me something that helps. Maybe you won't. But let's try it out and we can get back to catching murderers and you can get back to whatever it was you were doing.'

'I don't help no coppers.'

'You can say that again. I've seen your record.'

Gary shook his head and tightened his arms around his chest, as if to say, 'I'm certainly not gonna help you now.'

Foster looked over at Heather and nodded, before turning to the window and staring out at a miserable slab of concrete decorated by clumps of weeds pushing through the cracks.

'Gary,' he heard her say, her voice soft. 'The girl who was kidnapped is fourteen, like Leonie was. Now I know you hate the police and you don't want to help us, but you won't be helping us, you'll be helping this girl.'

Foster heard Gary shift in his seat.

'This girl who's missing, some really nasty things could be happening to her now,' Heather continued. 'Truly terrible things. If we can find her, we might be able to stop them happening. Help us. Please.'

Foster kept staring out of the window. There was a patch of grass at the perimeter of the yard, against the fence, which was littered with empty crisp packets, drink cans and other debris. Beyond that was a car park and a parade of shops, only one of which wasn't boarded up. There was little in the area to inspire the residents of this care home.

'OK,' he heard Heather say. 'Thank you.'

The kid must have nodded. Foster turned round, remained standing.

'In the days and weeks leading up to your sister leaving, do you remember anything out of the ordinary at home? Anything strange or different?' Heather asked.

Gary held the same pose, but Foster noticed his eyes had softened. He gave it some thought. 'Not really.'

'Did Leonie seem upset? Did she and your mum have a row or anything?'

Gary snorted. 'They was always fighting. Leonie didn't like her. She said we'd be better off wivout her. That she'd look after me.' The big eyes were wet. Foster could see him holding back the tears, refusing to allow himself to cry.

'She said that?'

He nodded. Bit his lip. Quickly wiped his eyes with his right hand.

'I know this is tough for you, Gary. But it all helps. Did your sister say anything, anything at all, before she left?'

Once again he shook his head.

'What about your mum? Had she been any different in the weeks before she died?'

'No,' he muttered. 'I didn't see her that much.'

Jesus, Foster thought.

'Leonie looked after you?' Heather asked.

He nodded. 'We wasn't a proper family.'

'Leonie said that?'

He nodded his head. 'The man told her.'

'What man?'

'The man what came to our house.'

Heather glanced briefly at Foster. 'What man, Gary? A friend of your mum's?' she asked.

'No. She was never there when he come.'

'A friend of Leonie's?'

He shook his head. 'He wasn't no friend. But she liked him. Said he spoke the truth.'

'The truth about what?'

'Dunno.'

'What sort of things did he say, Gary?' Foster asked, speaking for the first time in a while.

Gary gave him a hostile glance. He looked back at Heather. 'I'll speak to you but I won't speak to him,' he spat out.

'OK,' Heather said, nodding. 'That's fine. Tell me. What

sort of things did the man say to Leonie, Gary? Did she tell you?'

He shrugged. 'She said he told her we wasn't a proper family. He said some things about Jesus.'

'Can you remember anything else?'

Gary thought about it. 'Leonie said he told her that Jesus loved us. And that other people loved us, too. He told her one day our family could be together for ever and we would be happy.'

'Anything else?'

'No.' He brightened. 'He gave her a book.'

'Do you remember what that book was?'

'Dunno.'

'The Bible?'

'Dunno. It had pictures. Not like a cartoon. Old pictures.'

'What was it about? Do you remember?'

He scrunched up his face, gave it some thought. 'Dunno,' he said. 'There was a boy called Joe. He lived ages ago. He found a secret treasure.'

'What was it?'

'Can't remember. Maybe it was books?'

'Books?'

'Yeah. I think. She didn't read me no more of it. It was boring.' He sighed.

'How many times did the man come to the house?'

'Dunno. He always came when I was out playing.'

'More than once?'

'Think so. One time I came back and he was going.'

'What did he look like?'

He looked briefly at Foster. 'Like him.'

'What, tall and ugly?' Heather said instantly, and winked. Gary snorted with pleasure at the comment. A bubble of snot appeared in his nose and burst.

'Very funny,' Foster said, trying to play along.

'Seriously, how did he look the same as DCI Foster?'

'He was big. He was wearing one of them things,' he pointed to his neck.

'A tie?'

Gary nodded

'Did he have hair?'

'Black hair.'

'If we got someone to draw a picture of him, would you help him?'

Gary nodded. 'He patted me on the head and said hello. Then he got in a car.'

'What sort of car?'

'It was a blue Ford Mondeo. An old one.'

Kid knew his cars, Foster thought. He'd been the same when he was that age. Obsessed with cars. He hadn't known his times tables, but he knew the top speed of an Austin Allegro.

Heather glanced up at him. He mouthed for her to ask about Gary's mother.

'What happened on the day your mum died, Gary?' she asked.

A frown appeared on the boy's face. He started to scratch his left arm. He looked from side to side. Then he shook his head. 'No,' he said.

'No, you don't want to talk about it?'

'I don't remember,' he replied. He carried on scratching the back of his left arm, head shaking vigorously. His features changed. The menace returned. He began to glower. 'I don't fucking remember, RIGHT!'

Foster saw Heather flinch at the sudden rise in volume.

'That's OK,' she said softly. 'It doesn't matter.'

'I don't fucking remember,' he hissed, his legs jolting as if sparked by a current.

Heather said nothing for a few seconds, allowed Gary's anger to subside. Foster motioned to her that it was time to go. They had the post mortem report that said Gillian Stamey's death was caused by heroin toxicity, presumably self-administered. The only detail that intrigued him was the purity of the drug that killed her. It was high grade; junkie single mums on benefit would usually ingest any old smack, even if it was cut with rat poison and made them as sick as dogs. She'd been cremated so there was no chance of an exhumation. They could ask Gary about it another time if necessary, with the required psychologist present, but meanwhile there were other leads they could explore.

'Leonie isn't dead,' Gary said suddenly.

'How do you know?' Heather asked softly.

He looked at the floor. 'I just don't think she is,' he mumbled. Then he looked up, eyes brimming, anger on his face. A different kind of anger. Not hate but wronged. 'She said she'd look after me. She promised. She'll come back and get me one day.' The last sentence was defiant. His nose was running. He sniffed, then wiped a copious stream of snot on the sleeve of his sweatshirt.

Heather nodded, face sincere. She had yet to fully concede, as Foster had, that the world was a cold, indifferent place. And such a world threw up feral kids like Gary

Stamey who had no respect for authority. For anyone. His joyless life of petty crime might only be a nuisance to police forces now, but soon he would graduate to bigger and worse crimes.

'Gary,' Foster said, ignoring the scowl his voice provoked. 'If you're hoping she comes back and makes your life sweet, then why do you spend all your time robbing? How about keeping out of trouble?' He plunged his hands into his pockets. 'Listen to me – though you probably won't, because you've had a million talks like it and it's pretty clear from your record that you've never heeded a word. I know you hate me and people like me, but you're heading one way and one way only – a life in prison. What would happen if Leonie came back for you then?'

Gary stared at him. 'Fuck you,' he said, voice flat and emotionless. Then he looked down at his shoes.

Foster shrugged. I tried, he thought. This kid's too far gone.

I I

The warm smell of toasted sandwiches inside the café provided a perfect counterpoint to the wind and rain lashing High Holborn. Nigel, starving after his trip to and from Ealing, ordered one and gazed out of a streaked window and across the road towards First Avenue House, a grand if grey building, where he could see them gather: estranged men and women smoking furiously on the pavement, pacing back and forth, waiting for their time in one of the umpteen family division courts inside, summoning sinew before attempting to sort out their differences for the sake and welfare of their children. More than once on a visit here he'd seen violent slanging matches spill from the courtroom on to the street, or ambulances pull up to tend to those for whom the emotional trauma had become too much. Because of these animosities, those entering the courts were searched and scanned to prevent them secreting weapons in an attempt to murder their errant spouses; inside, drinks were dispensed from plastic jugs and glasses for the same reason.

Thankfully for him, when he had finished his coffee, the traffic through the main entrance was slight, with just a handful of glowering, fractious adults at the front of the building. He had managed to convince Foster to dispatch the DNA sample to Chris Westerberg. While that was being processed, he wanted to exhaust every line of inquiry. That included the paper trail that might have been left by either Horton or Sarah Rowley upon their death. Where there was a will, there was often a way to overcome a dead end.

Horton died intestate. But from online calendar indexes Nigel had discovered that his widow had left a will upon her death in 1913. It might contain very little, but it was worth a try. He hurried across the street during a break in the rain, made his way up the stairs to a brightly lit, spartan room decked out in calming neutral colours like the rest of the building. The place might house the wishes and last words of the dead, the physical debris left from their brief time on the planet, but none of that grave mystique was reflected in the sterile surroundings of the probate search rooms. A few other family historians had beaten him up the stairs. How the chattels of the dead were divided often gave a fascinating glimpse into family hierarchies, as well as offering an indication of how our ancestors lived, both rich and poor. The lord of the manor might bequeath half of Surrey to his children, but more evocative pickings were often gleaned from those with the least to pass on, but who still thought it right and proper to pass on their favourite flat cap or best milking cow.

He grabbed an order form and filled out the date of the will made by Sarah Rowley. While that was being found, he returned to his seat in the café for another coffee, taking time to watch the daytime television comings and goings outside the family court, before returning to collect a copy of the will. As he expected, it was hardly brimming with bequests. The deceased's wedding band was left to their elder daughter. Elizabeth inherited an oak table, while

Isaac received a set of carpentry tools Nigel assumed had belonged to Horton. Sarah also asked, intriguingly, that a locked metal box inscribed with her initials be buried with her. Those were the only possessions listed. A sum of ten pounds was left to 'the parish of St Bertram, East Ham'.

While there was no genealogical information that explained the Rowleys' obliteration from all records pre-1891, at least there was a trail that Nigel could follow. Perhaps Sarah Rowley did not want to divide a small sum between her children; maybe she felt they didn't deserve it. Whatever her reasons, the act of giving the money should have been recorded by the church, and if she was an active member of the congregation then there might be further records that could offer details about her and her husband.

He put in a call to the London Metropolitan Archives, where most of the records belonging to London churches were held. They had nothing for St Bertram's in East Ham. They suggested he try the Essex Records Office. He phoned them but was given a similar answer: they had no records. Anything the church had was still held in its own archive.

St Bertram's was a ten-minute walk from East Ham tube station, nestled away in a warren of Victorian terraced artisan houses. The church, as Nigel deduced from the lack of records in the LMA, was relatively modern. Perhaps no more than a century old, red-brick and functional unlike the Gothic splendours that decorated much of the capital. He wandered aimlessly around it a few times looking for an entrance, eventually discovering it in a modern wing of the church, a few years old at most, which appeared to act as a sort of community centre. Mothers and children milled around, either leaving or attending an afternoon playgroup.

He asked at a small reception area if he could see the vicar. A few minutes later he arrived, smiling broadly, not much older than Nigel, with a jolly, rubicund face. Nigel returned his handshake, made profuse apologies for not calling in advance and explained the reason for his visit, leaving out any mention of the murder and abduction inquiry.

'We have quite a few genealogical inquiries,' the vicar explained. 'Many of them from abroad. We're usually happy to help. What are you after?'

Nigel explained Sarah Rowley's will.

'When did she die?' the vicar asked.

'1913.'

'Really? That was only five years after the parish was formed and the church opened. She'd be among the first parishioners. What was the name again?'

'Sarah Rowley. Her husband died four years before. He was called Horton.'

The vicar glanced down at the floor. 'Something about that name rings a bell,' he said. 'I've only been here for a couple of years, so I haven't been able to familiarize myself completely with the church's history. But if you come with me to the vestry we can see if there's anything that can help you.'

Nigel followed the vicar through the main church, which also appeared to have benefited from a recent facelift. There was none of the mustiness – the smell of history, as he liked to think of it – which characterized the rare occasions he'd been allowed to rummage through the parish chest. He was led to a door to one side of the altar. The vicar produced a set of keys and unlocked three bolts.

'Some of our parishioners think the Lord turns a blind eye to breaking and entering,' he said with a wink. Inside he switched on a light, revealing a large room crammed with all sorts of church items. Old altarpieces, vestments, stacks of hymn books and pew cushions. 'Sorry, it's a bit more chaotic than you're probably used to. The archiving is pretty haphazard.' He pointed to a shelf at the back of the room, where several huge volumes of books were laid against each other. 'You can start there. Those are the parish registers. Sorry there's nowhere comfortable to sit.'

Nigel waved away the apology. He picked up the first ledger. It was the original, the spine battered and frayed, some pages becoming loose. 'Far be it from me to tell you how to run this place, vicar, but you really should think about getting these registers preserved in a local record office. There'll be a local family history federation or society that would probably be willing to transcribe the information from these books, so they don't even have to be touched any more.' He flipped it over for further examination. 'I'm not sure how long these will last otherwise.'

'You're quite right,' the vicar explained. 'It's on my to-do list.'

Nigel sat on a small wooden chair. Carefully he opened the first volume, beginning in 1908. Almost immediately he came across the burial entry for Horton Rowley in 1909. Simply the bare details, his name, age and date of burial. He continued through the volume and sure enough, in 1913, he found details of Sarah Rowley's burial. But the information gave him nothing new.

'You don't have a graveyard here. Where would these people have been buried?'

It might be worth a trip to see if there was anything interesting inscribed on the grave – but the weather and time might have claimed it, and he was not carrying the necessary materials to render epitaphs decipherable.

'East Ham cemetery on Marlowe Road. They have a register there, too.'

Nigel made a note of the address. Closed the volume.

'Do you have any copies of the vestry minutes?' These were the details of parish meetings; like many of their kind they recorded only the salient points, though they did occasionally yield a genealogical jewel.

The vicar shrugged. 'I think they're kept elsewhere, but I really must be honest and say that I have no idea where,' he said, face reddening. 'Our verger Audrey Cantrell might be able to help. Unfortunately, she's away on holiday with her family at the moment. Sorry about that.'

This appeared to be another cul-de-sac.

'However, there is one thing,' the vicar added. 'He stepped over a few boxes and pulled away a piece of dark blue cloth, of the type that might cover an altar. Beneath it was a large wooden chest. 'In here is a number of documents and packets of papers that belonged to my predecessors, going right back to George Burch, the first vicar of this parish. I haven't gone through it in any exhaustive detail but there are all sorts in there. Feel free to have a look.'

A rummage through the parish chest was a phrase used

to describe merely looking through church records, usually in an archive; never had Nigel literally hunted through one. The vicar unlocked a large bolt and lifted the lid. It was piled high with folders and boxes, barely a loose piece of paper.

'Most of the stuff in here is old hymn and prayer books, but there's some other stuff, too. It's not in date order, but you should find boxes or packets belonging to many of the vicars. Some accrued more than others.' A thin smile appeared on his face. 'It depended on how many press cuttings each of them kept.'

'I thought worshipping the Lord was reward enough,' Nigel said.

'Let's just say a few of those in my profession are not averse to the oxygen of publicity.' He glanced at his watch. 'I have a few small items of business to attend to. Feel free to have a look and take as long as you wish. I'll be back in an hour or so. If you need me in the interim, give Shirley a shout in reception and she'll call me on my mobile.'

A vicar with a mobile? It didn't feel right. Nigel thanked him and turned his attention to the open chest, leaning over and inhaling a familiar scent: the smell of old paper. He picked up the first packet. Clive Hawley 1956–72. He slipped a few of the documents out, just to see what sort of material lay within. There was a host of press cuttings, almost all from the local paper, yellowing, dry and faded. Very little else, save the odd hymn sheet. Still, he burrowed deeper into the chest searching for anything relating to George Burch, taking out and stacking old books that were falling apart at the seams.

Eventually he found a tatty file, bound with string. He opened it up. The first item he came across was a newspaper report. Dated 2 June 1908, it was a small report from the local paper noting the laying of the final brick of the church and mentioning the appointment of Mr Burch. The second consisted of several sheets of notes written in a neat copperplate hand, dated 7 September of the same year. It was a letter from a Mrs Winifred Shillingford of the same parish offering what seemed to be a critique of the vicar's performance during worship. It praised his delivery but complained about his frequent divergence from Bible scripture. 'I think you will understand that for many of your congregation such contrivances are not welcome. We come to hear and celebrate the word and love of Our Saviour. Not to be handed lectures on the iniquities of the modern world nor to gain a greater understanding of current affairs,' Mrs Shillingford fulminated. The world's first trendy vicar, Nigel thought.

Going through the collection revealed other personal correspondence; some seeking or offering help, giving praise or criticism, or merely letters of thanks for sermons delivered. Dotted among them were notes written in the vicar's hand. At first he took this to be a form of private correspondence with God, but then realized that they were actually rough notes for sermons and eulogies; words were crossed out, amended, barely legible scrawls placed in the margin. For many funerals there was a short biography of the deceased, in note form, listing several biographical details and personal achievements. He felt a sense of rising excitement; the premonition that he was nearing the critical point of the chase. He went through each clipping, letter and note. No mention of Horton Rowley, but in 1913 he came across mention of a woman named Sarah Read. Next to it, in brackets, was the name 'Rowley'.

A coincidence? He doubted it.

There was a page listing details: her children's names and ages, her age, even details of Horton, the date of his death. Reading the next page made his heart beat even faster, however. It was an outline of the eulogy the vicar must have delivered at her funeral, written in a light, almost delicate hand. The first paragraph or so contained the usual obsequies; loving mother of three, formerly loyal wife to her beloved Horton, with whom she would now be reunited, and dedicated member of the parish. There was little to distinguish it from most of its kind, either before or since. A passage lower down caught his eye:

Sarah was a loyal servant of God, as many among you will know. A more pious member of the community it would be difficult to imagine. Yet what was remarkable about her faith was that it remained so despite many trials and tribulations. I speak not here of the profound loss of her much-loved husband, hard as she found that obstacle. Many of you here who knew Sarah will know of her struggles to escape the clutches of cultists from across the ocean, an experience itself that would cause many of us to turn away from the Lord's loving embrace. Not Sarah Read, as we knew her. Her experiences had the contrary effect; far from rejecting the Lord after such an event, it brought Sarah and Horton closer to him, for they knew in truth the dangers of worshipping

*false idols, celebrating the occult and the wickedness of those
who stray from the true word of God. After Horton's sad
death, seeking sanctuary, shelter and safety, Sarah moved
from her previous home and into the bosom of our parish,
where she brought the certainty of her faith, despite all her
trials. For that she will live on in our hearts as surely as she
will in God's kingdom.*

Nigel read it through once more to allow the meaning to
seep in. 'Cultists from across the ocean'? The truth was
emerging from behind an obscuring cloud: the couple had
fled a foreign country. But what cult and where? One that
worshipped false idols and celebrated the occult like some
form of voodoo? And why had she changed her name?
Was she still being pursued?

At the back of the packet was a series of sepia-tinted
photographs. Two pictures of the vicar outside the new
building, looking awkward and aloof, a pose Nigel knew
well from the time, people still adapting to the novelty of
having their picture taken. Another appeared to be of a
parish ladies' outing – three rows of behatted ladies.
'Ladies' Temperance Outing to Margate, August 1911'
was noted on the back in writing similar to the vicar's.
Beneath it he'd scribbled the names of the featured parishioners. Nigel flipped the photo back over; but he didn't
need to find Sarah Rowley's (or Read's) name. He was sure
that was her, sitting tall and proud in the middle of the
front row. The family resemblance to pictures he'd seen in
the press of Katie Drake was startling; the same full lips
and proud pose. She would have been in her late thirties
when the photo was taken, and though the years had taken

some toll she was still a handsome and charismatic presence. She seemed to possess a darker skin than the other women present; duskier, more exotic, next to their porcelain pale skin. The more he gazed at her, the more indomitable she seemed. He could sense her strength, picture the way she moved, even assign her a voice.

It never failed to amaze him how an old photograph could summon the dead.

Foster fixed himself his first cup of tea of the morning, waiting for a murky dawn to emerge through the window of his kitchen. As the tea bag steeped in the mug, he wondered where to turn next. Harris and his crew appeared to be leaving him to his own devices. So far all the Gold Group and Senior Management Team meetings had been held without him; they were often held outside his restricted hours, either early morning or late evening, and he sensed Harris was happier calling the shots without him being around.

It was Friday. Naomi had been missing almost four days. Vickers had been dropped as a suspect, and the other source of likely suspects had grown scarce – every pervert and paedophile they dragged in had an alibi. Frustration had bled into desperation. The main investigative team had resorted to bringing in teenage youths who'd been collared for under-age sex, irrespective of the fact that most of them had been under the impression the lipsticked Lolitas with whom they were consorting were above the age of consent. Yet Susie Danson had been right in one respect. If this was a sex crime then they had three or four days. That was about to pass and the sense of despair was like damp, permeating all levels of the investigation and rising even to Harris at the top, who patrolled the main incident room with a haunted, hunted expression as the media continued to howl for the girl's safe return, or at least some evidence of a breakthrough.

Foster, hunched over his steaming cup, did not share their resignation. Something told him this was about more than sex. Something told him Naomi might still be alive.

He sipped at his tea, watching helplessly as the clock on his kitchen wall ticked past 7 a.m. Foster hated watching time slip away but he wasn't due in until nine, as advised by his action plan, and there was little he could do until then. He'd been up most of the night, digesting what Gary Stamey had told him about the man who had visited their house, in particular the book he had given Leonie featuring Joe and his secret treasure. He scoured the Internet for websites about comics and graphic novels but found nothing matching the description.

From the hall he could hear the muffled sound of his mobile phone vibrating as it rattled across the surface of the sideboard – he'd taken to switching it to silent, so irritated was he by the ring tone, or the way it bleeped chirpily whenever a message came through. He reached it just before the caller was diverted through to his voicemail. It was Heather.

'Hi, did I wake you?'

'No,' he said, feeling affronted. 'I've been up for a while actually.'

'Good. Listen, I've just got in and it's been logged there was a call for you last night. From Carol Stamey, Martin's wife.'

'What time?'

'Just after eleven.'

He cursed. He'd still been up then. 'Why didn't they pass it on to me?'

'They've been instructed not to bother you, remember? They said you were off duty and asked if she was willing to speak to someone else, but she hung up. I thought you might want to follow up this morning.'

He thanked her and ended the call. Back in the kitchen he drank his tea and then called Carol Stamey back. No answer. Probably still asleep. He had no mobile number for her. Why had she hung up last night? Maybe she was calling without her husband's knowledge and he'd walked in and caught her. Or what she wanted to say was for Foster's ears only.

If it was the former, he didn't want to make it awkward for her by phoning, in case Martin Stamey answered. So he showered and dressed, got in his car and drove out to Purfleet. He doubted he'd be missed, and if they did call him then he'd make up an excuse about being at a physio-therapy session, which wouldn't be much of a lie since he did have an appointment that afternoon.

A fine drizzle was falling as Foster pulled up outside the house at 8:15 a.m., the beam of his headlights still strong. The sort of day when morning and dusk were inter-changeable. He cursed when he saw two cars parked in the driveway, a silver Jaguar at the front. He'd hoped Martin might be out at work and the kids on their way to school. A red Alfa Romeo that presumably belonged to Carol was parked behind the Jag.

He got out of the car and straightened his jacket. He could always call on the pretext that he had a few more questions. She would tell him if it was no secret from her husband. If it was, he would leave his mobile number and hope she called him on it later. He walked up the drive. Despite the gloom, there was no light on in the house. He rang the doorbell, expecting to hear the frantic barking of the dog. Instead there was silence. He rang the bell again and waited. No answer.

Foster stepped back from the house, looking at the upstairs windows. The curtains were drawn. Had they gone away? Yet Carol had called from the house late last night.

He wandered across the front lawn to the side of the house where there was a wooden door. He gave it a firm push. It swung open to reveal an alleyway leading to another wooden door. Along the side of the house were two dustbins, a few crates filled with empty wine and beer bottles and a stone flower vase teeming with spent cigarette butts. He walked along the alley, expecting at any moment to hear the dog, wondering what he'd do if it took him as an intruder and set about him. He'd not seen it the other night, merely heard it. And it sounded the size of a lion. He was not a dog lover and, from the attitude of most dogs he'd met, it appeared the feeling was mutual.

The heavy wooden door at the far end of the alley was open, too, sitting slightly ajar. Odd, he thought, for a crook like Stamey to leave the entrance to the back of his house so accessible. He looked back at the first of the doors. A Yale lock and two deadbolts, neither of which had been used. He walked through and found himself at the far corner of an enormous garden secluded by a high wall that ran around its entire perimeter. In the centre of a huge expanse of lawn was a swimming pool, covered by boards for the winter. To his right was a conservatory, beyond it a large, raised stone patio studded with garden furniture and a cover that shrouded a barbecue. At the opposite side of the garden was a stone feature or a fountain, which was switched off or no longer worked. But his eye was drawn back to the lawn.

Two bodies lay face down.

Foster hurried over. Both were dead. The first, arms out by his side, face down, was Martin Stamey, naked. The back of his head missing, ravaged by a bullet. Five yards to his south lay the body of a young boy in pyjamas – presumably the son, though his face had been almost destroyed by being shot at close range. From each body lay twin trails of blood that slicked the lawn, leading to a set of French windows. One of the doors was wide open.

Using his mobile, he called Heather, told her where he was and to get in touch with the local force.

'What's happened?' she asked, bewildered.

'I don't know,' he said and put the phone down. That's what he needed to find out.

He went to the open door, stepped inside, parting the curtains. It was the room where he and Heather had sat and spoken to Stamey the other night. He glanced around. Nothing out of place. A door to the right led to the conservatory. Again, everything was intact. The large adjoining kitchen, too. He wandered back into the room, then into the hall, which led to the front door. There was another room to the right. A sort of dining room with a large antique table, and a grandfather clock that ticked loudly. It smelled and looked as if it was rarely used.

He followed the trail of blood. It went from the French windows to the hall and up the wide, gradual steps. Foster's feet were cushioned by the thick carpet. At the top he stopped. He listened. No sound, save the hushed sweep of traffic along the nearby dual carriageway and the ticking of the downstairs clock. In front of him was a bathroom. Empty. He turned left. There was a door on the right. From the picture of a young pop star on it he guessed it was the daughter's, a feeling confirmed when he opened the door and was met by the sort of paraphernalia he'd last seen in Naomi Buckingham's room. The bed was neatly made but empty. No blood trail.

A scarlet track led to the last door on this landing while another splattered path went up a set of stairs to an upper floor. The door was ajar. He opened it and caught a sight of the reflection in the mirrored doors of a set of floor-to-ceiling cupboards. He took a deep breath and turned into the room.

Carol Stamey, spreadeagled and naked. At first he thought the sheet beneath her was scarlet but then realized from one clean corner that it was white and sluiced in her blood. There was a matting of red blood in her hair where the bullet had entered the back of her head. From the amount of viscera spread across the sheets he could see her husband had been killed beside her then dragged outside. He went upstairs; the boy's stained sheets told a similar story.

*

A few minutes later Foster stood in the garden as the crackle and bustle of a murder-scene investigation went on around him. He was oblivious to the fuss. As he stood there, trying to absorb what he had seen, a jet-black 4 x 4 pulled up as near to the house as it could. The young girl he'd seen watching television at the Stameys' house two nights before jumped out from the vehicle, dressed in her school uniform, worry and panic etched on her face. She began to run towards the house, followed by a dark-haired woman in her late thirties, who began screaming at her to stop.

As she rounded the top of the drive, Foster moved forward to intercept her. Her eyes caught his and she saw something there that brought her to an abrupt halt. Her face was pale, her eyes wide and brimming with tears. She pushed a wisp of brown hair from her face with a trembling hand, her mouth contorting. Christ, she can't be more than twelve years old, he thought.

'What's happened?' she said, her voice trembly and edgy. The brunette had caught up with them, throwing an arm around the girl.

Foster put his hands up. 'What's your name?' he said to the woman.

'Amber Davidson,' she said. 'I'm the mother of Tracey, Rachel's best friend.'

'What's HAPPENED?' the girl screamed. She tried to free herself from Amber's grip but it was too tight. Foster was grateful she was there.

'Rachel, there's been an incident.' He looked at Amber. He hoped she was supporting the girl's weight as well as preventing her running away. She seemed to read his mind and brought Rachel closer into her. Given the number of policemen and the throb of activity around the house, there was no way he could delay the truth or let her near the scene. 'Your mum, dad and brother have been attacked,' he added.

'Are they OK?'

He looked at the woman holding her. Then he looked back at the young girl. The words wouldn't come. But he didn't need to find them.

She guessed. 'Are they dead?'

He nodded his head slowly, sadly.

She continued to stare at him for a few seconds, saying nothing. 'No,' she said, shaking her head. 'No,' she repeated – louder this time, swinging her head from side to side vehemently. Her body began to convulse, her arm flailing into Amber's face, drawing blood from her lip. Foster moved forward to help restrain her. He felt her nails rake down his cheek but he managed to wrap his arms around her. Two uniformed constables joined the struggle. Rachel started to scream wordlessly; then the fight and anger drained from her body and she fell limp. Amber held her and hugged her tight, allowing Foster to let go. He took one of the constables to one side. 'Get me a WPC and a doctor as soon as possible.'

Five minutes later Rachel was staring numbly out of a squad-car window with a blanket around her shoulders, a WPC at her side while they waited for someone to come to sedate her. Foster took Amber Davidson to one side.

'What happened?' she asked, her face streaked with mascara. She was tall and lithe, and her face tanned and healthy.

Foster shook his head. 'They've been murdered. We don't know the details,' he lied. 'Where was Rachel last night?'

'With me. She slept over. The girls had a dance class. They often sleep over afterwards. Sometimes they sleep at ours, sometimes they sleep here . . . Oh, God.' She brought her hand to her mouth and her voice cracked as she contemplated what might have been.

'Why isn't she at school?'

'We got there and she remembered she'd forgotten her art project. We dropped Tracey off and came to get it.'

Out of the corner of his eye Foster saw a short but wiry old detective wander over. He did not look too pleased. Foster ignored him.

'And everything was normal here yesterday?'

'Not really,' she said.

'How so?'

'The dog had been taken ill. He'd been violently sick. Rachel was very worried when I picked her up because her dad had taken him to the vet's. I called later to find out what was going on, and they said the dog had died. They didn't want me to tell Rachel because they thought it might upset her and they wanted to tell her themselves . . . This. It's just awful.'

'How old is Rachel?'

'How old is she? She's twelve, same age as my daughter. Why?'

'Just wanted to know. And when you picked her up yesterday, did her mother say anything to you about the dog or anything else that was bothering her?'

'No, she was just worried about the dog. Carol was the

one who told me later last night that it had died. She said it had been poisoned.'

He knew the reason why she had called him last night. The dog had been killed to make an attack on them in their house easier. She had sensed the danger. Why had she not called the local force? Perhaps, given Stamey's life-style, she guessed they wouldn't be too sympathetic to her plight. But he had not been available. Had she been put through he might have prevented this happening. That damned action plan had contributed to these people's deaths.

The detective was at his side. He introduced himself to Amber Davidson as Chief Inspector Dave Alvin of Essex Police. His voice was a gruff rasp, as if he'd been gargling with gravel. 'Madam, I'd be grateful if you could spare me a few moments with my colleague here.' He broke into one of the most insincere smiles Foster had seen.

'Of course,' she said. 'I really should go back to Rachel anyway.'

Alvin continued to smile. They watched her walk back to the sanctuary of the squad car. Once she climbed inside, Alvin turned to him, still wearing the smile. He was a few inches shorter than Foster, with a flat pugilistic nose and a thatch of thick grey hair. Foster guessed mid to late fifties, old school, not the sort to mince his words.

'Could you precis exactly who the fuck you are and what the fuck you are doing questioning my witnesses?'

'Detective Chief Inspector Grant Foster, Metropolitan Police,' he said, thrusting out his hand.

'You're going to have to give me more than that, young man,' Alvin added.

Foster put his hand back in his pocket. 'I'm the man who found those people dead.'

'So I'm told. You're a long way from home. Satnav knackered, is it?'

'Carol Stamey tried to reach me last night. I paid her and her husband a visit on Wednesday. In relation to a case I'm working on.'

Alvin pulled a long cigarette from a pack in his pocket and lit it. He exhaled copiously. 'What case would that be?'

'Fourteen-year-old girl abducted in London, her mum murdered.'

Alvin's bushy grey eyebrows rose perceptibly. 'The one on the news. The blonde girl?'

Foster nodded.

'You think this is related?' His rising intonation betrayed his scepticism.

'I do,' Foster said.

Another loud exhale. 'Care to tell me why?'

Foster paused. A light rain had started to fall. 'Quid pro quo. I'll answer your questions if you answer mine.'

'Fire away.'

'What sort of person was Martin Stamey?'

'A reprehensible piece of shit.'

'Big time or small time?'

'Small time but thought he was big. I think he's rubbed someone even bigger up the wrong way.'

'What sort of game was he in?'

'Smuggling fags, fencing, wee bit of extortion. My turn. Why do you think this is related to your kidnap and murder?'

'Stamey and my victim were related.'

'In what way?'

'Cousins.'

'Close?'

'Distant.'

'And? Was your victim shot?'

'Strangled. But the body was dragged outside. Throat slit. Did Stamey have any obvious enemies who might do this?'

'He wasn't a popular man. We'll have a task narrowing them down to single figures. Was your victim done like this? Forced entry in the middle of the night?'

'No, we think she invited the killer in. He took the girl when she came back from school. Carol Stamey tried to call me last night. Did she try and call your lot, too?'

'No. And it sounds to me as if there's fuck-all similarity between the two murders.'

'What about the girl?'

'What about her? She was staying at a friend's. Had she been here, she'd be worm food, too.'

'Perhaps. Maybe they would have kidnapped her.'

'Maybe. But maybe is not enough. If you want to take this case over, you're going to have to give me a damn sight more than that, mate.'

Foster looked away. The rain was now slanting down in sheets, pouring off his shaven head. It had got darker. His opposite number was right: Foster knew this murder fitted in, but he did not yet know how. A thought nestled at the back of his mind, but he would need to be alone to tease it out.

'Look,' Alvin said, his tone softening. 'A fourteen-year-old kid is missing and we can't ignore that. I'll personally let you know how we're progressing. But, if I'm right and this is a contract job, then you know as well as I do how difficult it is to nail someone for it. But if it wasn't a hit, I'll let you know and we can talk some more. Deal?'

Foster nodded. It was the best he could hope for. 'What about the girl?'

'We'll make sure she's safe, that's she's watched. Maybe see if there's any other family that can take her in the long run.'

'There isn't. I know the family history.'

'OK. Maybe a friend. But that's for the future. I'll bear in mind what you said and make sure she gets the protection she needs.'

He pulled his car keys from his pocket. 'The dog was poisoned,' he told Alvin. 'Last night. You might want to get on to the vet's and get it autopsied before they sling it in the incinerator.'

As he drove away, windscreen wipers flailing back and forth, he went back to the thought that had passed through his mind when he was speaking to Alvin. Did the killer expect the daughter to be there? She was spared because she was elsewhere, from either being murdered or kidnapped. If he was right, surely the killer would've been watching the house and seen her go? He pictured the Stamey boy dead in the garden. He hadn't been kidnapped. If he was right and this was related, what was the pattern here? Like an early childhood memory it was hazy, just out of reach.

He left the thought for a while and flicked on his stereo, wired up to his music player, set to play randomly. A song he didn't recognize came on and he hummed along absent-mindedly despite not knowing the words. His mind refused to be diverted.

He hoped Alvin kept his word and Rachel was made as safe as possible. The killer might be back. Apart from her and Leonie, there were three male descendants still living in the UK. One, a Stamey, was in prison. Safest place to be. Another, Anthony Chapman, they knew little about. They needed to find him. Quickly.

The last was Gary Stamey. He remembered the body of the other young Stamey boy in the garden. Something clicked.

He needed to make Gary safe.

13

That Friday morning had gone badly for Nigel. A girl was missing and her life in mortal danger, yet he spent precious hours stumbling through another screen test with predictably dire results. This time the show's producer Lysette, a fresh-faced, enthusiastic brunette in her mid-thirties had been there along with Guy, the glum cameraman, yet despite her exhortations and encouragements Nigel simply couldn't get it right. Partly because his mind was elsewhere, partly because the scripts they kept giving him to read were so dire. He simply could not rid himself of self-consciousness. When they'd watched the final playback before lunch, Nigel had winced at his stilted voice and nervous, flicking eyes. Lysette made some positive noises but he knew that was to protect his ego. Guy's world-weary sighing offered a more honest assessment. He felt certain that the next few days would bring a phone call putting him out of his misery, announcing they were going to look for another presenter.

Foster's panicked call was welcome, despite the detective's agitated state. 'You remember that list you gave me?' he said. 'The one with all the descendants? Presumably it was so small because you couldn't trace the maternal line back beyond this couple.' Nigel agreed it was. 'Well, two of the people on that list were murdered last night, as well as another connected to them. Katie Drake is dead, too.

Naomi Buckingham is missing. Another girl on the list is missing and her mother dead. We know from our records that a family of four emigrated to New Zealand seven years ago. That leaves three people, one of whom Heather and I spoke to yesterday. His name is Gary Stamey; it's his sister Leonie that's missing. The mum died of an overdose, apparently. He told us that a man visited his sister shortly before she vanished. This man wore a suit and gave them a book about a boy called Joe and his secret treasure. Can you see where I'm going?'

Nigel did. The past was invading the present.

'I'm thinking the past has finally caught up with this family.'

'What about the people left on the list?'

'Don't worry about the Stameys. One's in prison. One girl is missing and the other girl is safe. At least, I hope she is. Leave the eleven-year-old boy to me. I want you to find the non-Stamey. He's called Anthony Chapman, born in East London in 1964. I've asked for a search of all the databases we use and so far we can't find any record of him. None whatsoever. I was hoping you might be able to work your magic and see what you can find out about him. Because if I'm right, and someone's working their way through the bloodline, then he could be next.'

With that, he rang off.

Nigel already had Anthony Chapman's birth certificate. He worked forwards from that and searched for death and marriage certificates but found neither. He was the only child of Reginald and Edith Chapman, both of whom were dead. Edith was the last to go in 2003, aged 72. She died at her home in Selby Street, Bethnal Green. The same address that was supplied on Anthony's birth certificate. That gave him one route to explore. In the absence of any others, he rode the tube to Bethnal Green, finding the street tucked away off Vallance Road, a winding old Victorian terrace that was once home to the Kray twins. The area still carried the flavour of the old East End. Selby Street was small and almost traffic-free. The front doors opened straight out on to the street. Neighbours stood chatting to one another. All it required was a few children kicking a ball back and forth across the road – but they were in school, and he doubted the nostalgia would stretch that far.

The Chapmans' former home was at number 17. He headed towards two women standing talking outside number 11; both turned to eye him suspiciously as he approached.

He smiled. 'Sorry to bother you, ladies. This might seem rather impertinent, but I'm looking for some information you might be able to help me with.' His manner and voice appeared to make them soften, but a glint of suspicion remained. 'Did either of you know old Mrs Chapman who used to live at number 17?'

One of the women, who had been pulling furiously on a cigarette, let a stream of smoke out of her nostrils. 'I did. I live here.' She gestured to the door at her back. 'I knew old Edith pretty well. Lovely old lass. She died a few years ago. Why do you wanna know?'

Nigel was prepared for that question. He was a dreadful liar but he feared the truth might persuade people to clam up. 'I'm researching my family tree. It turns out that I'm related to Mrs Chapman. Of course, she's dead. But I'm very keen to trace her son, Anthony.'

'Son,' she said, disbelief in her voice and written across her face. 'There was no son. She and Reg didn't have no kids.'

'Are you certain of that?'

'Yeah. I moved in here twenty-odd years ago. There weren't no son then and she never mentioned none. You sure you got the right person?'

Nigel looked at his feet. 'I think so. Anthony Chapman was born to Edith and Reginald Chapman of this address back in 1964.' From his pocket he produced a folded copy of the birth certificate. Both women leaned in to see, trailing with them a combination of perfume and smoke.

The resident of number 11 peered at it for several seconds, then looked at Nigel. 'Well, you learn something new every day, don't you? She never once mentioned a son. We just thought they never had any kids. Medical reasons or something. And all that time she had a boy she never mentioned. Wonder what happened to him?'

'That's what I'd like to know,' Nigel replied. 'Is there anyone around here who might know? Another elderly resident who might have lived around here then – or the people who now live at number 17, perhaps?'

'No, it's a bloke, out-of-towner. Not from round here.' She thought for a few seconds. Pulled hard on her cigarette and thought some more. Nigel noticed for the first time that she was wearing a pair of carpet slippers on her feet. She pointed her finger at him and started nodding her head. 'You know where you could try? St Matthew's Church. It was her life, that place.'

The church was deserted. He idled away the afternoon until it came to life, as the early winter light closed in and the temperature, barely above freezing anyway, began to plummet. At least the rain had stopped. St Matthew's, despite having almost been flattened by the Luftwaffe, was the focal point of the local community, and shared its rich, villainous history. It was here that the funeral services of the Krays were held. In the gathering gloom, silhouetted against a clear dusk, the old church, still surrounded by the churchyard that afforded it a distance from the hurly-burly, seemed to loom in judgement over the area.

The vicar was inside, laying out hymn books. Nigel strode down the aisle and introduced himself.

'You better be quick,' he said, eyes twinkling cheerily.

He was in his late sixties, Nigel guessed, florid face, rheumy eyes, exuding a gentle, avuncular warmth. Nigel could imagine parishioners queuing up to share their problems with him.

'It's about one of your former parishioners actually. An Edith Chapman?'

He looked up. 'Edith? Dear woman. What about her?'

'Well, I hope you'll excuse me prying like this, but I'm a genealogist.'

'Fascinating! I'm a bit of an amateur myself.'

Yes, Nigel thought, seems like everyone is these days. 'Really? Excellent. But going back to Mrs Chapman . . .'

'My mother's side is easy,' the vicar continued. 'I'm back to parish registers. But that was where I inherited the ecclesiastical calling from. So there's a record there. But my father's is a mystery beyond about 1878 or something. Bizarre how the trail goes cold, isn't it? Perhaps I should employ you?'

'My rates are good,' Nigel said. 'Mrs Chapman . . .'

'Yes, a dear old woman. A valuable member of the parish. What is it you want to know?'

'The records say she had a son.'

His face changed. The twinkle departed. 'Do they now,' he said. He continued about his chore for a few seconds without speaking.

'Sorry, I don't meant to pry.'

'Just on whose behalf are you carrying out this research, Mr Barnes?'

Nigel weighed up his options. It was the question he feared. He knew he would not be able to lie to a man of the cloth, regardless of his atheism. It was not right.

'The police.'

The vicar's eyes narrowed, their friendliness all but vanished. 'And what would the police be doing seeking the son of a harmless old lady? She was never in trouble for one second of her life.'

'I know. We're trying to find her son. We think he may be in danger.'

'What sort of danger?'

'I do apologize, but I'm not at liberty to say.'

The vicar chewed the inside of his lip, sizing Nigel up. He could feel his cheeks redden. He could hear voices behind him, the sound of footsteps on the stone floor.

'Tell me, Mr Barnes. Do you pray?'

Nigel was momentarily taken aback by the question, wondering if it was some sort of trick. 'No, not really,' he said eventually.

'Well, you will this evening.' He handed Nigel a prayer book. 'Evening service is about to start. Once that's completed and I've finished attending to the parishioners, we can have a chat and I'll see if I can help.'

Nigel waited. Once the service had finished and the congregation cleared the vicar invited him through to his office at the back of the church. He asked him to take a seat, offered a hot drink that Nigel refused, requesting just a glass of water.

He eased himself into a chair behind the wooden desk and sat back with a sigh. 'It's good to take the weight off after a long evening. Now, tell me, why do you want to find Mrs Chapman's son?'

'There's a chance his life could be in danger.'

The vicar nodded. The rosiness of his cheeks, a hooked nose and twinkling eyes gave him the look of a kindly Mr Punch. 'Well, if you're correct, then she was right all along,' he replied.

'Who was? Mrs Chapman?'

'Yes.' He took small sip of his coffee. 'Presumably as a genealogist you're fully aware of the Church's role in the community. With adoptions and suchlike?'

Nigel was. There were many agencies that had arranged adoptions in the past, the Church being the most prominent, mostly in transferring the unwanted offspring of the poor to the rich. 'Yes, I am.'

'Well, my predecessor, the Reverend Robert Daedulus, was particularly active in that regard.' He peered over his glasses at Nigel. 'And he was not a stickler for record-keeping, if you get my drift.' The vicar took off his glasses and began to suck on one arm. 'Some years ago, when her husband died, I spent a fair amount of time helping Mrs

Chapman deal with her loss. She told me my predecessor had arranged the adoption of her son in November 1964. He was only two months old.'

The only reaction Nigel could think of was blasphemous, so he remained silent.

'Was he troublesome? In some way damaged?'

'She was adamant that any problems with the boy were not behind her reasoning. Neither did she want any payment. She said she simply wanted the boy to be safe. She told me that Reverend Daedulus had arranged a private adoption. She told me the son was a mistake. That she never planned to have children. Obviously, she did not believe in termination so she had the child, and nursed him through his first weeks. But all the time she wanted to get rid of him.'

'That sounds very cold.'

'Doesn't it just? I felt that myself. But another thing about my job is that you learn not to judge. I leave that to my boss.' He winked, took another sip of coffee before continuing. 'I think she must have sensed my own shock. She was not a drinking woman by any means, but she'd taken a few glasses that evening. She leaned over her kitchen table and fixed me with a beady stare.' The vicar did an approximation of her, leaning forward towards Nigel. 'She said, "If the boy had stayed with me, they would have got him. Eventually. Just like they might get me. I couldn't take the risk of them coming and what they might do. So I did what any mother should do and made sure he was safe." I asked who "they" were. She wouldn't say. I also asked her why she and her husband didn't move, or change their name or emigrate even. She said it didn't matter.

'She told me her Aunt Margaret said that no matter what she did, they would find her one day. Her aunt kept screaming, "They will never relent . . . Protect yourself as if from the Devil himself." She told her to never, ever have children. Her grandmother had told her all this on her deathbed. Margaret believed every word and so did Edith.

'Her grandmother told no one else. Margaret did, but her family didn't believe her. She was mad, they said. They put her away in the loony bin. Left her there to rot. Edith said it was an awful, awful place. She was the only person who ever went to visit her. She would go there without telling anyone. Only her husband. Until Margaret died. She believed her aunt. She told me, "Maybe I was wrong, maybe I was right. I couldn't risk it. 'They will not relent!' she said. Margaret saw something, something awful that persuaded her." And that was it – she said no more about it.'

Nigel wondered who 'they' were. Someone or something so unspeakable that a woman would rather give away her firstborn to strangers than risk him coming to harm.

'That night was the only night she spoke about it,' the vicar added. 'She knew her son was all right and was doing well. That was comfort enough.'

How? Nigel thought. How could that possibly be a comfort? Here was a woman with no family, just a husband, who died well before her. Who had no other family. Who had given away her only child. Whoever 'they' were must have terrified her to make such a sacrifice. The vicar appeared to read his mind.

'She was a very solitary woman. Happy keeping to herself. The church was her life, but she played no active part in it, to be honest. There were friends, there was the bingo hall and that was it. A woman of very simple tastes.'

'Did you ever speculate yourself about who the people were she was hiding away from?'

'Sure, but I came up with nothing other than a few wild ideas.' He drained his coffee mug. 'Who are the people putting his life at risk?'

'We don't know.'

'Well, then. It's a mystery all round, isn't it?' He checked his watch. 'I better be getting back or my wife will be starting to worry. Pains me to say it, but there are parts of my parish where it's best not to be after dark.'

Nigel stood and put on his coat. 'Your predecessor left no note or record as to who the adoptive parents were?'

He shook his head dolefully. 'No, and to be fair to you, Mr Barnes, I wouldn't pass it on even if he did. Look at it this way: you show up and tell a man in his mid-forties that not only was he adopted, but there are nameless people out there who want to kill him. I don't think that'd be wise, do you?'

'No, but he might prefer the truth to death.'

'Fair enough. But it's academic. There are no records. Or at least, none I'm aware of.'

Nigel sighed. Without that there would no chance whatsoever of them tracking down Anthony Chapman or whoever he may be now. That also meant any pursuers would struggle, too. He started to head for the door, then stopped. 'The aunt who told her to give away her child. Did Edith say which asylum she was held in?'

The vicar nodded. 'Colney Hatch. She said it was hell on earth.'

14

Light beamed through the bay window at the front of Susie Danson's house, though Foster could see the room was empty as he walked up her path. At least it told him someone was home. He could see a piano and a violin on the stand. He'd never had her down as a music lover. Did she have kids? He was ashamed to say he couldn't remember. He'd probably never asked. She was separated, he knew that. He was at the door by now, so rang the bell.

Ten seconds later Susie Danson opened the door, broad smile, lipstick blazing bright as ever. Her hair was up, gold earrings dangled from her ears and she was wearing a black dress that fitted snugly.

'Oh,' she said, her smile fading, replaced by a puzzled look. 'Grant.'

'You look fantastic,' he said genuinely.

'Thanks.' She sounded nervous, looking more than once over his shoulder.

'Sorry to turn up unannounced. I did try calling, but no answer.'

'It's actually not the best time. I'm expecting someone any minute.'

'I won't take long,' Foster replied. But it was only then that he appreciated what was happening. She was waiting for a date. He felt a pang, a twinge he didn't recognize, deep in his stomach.

Jealousy. It had been a while since he'd felt anything like that. 'Oh,' he blurted out. 'I'm sorry.'

She shook her head, as if remonstrating with herself. 'Look, come in,' she added and grabbed his shoulder and pulled him inside.

The house was warm and he could smell her scent heavy in the air. He watched her walk away down the hall and the pang grew stronger. Why didn't he ask her out all those years ago when he had the bloody chance? Because you're a cretin, he answered. And there was every chance she'd say no. As he followed, he put all that to the back of his mind – there was a job to do and he needed her help.

In the kitchen, bare yet beautifully furnished and lit, she went straight to the fridge and pulled out a beer, handing it to him with a smile. 'If I remember rightly, you like a drink or two. Red wine, isn't it? "As long as it ain't white," you used to say. I don't have any red, but is beer OK?' He nodded, impressed at her recall. White wine was for women and Antipodeans. As if to illustrate, she pulled out a bottle of white and poured herself a large glass. 'I don't like drinking alone and your arrival has made me suddenly very thirsty.' She chuckled to herself.

'What's the joke?' he asked, taking a swig of beer.

She shook her head. 'Nothing,' and let out a sigh whose meaning he couldn't decipher. 'What's the emergency? I'd like you to tell me you've found Naomi.'

'No. Still missing.'

Susie grimaced.

'You think she's dead, don't you?'

'I think there's a good chance she is,' she replied. 'If she's not, she very soon will be.'

'What if I told you that I think there's much more to this case than meets the eye?'

'Like what?'

'I've just been to a homicide in Essex. Three people murdered – father, mother and son. Young daughter spared, though probably by accident because she was elsewhere.'

'I don't see the link.'

'They were distant relations to Katie Drake. I think this all has something to do with what happened in the past.'

Susie took a small sip of her drink, looked Foster in the eye. 'Everything has something to do with what happened in the past,' she said. 'Tell me about the crime scene.'

'The father and the son were shot in the head in their beds and dragged out into the garden. The mother was shot but left in her bed.'

'Shot? Completely different method of killing to Katie Drake.'

'I know. But dragged out into the garden?'

'I'd need to see the pictures, Grant. Visit the crime scene, look at post mortem reports.'

'But let's just say they were related. Let's just say that the man who murdered Katie Drake and abducted Naomi also killed these people. What would you say then?'

She shrugged. 'OK, I'll play along. The father and son, were they the related ones?'

'By blood, yes.'

'Then you might say that by dragging their bodies into the garden the killer is in some way showing what he has done to the world. If there is some dark secret in the past, then he's dragging it out into the light for all to see. But why he would choose to kidnap and not kill – or at least, not kill Naomi – if he is avenging some past wrong is less clear. Maybe there is some information he wants to extract from her before he kills her, or she represents something.' She held her hands out. 'Sorry, Grant. Get me some info from the crime scene and I'll be able to do a better job than winging it in my kitchen.'

Foster put his hand up to stop her apology. 'You've been a great help already. It's not my case so the info might not be too easy to get hold of, but I'll do my best.'

She grabbed her handbag and fished out a business card. 'They're the best ways to contact me, particularly the e-mail.'

He was just about to ask her what the occasion was that evening when the doorbell rang. She jumped almost a foot. 'Sorry,' she said. 'I'm not used to all these surprises.'

'Should I make myself scarce?' he joked. 'Leave by the back door?' He checked his watch. 'I need to leave anyway. I'm collecting an eleven-year-old boy from a care home.'

She didn't appear to hear him. 'Hmmm, wait here,' she said distractedly.

She went to the door. He heard her open it, a few muffled words being said, and the smack of lip being lifted from lip. Footsteps down the hall. Susie explaining she'd had a visitor, walking back in slightly red-faced.

Followed by DS Brian Harris.

Neither of the men spoke for several seconds. Foster knew Harris's marriage had been in trouble, but not quite this deep.

'My life was very simple before I got involved with the Met,' Susie said. 'Drink, Brian? Lemonade or Coke.'

'Just water,' he said, eyeing Foster coolly.

He'd forgotten Harris was teetotal. It explained quite a lot.

She waved another beer at Foster but he declined. She topped up her own glass and let out another barely perceptible chuckle.

'So what are you doing here, Grant?' Harris said wearily. He looked worn, the events of the previous days having taken their toll.

'Running an idea past Susie. It's a slice of luck you're here, actually. I was about to go to the office and catch you there, but I would've wasted my time. The triple murder out in Essex this morning. Have you heard about it?'

Harris took his water from Susie, nodded his thanks and plunged his empty hand into his pocket. She left the room. Both men watched her go.

'Heard about it?' Harris replied. 'Unfortunately, yes. It's threatening to take away some of the TV exposure and column inches we hoped to hog with Stephen Buckingham's appeal tomorrow. Time's running out. It's our last throw of the dice. Let's hope the media still think the story of a missing fourteen-year-old is more newsworthy than the murder of a family of a well-known gangster.'

'I think they're connected,' Foster said bluntly.

Harris looked amused. 'Are you being serious?'

Foster nodded. 'Yes, sir. I was there.'

Harris's expression changed to bemusement. 'So that's where you were. I could have done with you pounding on a few doors.'

Foster ignored the slight.

'On what basis do you think the cases are connected?' Harris asked.

'The victims were related.'

'How?'

'Distant cousins. They shared a common maternal ancestor.' Before Harris could intervene, he continued. 'The hair left on Katie Drake's clothing belonged to a male. You know they couldn't obtain anything other than an mtDNA sample. It turns out that the person who owns that hair and Katie Drake shared a maternal ancestor. Could have been ten thousand years ago, could have been a hundred. Forensics knew that and didn't deem it useful. I thought about it and decided to ask Nigel Barnes, the genealogist who worked on the Karl Hogg case, to discover just how many maternal relations of Katie Drake were still alive. Turns out he can't trace their ancestry back beyond about 1890, which means there weren't many. I fed the names into the database and I came across the Stamey family.'

He paused for breath. Susie had walked back into the room. Harris's face wore an inscrutable look, but Foster knew he was listening. 'Go on,' he said.

'Leonie Stamey's mother was found dead of an overdose. She was a junkie. On the same day, Leonie disappeared. She was fourteen.' He let the words hang in the air for a few seconds.

'She was kidnapped?'

'The local force looked into it. They decided she ran away.'

'Sounds like valid reasoning to me. There was hardly any attraction for her to stay.'

'Then we have the slaughter of the other branch of the Stamey family.'

'Which has all the hallmarks of a gangland slaying, Grant. I see where you're going with this but I don't see anything but coincidence. They were related. So what? I'm not an expert in genealogy but even I know that you and I could share an ancestor way back in the mists of time.'

Foster expected nothing less. 'I know, sir. I don't expect you to give me teams of men and resources to spend time on it. But I think there's a link. I'm in contact with the SIO on the Stamey family killing.'

'What does he think?'

'That Martin Stamey was a naughty boy who crossed the wrong person.'

Harris gestured as if to say, 'There you go.' Then he admitted, 'Look, Grant, you know as well as I do that we aren't making a great deal of progress on finding Naomi, dead or alive. You keep pursuing this link if you want. But I need something far more concrete if we're going to invest some manpower in it.'

Foster nodded. 'I need some help. There are three living relatives from that maternal bloodline. The Stamey's daughter, who was at a friend's when they killed her family; she's under protection. There's a man in his forties who may or may not exist. And there's Leonie Stamey's younger brother. If I'm right, he might be next. I'd like to put him in a safe house.'

'Where is he now?'

'In a care home. He's a walking crime wave. I'm on my way to get him now.'

'You're talking about taking him out of a home and putting him somewhere safe on the basis of a hunch? Sorry, Grant. Essex murder squad has reason to protect the girl. I can't see the justification for protecting this boy. Anyway, how can anyone know he's in the care home? The details of who's there aren't public knowledge. He's as safe there as anywhere.' He looked back at his watch once again. 'Look, I must shoot. Keep me informed how this line of investigation goes. Find me some proof of a definite link and we'll have a chat about this again. We're desperate for some kind, any kind, of breakthrough.' He looked at his watch. 'The performance is due to start in half an hour,' he said to Susie.

'I'll phone a cab,' she said.

'No need. I'm driving.'

'OK, give me a second.' She left them alone once more.

Foster drained his beer. 'Going anywhere nice?'

'The opera. *Don Giovanni.* You seen it?'

'Not recently, no.' He put the beer down on the side. 'I'll leave you to it then.'

Harris nodded. 'Enjoy your weekend.'

Fat chance of that, Foster thought as he made his way down the hall and out. The sound of your slurping lips kissing Susie will be echoing through my mind.

'Do you have satellite TV?'

They were the first words that Gary had spoken since Foster collected him from the care home. All the way back he sat sullenly staring out of the window, his desire to be hostile quenching any curiosity about where he was being

154

taken. Foster had turned on the radio, found a station that was playing something urban and gritty that he believed Gary might like, but eventually turned it off after he found the beat so banal and repetitive that he'd switched back to a station playing classic hits. Gary did not stir.

'You're coming to my place. Not for long. Just until we get something else sorted,' Foster had told him. Again, no response.

It was late when they got back, and Foster took Gary into the lounge and introduced him to the television.

'Yes, I do,' he said in reply to Gary's query. 'God knows why. Just more channels with nothing worth watching.' He handed Gary the remote. 'Find yourself something to watch. As long as it's not pornographic or violent.'

There was a childlike glimmer of excitement in Gary's eyes as he took the thick piece of plastic from Foster. He turned the television on and went straight to the screen listing the available channels.

'You know what you're doing then,' Foster said.

Gary shrugged. 'I've stolen loads of these. Is that the new Sony plasma?' he added, nodding towards the television.

'It is, yes,' Foster said.

'Thought so. They're the lick,' he said enthusiastically. He looked at Foster for the first time with something other than disdain. 'You must be loaded.'

'Well, I had a bit of time off work recently. Upgraded my home entertainment system. Which reminds me.' He grabbed the remote off Gary, hit mute then handed it back. 'If one item from this house goes missing then I'll find you and make sure you go to a young offenders' institution for a very long time. A really nasty one. You get what I'm saying?'

Foster had already performed an inventory in his mind of all the possessions Gary might steal, and the TV and stereo were the only likely ones. They were both insured, so that didn't matter. His father's cellar, or what little remained of it, wasn't, but he guessed Gary had not yet developed a taste for vintage claret.

Gary hit mute and the sound returned. 'I ain't gonna nick nowt off no copper.' His eyes locked on the screen then glanced back at Foster. 'Just why's you brought me here anyway? You not a fucking nonce, are you?'

'No,' Foster said wearily. 'I'm no nonce. And when you're here in my house I'd be grateful if you watched the language. I brought you here because I'm interested in keeping you out of trouble. I think you can help me with the case I'm working on, and you can't do that when you're up to no good.'

'I ain't fuck . . . I ain't helping no police, man.'

'Even if it helps find your sister?'

Gary paused. His eyes went back to the screen. He scrolled down to the movies and brought up the options. Foster left him to it and went into the kitchen, rustled around in a drawer, pulled out a pile of takeaway leaflets and went back to the room. Gary had settled on an action movie. Foster really couldn't be bothered acting as censor. The kid was beyond being corrupted anyway.

'Pizza, Chinese or Indian?' he said, brandishing the menus. 'There's even one that delivers all sorts: burgers, pizza, chicken, pasta, you name it.'

'Burger,' Gary said without hesitation. 'Don't want

nothing that stinks. Can I have it with cheese? No onions, though.'

'One cheeseburger,' Foster said. He took the phone from its cradle in the hall and wandered through to the kitchen. He dialled the number and while he waited for an answer he took the cork from a bottle of Bordeaux and found a glass. He was about to fill it to the brim, remembered he was in effect responsible for a child, and poured himself what he considered a half measure. A heavily accented young man took his order for two cheeseburgers and two small bottles of Coke and said it would be with him in forty-five minutes. Foster took his wine and went back to the sitting room.

Until the doorbell rang with their food, they didn't speak a word. Gary stared at the screen as if in a daze, a stray finger occasionally wandering distractedly up his nostril en route to his mouth. Foster resisted the temptation to say that he should save his hunger for his meal and instead sipped at his wine and tried to work out what the hell he was going to do next. Gary was here. Safer, he felt sure, than at the care home. But he could not stay here indefinitely. Tomorrow was Saturday and Foster wasn't supposed to be working. He could have Gary for the weekend but he'd need a plan for the week. If it came to the worst – if Naomi hadn't been found and there weren't any new leads – he could drop him at the care home during the day and then pick him up after work.

There was also the small matter of how he was going to tell him about the murders of his aunt, uncle and cousin.

That could wait.

They ate their burgers in silence. For such a small,

skinny boy he knew how to put away his food. Must have hollow legs, Foster thought, immediately hearing his mother's voice, which used to level the accusation at him. Gary hoovered up his burger, all his chips and didn't refuse when Foster offered him a few of his. He also guzzled the Coke and belched loudly and without apology when it was finished. Foster cleared away the detritus. When he returned, the film was over. Gary was already flicking through the various screens to see what was up next. He looked up at Foster.

'You live here on your own?'

'I do, yes.'

'You got no wife or kids?'

'No, I don't.'

'Why not?'

Foster heard his mother's voice again. Disconcerting when it was conjured up by the voice of an eleven-year-old boy.

'Let's just say that I'm not the marrying kind.'

'You're a cockmuncher?' A look of horror spread across his face. 'Man, I knew you was a nonce.'

'Listen, I'm not gay. Not being married doesn't mean you fancy men. I've had lots of girlfriends. I just haven't settled down with any of them. And don't use words like cockmuncher. It's disrespectful.' Have you heard yourself? Foster thought. Allowing yourself to become affronted by a child. Great. Now I've managed to sound like both my parents in the space of two minutes. 'I've got a daughter, actually.'

'Where is she?'

'What is this, twenty questions?' He saw Gary's face

darken. He felt a twinge of guilt. The kid was at least beginning to communicate with him. He softened his tone. 'Sorry, sorry. She lives in Scotland with her mother. I've not seen her since she was a baby.'

'How old is she now?'

'Fourteen. Fifteen in December.'

Gary's eyes widened. 'You haven't seen her in all that time? Man,' he added, shaking his head. 'If I ever have a kid then I'll never let it go anywhere. I'd keep an eye on it all the time.' He looked down at his hands. 'I know why you brought me here.'

'You do?'

'Yeah. You think I'm in danger.'

Foster paused. There was no point lying to the kid. He was hardly naive. 'How close were you to your Uncle Martin?'

He wrinkled his nose. 'I met him a few times. And my cousins. But I haven't seen them in ages. Mum took us round there once before she died. Why?'

'They've been found dead. All of them apart from Rachel.'

'Oh.' He didn't seem to know how to take the news.

'We think your uncle got mixed up with some bad people. We don't think you're in danger, too. But we want to keep you safe for a few days, just to make sure.'

'Were they murdered?'

'Yes, they were.'

'And you're going to catch the people who killed them?'

'I'm going to help catch them. Another police force is working on it.'

Gary looked away at the far wall, absorbing what he'd been told, the hard carapace falling away to reveal the child once more. Foster felt an inkling of sympathy. This kid has faced nothing but woe and misery. Who could blame him for kicking against the pricks the way he did?

He halted that line of thought. Is that what looking after a kid does? he wondered. He'd only had one under his roof for a couple of hours and already he'd turned into a politically correct hand-wringer; the sort who excuses vile behaviour by bleating about the troubled backgrounds of those who commit it.

He was on the verge of delivering a lecture, something sanctimonious about how the tough hand life had dealt him didn't mitigate all his crimes and it was time to take responsibility, when he saw the kid was about to say something. He saved the sermon.

'Leonie knew this would happen.'

'She knew what would happen?'

'That something would happen to Uncle Martin.'

'She did?' He edged forward on the armchair. 'What did she say, Gary?'

The boy sat in silence, eyes downcast now. Foster restrained himself, trying not to bully the kid, force him to clam up.

Eventually Gary spoke once more. 'She said it was a secret. That I couldn't tell anyone.'

'Something has happened to your Uncle Martin, though. And your aunt and cousin, too. Something bad. I need you to tell me so we can help find who it was and stop them before they do it again, and so we can keep Rachel safe.'

Gary continued his silence. It was clear to Foster he was weighing up breaking his sister's confidence. Foster tried not to appear too desperate, though he felt like shaking him to get at the truth. Gary knew more than he had let on, he was certain. By yielding this once, Foster hoped it might break the seal and the rest of what the boy knew would seep out.

'Leonie said that we'd strayed from a path. Because we'd strayed we was to be punished unless we got back on it. She said I would be all right because she was back on it soon and I would be, too. But Mum, Uncle Martin, Uncle Dave, they wasn't and they was gonna suffer.'

'Did you ask her what she meant by suffer?'

He shook his head. 'I just knew it was bad, innit? Then Mum died . . .'

'Do you know who she meant by "we", Gary? When she said "we" had strayed from a path?'

He shrugged. 'Our family, I think.'

'Did she say what this path was? Was she talking about Jesus?'

He nodded his head. 'It was all about Jesus. Jesus was gonna come back. I didn't understand it but he was gonna come back and some people wouldn't be OK because they weren't ready but we'd be ready.'

Foster knew the key to all this lay tangled in the details of the man who had visited Leonie Stamey – the same man he suspected had visited Katie Drake.

'Do you remember anything else about what she said, Gary? Anything at all?'

The boy thought for some time. Foster could see he was tired and it was getting near midnight. He would desist in a minute, let him get some rest. He'd made up the spare bedroom, his old room when he'd lived at home as a kid.

'I can't remember,' he said sullenly. Then he smiled. 'She started dressing funny.'

'Really? How?'

'She just started dressing funny. Like she used to wear short skirts and tops and things like that. But then she stopped. She wore like long dresses and tops. There was some girls who was her friends who kept teasing her about it and stuff. Then she wasn't friends with them no more. Said they was wicked and she didn't mean good wicked, she meant bad. They said she was a stuck-up bitch. One of them punched her and she didn't fight back. I was amazed because she was a good fighter, Leonie. No one used to mess with her before then.'

'Did she tell you why she changed the way she dressed?'

'No. Think it was something to do with what the man said. She changed a lot,' grinning almost, putting much emphasis on the last word of the sentence. The smile disappeared from his face. 'She said she'd make sure I was safe,' he added softly.

'Well, she's not around, Gary. It's up to us to keep you safe.'

The eyes burned with hatred. 'You think she's dead, don'tcha?' Voice rising with anger.

Foster held his hands out. 'I don't know, Gary.'

'Well, I know. She isn't.'

'Because she promised to come back for you?'

'Because I've heard from her.'

Foster almost did a double take. 'Since she disappeared?'

No response.

'Gary, if Leonie has been in touch with you then I need to know.'

Again, the boy didn't speak but stared ahead at the wall.

Foster rubbed his face. 'People have died, Gary. You can help me find the people who are doing this. You can help me find the fourteen-year-old girl who went missing last week.' Still no reaction. 'You can help me find Leonie and stop anything happening to Rachel.'

Gary shook his head slowly; he looked as if he might cry. 'I promised.'

Foster sighed. 'Please, Gary.'

Another slow shake of the head. The kid was a stubborn mule.

'If you don't, I'm going to have to take you in for obstructing the police.'

'You don't scare me. You think I've not been arrested before?'

The kid had a point. More than a hundred times, if his charge sheet was to be believed.

'I can help you find Leonie, Gary. Then you'll be safe.'

Silence. His eyes appeared to brighten, as if lit by hope. But he still wouldn't talk.

'Sleep on it. Let's talk in the morning.'

Her mother forced the corners of her mouth into a smile but she could not hide the sadness that seeped out from her sorrowful eyes, like gas from an unlit lamp. Sarah stood in the heavy dress; despite its prettiness, for all she cared it could have been a suit of tar and feathers. Her younger sisters twittered playfully around them, delighted at the prospect of a wedding and an open house.

'Will there be dancing?' Henrietta asked excitedly.

'Will there be food?' asked Emma, who, at six, was still to lose the puppyish layer of fat that encased her body.

At least the open house might involve some laughter, though not hers. In the pit of her stomach she felt nauseous. The prospect of the house emptying and of being taken to his chosen place to consummate the marriage — the bile and terror rose just thinking of it. The last few nights the dream had been the same. He leaned in for a kiss. Those rotten teeth, those stained yellowing whiskers, the hairs like spider's legs protruding from his fleshy nose, the sickly sweet odour that filled the room, it was like no nightmare she had ever had before. Yet soon it would be real.

She could tell that her mother saw it all. But she could not question it. She was to be her father's gift to the most respected man of the town and there was nothing that could be done to change it. Her mother tried to explain what an honour it was. How she was serving the calling of the Lord. But she cared nothing for this Lord that tore her away from the people she loved and turned her into a breeding mare for some slovenly old fool. She had never been the most

164

pious of children, though she had tried. She read the book, she memorized the doctrine and covenants, she listened to the Gospel in church, and all the time closed her eyes, willing herself to submit, to believe, to make it all worthwhile, but the nagging doubt and injustice that lodged like a tick in the back of her mind refused to be quelled.

'I, too, stood where you are now,' her mother intoned. 'I, too, experienced the same fears and doubts that you are feeling. You are but a child, albeit a strong one, Sarah. He is a good man who will make sure you are very comfortable. Far more comfortable than I ever was. Particularly back then. In your own way, you will come to love him.'

Sarah swallowed the urge to laugh, to bellow, to scream, 'No, I WON'T!' Instead she looked at her mother, at that dark-skinned mournful face, lined with hardship and struggle. She had been found as a young girl, left for dead at the massacre of Bear River, buried under the carcasses of her kith and kin. A kind man of the faith, not long since off the boat from the old world, had found her. She had been taken back to his family, newly settled, where she had worked as a domestic servant but been cherished like one of their children. The faith had saved her, offered her hope, a new family, a fresh start. No wonder she agreed to be wed to Sarah's father when she was chosen. It was time to repay the debt.

They hugged. Hot tears stung her eyes but she kept them in. 'Oh, Mother,' she said. Her mother's hands ran down the back of her head, like they had many times before, as a means of comfort. She wondered if it was to be the last time they would do that. She could not help it. The tears broke free and she began to convulse, to sob. Her mother gripped her tighter.

'Shhh,' she said softly. 'It will be all right. It will be all right.'

Sarah could not admit why she was so sad. That it was nothing to *do with that sweating warthog she was supposed to marry. That it was because she would never see them all again. She knew it would be all right.*

She knew he would come for her.

15

A shot of pain woke him. One leg was curled underneath the other and he'd tried to straighten it in his sleep, but the arm of the sofa was in its way and a gentle collision was enough to cause him discomfort. Foster rubbed his face, preparing himself. A chink of light through the curtains told him it was morning, the end of one of the longest nights of his life – and there had been many. He knew when he sat up his aches and pains would scream for attention and the stiffness would be with him for a few hours afterwards. His battered body was no longer fit for sleeping on couches, but with Gary upstairs in the spare room, he wanted to be ready if the boy tried to run away. As a result, he'd spent most of the night awake, primed to react, listening to the wind in the leaves and the clank of the central heating system shutting down slowly and then later, much later, shuddering to life.

He rose groggily to a sitting position, a dull ache behind his eyes.

'Brian Harris,' he thought to himself for the hundredth time. 'Of all the bloody blokes in the world.'

After a few more moments summoning the will, he stood, wincing with discomfort. All told, it wasn't too bad.

He made his way gingerly upstairs to the bathroom and splashed some cold water on his face. He dried off and went to the spare bedroom. The door was closed. He knocked. No answer. He knocked again. Silence. That meant nothing. When he was a kid that age, he could sleep through a marching band passing his bed. He eased the door open and popped his head round.

The bed was empty.

The window was open, the curtain billowing in the breeze. Foster went over and looked out. It was a sheer drop into the garden. That wouldn't have fazed Gary. He remembered one of his previous convictions for escaping from police custody. He'd scaled the high, flat wall of a magistrates' court and got out through a ceiling window, down the side of the building and away. A mini-Spider-Man.

Looks like I slept more than I realized, he thought.

He went downstairs and filled the kettle. His mobile phone, charging on the sideboard, showed a missed call. Nigel Barnes.

Foster struggled to understand. Barnes was babbling about a breakthrough, so he agreed to meet him in Farringdon near the London Metropolitan Archives, in the same café where he and Heather had approached him about the Hogg case earlier that year. First he phoned in a missing persons report for Gary, giving a description and asking anyone who found the boy to call him immediately. He phoned the care home. No sign of him there. Please stay out of trouble, he thought. If he starts robbing after I signed him out of the home then my arse will be toast, he thought.

Barnes was waiting, hair mussed and wild, running his

hands frantically through it. He was wired on coffee and adrenaline. It turned out he'd barely slept. That makes two of us, Foster thought. He ordered a black coffee, sat down and emptied two sachets of sugar into it. Barnes must have spent most of his night smoking, because he reeked of tobacco. His experience with Karl Hogg made him very sensitive to the smell, plunging him right back into the box-filled room, the pain, the sickly sweet nicotine breath of his tormentor . . .

'Come on then, what's the news?' he asked, snapping himself out of his brief, unpleasant reverie. 'Barely understood a word of what you said on the phone.'

Barnes drew a deep breath, pushed his glasses further up the bridge of his nose. He told him about Anthony Chapman, how his mother gave him away shortly after his birth because she believed that his life was in danger if he remained in the family bosom. The Church privately arranged the adoption and all details of it were erased. After her husband died she had confessed to the new vicar of her parish that it was the word of an aunt that convinced her to take such drastic action. That aunt had been locked up for most of her life in a notorious mental hospital, Colney Hatch. It had retained the old moniker informally despite changing its name to Friern Hospital in the 1930s. The hospital was long gone, demolished to make way for luxury flats, though the old façade had been retained. Princess Park Manor. Foster knew it as a haven for city boys, football players and minor glitterati. He chuckled inwardly. Did they know their pads were built on the drool of tens of thousands of raving nutters?

'All very interesting, but how does it help us?' he asked.

'The records for Colney Hatch are in the London Metropolitan Archives. Case notes, admittance registers, that sort of thing. This aunt may well have told the doctors about her fears. Who these people were that sought some sort of revenge. In which case, they may have made a record of it.'

'Back up,' Foster said, holding up his hands. 'You're telling me there might be something in the delusional rantings of a woman so mad that she spent her life in the nuthouse, the same woman who was ignored by her entire family bar one for being completely doolally?'

Barnes shrugged. 'Well, I'd put it in slightly more sympathetic terms, but yes, I am. What this woman said so spooked Edith Chapman that she gave away her child. From what I know, Edith Chapman was a decent, upstanding member of the community –'

'She gave away her child,' Foster interrupted. 'Hardly a decent and upstanding act, is it?'

'No. But we know that someone appears to be tracking down and killing the descendants of Horton and Sarah Rowley. We don't know why. This aunt prophesied all this. OK, she was a few decades out, but what's to say she wasn't right? From where I'm sitting, it certainly looks like she might have been.'

Foster sipped at his coffee. He knew Barnes was on to something – this was a lead worth pursuing. If they could work out why this was happening, finding out who was behind it would become a damn sight easier. He could only imagine what Harris might say when he went to him claiming the words of a long-deceased mental patient marked a breakthrough.

Were Harris and Susie going out? Was it a one-off? Did he stay the night? No, stop it, he thought. Don't think about Harris.

'OK,' he said eventually. 'What do we do?'

Nigel flicked open his notebook. 'The patient's name was Margaret Howell. She was born in 1909, first child of Emma Howell, née Rowley, the elder daughter of Horton and Sarah Rowley, the couple who moved here in 1891 from regions unknown. She died in 1964, aged 55, in Friern Mental Hospital from a "seizure", though what sort it doesn't say. Epilepsy, perhaps.'

'Doesn't tell us much,' Foster said.

'No, but her case notes might. There's one problem: patient records are usually subject to a hundred-year closure rule. Unless.'

'Unless what?'

'Unless the police make an application.'

'That could take days, even weeks,' Foster replied. He rubbed his chin. It had been a few days since he'd last shaved. 'You said the archives have the records for the mental hospital?'

Barnes nodded.

'They have them even though they're not available to the general public.'

Nigel nodded again.

Foster drained his coffee cup. 'In that case, follow me.'

Nigel sat at the desk waiting for Foster. He'd been invited into the back office where he'd been sitting patiently for the best part of an hour. The archive was sparsely populated, just a few dedicated researchers, most of them students, he guessed, going quietly about their task, alongside the occasional amateur. Foster returned clutching a faded brown packet.

'Here you go,' Foster said, dropping the bundle on the desk in front of him.

'I'm impressed. Thought they'd want a written application.'

'They did. But I made it clear there was little time to waste. They want one sent retrospectively.'

Nigel picked the packet up. Closed documents. It was rare that a researcher like him got his hands on them, and he couldn't deny the thrill. The front bore Margaret Howell's name, date of birth and patient number. It was, to his disappointment, surprisingly thin.

He pulled out the records, a sense of rising excitement. Foster sat down opposite, watching him closely.

The first document was Margaret Howell's admittance papers. The date was 29 May 1924. She was just fifteen years old. 'Looks like she spent her whole life in an asylum,' Nigel murmured to Foster as he scanned down the document, which covered two pages.

The first part was biographical information. Age, occupation, religion, address, none of which seemed remarkable. Then it mentioned 'Age on first attack . . . 11' before going on to state that she had had several more attacks.

In legible hand, under the heading 'Facts Specified in Medical Certificate upon which Insanity was Founded', the reasons for her being deemed insane were listed.

She says that she and her family are cursed by a past event. She believes they will be hunted down and killed

*for the deaths of others. She exhibits strong symptoms
of paranoid behaviour, which often degenerate into
seizures and fits. Her next of kin dismiss the idea that
they are in any way in danger and deny any knowledge
of past misdemeanours that may explain Miss Howell's
behaviour.*

Nigel read it out to Foster, together with another para-graph under 'Other Facts Indicating Insanity' in which the doctor, presumably the one who committed her, noted that her family were frightened by her frequent mood swings, her delusions and her constant reiteration that they would all die for their sins. In their view she had become a danger to herself and a nuisance to them.

The second page carried a black and white photograph of a terrified and bewildered-looking girl. Her eyes were hollow, her cheekbones sharp and her face devoid of any discernible tone. He showed it to Foster.

'Jesus, that's a kid. How many people were in this place?'

'Back then? Around three thousand people.'

'What exactly was wrong with her?'

Nigel scoured the page. Alongside the photo was a line stating 'Form of Disorder'. Next to it were written the words 'Paranoid Schizophrenia'.

There followed a more detailed physical description. Her physical condition was 'feeble'. Her temperament 'volatile'. Her skin also showed bruises from her latest 'attack'. There were more details of the history of her condition – a series of attacks between the age of eleven and her admittance, of increasing severity and duration.

No mention was made of any paranoid behaviour. She was admitted to Ward 4.

The next set of case notes was dated little more than a year later. It noted the effects of treatment on Margaret. The handwriting was, even for a physician, almost impossible to decipher despite Nigel's years of practice in the art. There was one phrase he could make out and it made his stomach turn. Electroconvulsive therapy.

'They gave her electroshock treatment,' he told Foster.

'When?'

'It had started by the time these case notes were written, just over a year after she was admitted. The handwriting is difficult to make out. But there's a sentence here that says she was responding well to the treatment and her delusional episodes were getting more infrequent.'

'Let's hope someone made a note of what those episodes were before they shocked her into becoming a zombie.'

'She must have retained some lucidity if she was able to scare Edith Chapman.'

'Do we know when Edith Chapman visited her?'

'I presumed it was over a period of time, and sometime near the birth of her son. But we have no way of knowing. I suppose she could have come to see her aunt when she was younger and whatever she heard and saw stayed with her.'

'That would make sense to me,' Foster said. 'I can see why a kid would be scared by the rantings of a mad woman, particularly if she visited her in some Gothic madhouse where people screamed and climbed the walls. But as she grew up, got older, why would she believe the words of a schizophrenic?'

'There's a long history of people who suffer from mental illness being viewed as possessed, either by spirits but more often the Devil. Edith Chapman was a religious woman. Perhaps she believed God was sending her a message. I don't know. Maybe her aunt was so convincing she couldn't believe it was anything other than true.'

He ploughed on through the file. Nothing for several years, until 1947, more than two decades after she was admitted. A different doctor this time, thankfully one with decipherable handwriting. Nigel scanned it first, but as he realized its importance he began to read out loud to Foster.

The patient continues to make slow yet gradual progress. Discussion was taken about whether to carry out a surgical operation but rejected in favour of continued electroconvulsive therapy. The patient last experienced a seizure more than a year ago, an encouraging sign. A possible discharge has been discussed but the patient herself states that she would rather stay where she feels safe. It is her delusion that she and members of her family are at risk from persons unnamed for acts perpetrated towards the end of the last century. The patient swears that on her deathbed her grandmother informed her of a horrible family secret. According to the patient, her grandfather was eventually found and killed by people seeking revenge for the deaths of the innocent, and that they would not stop until every descendant of the family has been dispatched in a similar manner. She is convinced that if she were to return to the outside world she would fall victim, so asks to stay. She can provide no proof of this wild story. She says her grandmother took the secret to the grave with her.

Very few of the family, apart from her young niece who comes once or twice a year, call in to visit her. When I approached them to test out the veracity of Miss Howell's claims, they insisted there was no truth in them whatsoever. No matter how well she responds to the ECT treatment, her paranoia shows no sign of subsiding. I fear Miss Howell will be in our care for most of her life, unless she desists in making these wild claims and seeks to live a life in the outside world. Alas, she is showing every sign of becoming institutionalized.

Nigel felt like punching the air. A breakthrough. Here was the first mention of a past crime, the 'deaths of the innocent', that could provide a motive for the present-day murders. But what was the horrible crime that left so many dead, if indeed it did exist? Foster was more concerned with a different unsolved crime.

'What did Horton Rowley's death certificate say?'

'Killed beneath an omnibus.'

'There was no indication of foul play?'

'None mentioned on the death certificate. They held an inquest but the coroner must have deemed it was an accident. I would get the records from the inquest but I know for a fact that no records exist from 1909. They tended to destroy them when a coroner stood down, or kept many of them for fifteen years afterwards. Not much help to us. There might be a few newspaper accounts, but omnibus accidents were not rare occurrences and we'd be lucky to find more than a news item in brief. Might be worth a try, though.'

Foster didn't respond. He took the records from Nigel and read the entry again. He put it down. 'Then we have absolutely no proof this woman was telling the truth. This isn't enough. Her words alone won't help us. We need to corroborate her story if we can. If not, it's just a mad woman ranting. What else is in here?'

In 1950 Margaret was admitted to the infirmary with a fractured pelvis incurred when she was being pinned down during her ECT treatment. Her treatment was altered in 1952, when a medical note stated that she had been given a leucotomy. Nigel took off his glasses and rubbed his brow wearily.

'What's that? Foster asked.

Nigel knew exactly what it was. He remembered tracing the family history of one client, which had led him to the asylum and the depredations that took place there in the name of treatment. 'A lobotomy,' he said.

'Jesus.'

'They went into the brain under the eyelid with an instrument shaped like a small ice pick. Then they cut the nerves at the front. It was very quick. Some surgeons prided themselves on how many they could do in one shift.'

'But what good could it possibly do?' Foster asked.

'Who knows? I suppose you might be less inclined to have a fit or a bout of hysteria with half your frontal lobe severed. It was quite popular for a time. Particularly on women.'

A short note from 1954 described the earlier operation

as a success. Both her anxiety and obsession had been brought under control. The same doctor mentioned that from then on she would be prescribed thorazine. Her discharge had been discussed but as there were no family members wishing to take her in, and there were fears about how she would cope in the outside world after so long in an institution, it was decided she should stay.

From that point on the notes were infrequent and terse. In 1959 she was hospitalized with a bout of pneumonia. No one revisited her case, or commented on her treatment. She existed until 1964 when a small paragraph noted matter-of-factly that she experienced a seizure, fell and as a result of her injuries was taken to an infirmary where, Nigel knew from her death certificate, she later died.

They sat in silence for a few seconds, each lost in their own thoughts. Nigel pictured a frail young woman, terrified by life, scared of what lurked round every corner, strapped down, electrodes attached to her body, in an attempt to divest her of a mania that may have had a grounding in truth, before severing the nerves in the brain that connected her cortex to her thalamus and then anaesthetizing her further with strong medication. Little wonder her condition 'improved'. In his mind's eye she sat, childlike and silent in the corner of a crowded ward, ignorant of the wailing and gibbering, a numb, muted life. He only hoped the treatment she'd endured rendered her oblivious to the horror of her situation.

At the same time, he wondered if he would ever be able to discover where Horton and Sarah Rowley came from and the truth behind the cataclysmic event that their granddaughter spoke of, the distant echoes of which were still being felt.

Nigel remembered a programme he once caught on the radio, about the effects of nuclear fallout. The fusion products from an air burst are sucked up into the stratosphere, dispersed by the winds, eventually settling across the wide earth in rainfall for years to come, with unpredictable effects that would only later be known.

Much like the past.

The problem appeared insurmountable. As Margaret Howell told the doctors, her ancestor seemed to have taken the secret with her when she died.

Then he remembered. He grabbed Foster's arm, causing the detective to stiffen.

'What?'

'I think I know where we might find out more about what Sarah and Horton were running away from.'

'Where?'

'In Sarah Rowley's grave.'

16

'You want us to dig her up?'

Foster thought Nigel was joking at first, but the zealous gleam in his eye indicated otherwise. He was being serious.

'Do you know how difficult it is to get an exhumation done? The Home Secretary has to grant it. You need a very, very good reason.'

Nigel kept on nodding, eyes ablaze.

'What do you think we're going to find – a document that conveniently explains what happened to her, and therefore what happened to Naomi Buckingham?'

'I don't know. But she asked in her will that she be buried with a metal box. Why would you insist on being buried with something unless you didn't want people to get their hands on it? It might not lead us to Naomi Buckingham or her mother's killer, but it might move us closer.'

Foster rubbed his chin. It wouldn't be an easy ask. For a start, the main argument for exhuming the body came from the mouth of a certified lunatic. The mention of the box in the will altered things slightly, but he knew there was no way Harris would sanction it as part of the investigation.

'The will said it was metal?'

Nigel nodded.

'Well, it may have survived, then.' He continued to stroke his chin. 'Do you know where she's buried?'

'East Ham cemetery. I can find the location of the grave.'

Nigel was still wild-eyed. Hidden secrets in a grave. Foster could see this must be a genealogist's wet dream. That would change if he ever attended an exhumation and saw that the reality was less romantic. Foster sighed, not quite believing what he was about to do.

'I might be able to swing this,' he said. 'However, if I do, you'll need to be there with me. She comes out of the ground and goes back in. We have a look in situ.'

He could see the excitement bleed from Nigel's face, along with all the colour. Not quite as thrilling now, he thought.

They drove towards Colchester through driving rain that pelted the windscreen like tiny stones, to the home of the Chancellor of the Diocese of Chelmsford, Kenneth Brewis. Foster had called ahead to check Brewis was in, and got the man himself, who issued a polite if curt invitation to drive to his house and explain the urgency. Foster knew there was no point wasting time, even if it meant a lengthy drive – it was just their luck that the chancellor happened to live in the most distant area of the diocese from London. Brewis was a QC, and the prospect of some pompous lawyer boring him rigid with the arcana of ecclesiastical law caused Foster's heart to sink. Church bureaucracy was even more labyrinthine than that of the modern police force. But to wait until after the weekend was not an option.

'Can't the police just go ahead and do it?' Nigel asked. 'Why does the Church have to be involved?'

'It's in consecrated ground so we'd need their help anyway. True, if there was a compelling case to dig up the body then a warrant signed by a coroner would be pretty easy to obtain and they'd allow us to bring it up without any protest,' Foster explained. 'But we're not interested in the body, or the little that would be left of it. We need to know what lies with it and for that we need permission to disturb the grave, and not actually exhume, which is down to the individual churches – and in the case of the Anglican Church, it's down to the diocese. At least, I think it is.'

'I didn't know that,' Nigel replied. 'You done this before then?'

'No. I just know the right people to call to find out. A grave is sacred ground. It's our job to make sure our case is compelling enough for us to be allowed in there with an excavator.' He knew that requests like the one he was about to make were measured in weeks and days, not hours, which is why he hoped a personal visit might speed the process.

Brewis's house was a grand one in the countryside on the edge of Colchester, an old stone former vicarage decorated with creeping ivy. A sleek grey Jaguar was parked in front of the house, Foster noted admiringly, as he pulled up alongside. The rain had subsided to a murky drizzle as they climbed out of the car and made their way to the front door, adorned by an elaborate brass knocker bearing the fleshy head of a cherub. He let it fall against the door and it made a profound thud that echoed through the house. Beside him Nigel shifted uncomfortably from foot to foot. 'Don't worry,' Foster said, trying to put him at ease. 'I'll do all the talking. Just smile, look well educated and drink all the tea they give you.' Barnes gave him a watery smile back and flapped away a curl of fringe that had fallen over his forehead.

The door opened to reveal a well-fed man in his fifties, dressed in cardigan and slacks, reading glasses perched on his nose. He looked at them both with some curiosity.

'Detective Foster?' he said expectantly.

'That's me,' Foster replied, thrusting out a large paw. 'Mr Brewis?'

'Come in, come in,' he said, gesturing for them to follow.

'Sorry to barge in on a Saturday,' Foster remembered to say.

'Don't worry. This bloody weather, what was I going to do?' They followed him into the hall, and he ushered them towards a large drawing room. 'The family are all out, so I was catching up with some paperwork and a bit of diocesan business.'

As they took a seat on a large sofa, Foster introduced Nigel as someone who was helping their investigation.

'Yes, what is the investigation? I have to say I'm intrigued what it could be that draws you out from London to Colchester on a foul Saturday afternoon. I've been puzzling it over ever since you called.'

'And did you manage to come up with any conclusions?' Foster asked, smiling.

'I don't know. But the police are rarely interested in diocesan business unless they're after an exhumation.'

'Got it in one.'

Brewis's eyes lit up. 'I thought so.' Then he moulded his features to fit the more serious mood he believed discussion of an exhumation required. 'Of course, you're aware of the usual processes involved with such requests?'

'I am.'

'But obviously this is urgent, otherwise you wouldn't be here personally.'

'It is extremely urgent. We have reason to believe that the grave of a woman buried in East Ham cemetery, and a parishioner of St Bertram's in East Ham, contains something that will help us in the course of a current investigation.' Foster was proud of the way he could slip into formal copper speak even after all these years, but he could see from the gleam in Brewis's eyes that he would have to give more. 'Of course, I can't go into details, but what is in that grave might help us catch a killer.'

He saw Brewis's eyebrows soar. He could picture him picking up the phone to his diocesan pals as soon as Foster's car wheels crunched away down the gravel drive to share the information.

'Ah,' he said. 'In that case, we'd better get a wriggle on and help you out. I need some details, of the deceased of course, any next of kin who need to be informed . . .'

'She died in 1913.'

'I see. Well, the ownership of the grave is passed on down the line. We will need to seek out any descendants . . .'

Foster leaned forward. 'We can help you with that – my friend here is a genealogist. We have traced her ancestry. There are no living descendants.'

Hidden from Brewis's sight by a large coffee table,

Foster put his foot on top of Nigel's and held it down firmly. Nigel's eyebrows furrowed and he appeared to be about to speak when he felt the pressure, and looked quizzically at Foster for a few moments before getting the message.

'That's right,' he murmured. 'No, er, living descendants.'

Foster nodded and removed his foot from Nigel's brogue. 'So you see, the only permission we seek is that of the diocese. Give us the faculty document and allow us to perform the exhumation – well, I say exhumation, but we don't intend to move the body. We simply want to open the coffin, look inside and remove what we find, before sealing the coffin shut and piling the earth back on top.'

Brewis fell silent. 'I don't see a problem, if it's in the course of your investigation, but I'll need to gain the consent of the other members of the diocese. And I'll need you to send me the relevant paperwork and details.'

'I can do that, some retrospectively. It really is very urgent.'

'When do you want to perform it?'

'Tomorrow?'

'A Sunday?' Brewis looked as if Foster had just introduced his daughter to the delights of sex and drugs. 'That isn't possible. Monday yes, but not the Sabbath.'

'I understand,' Foster said, standing up. 'These things are best done at night. So 12.01 on Monday morning it is.'

On the way back to London, Foster took two calls. The first from Dave Alvin agreeing to forward details of the crime scene and autopsy to him, so he could pass them on to Susie Danson. Alvin made clear his belief that it was a gangland killing; Martin Stamey, apparently, had no shortage of enemies. The second came from Heather. Foster had asked her to make a few inquiries about the four Robinsons who had moved to New Zealand seven years previously.

All of them had died in a house fire two years ago, apart from a nine-year-old girl, Louise Robinson, whose name Heather remembered from the list Nigel had produced. An inquest ruled it was accidental death. The files were being dug out and faxed across.

Foster had his doubts. The girl had been in the house but escaped with minor injuries. She had since been taken into care. She, Rachel Stamey, Anthony Chapman, wherever he may be, and Gary Stamey were the last of the line. Then he remembered David Stamey, incarcerated in jail. Should he get him protection? He decided he was probably out of harm's way behind four walls and bars.

It was dark when he reached home after dropping Barnes off at his flat. Foster unlocked the door and headed straight for the kitchen, where he poured himself a glass of wine, before turning to the fridge to see if there was anything he could eat. The selection was uninspiring so he decided to keep it liquid for the time being. He went through to his sitting room and flicked on the light.

Gary Stamey sat rigid on the sofa, coat still on, hands plunged deep into his pockets. Foster was startled, jumped almost a foot in the air, but managed to compose himself.

'Couldn't keep away, eh?' he said, heartbeat returning to normal. He went over and felt the radiator. Cold as ice. Bloody boiler, he thought.

Gary didn't say a word. Or even move.

Foster went over to the armchair and sat down, watching the boy from the corner of his eye. 'Out of interest, and for my peace of mind, just how the hell did you get in?'

Gary shrugged his shoulders. 'You said this place was safe. It ain't. I came in through the kitchen window at the back. No lock on it.'

'I should hire you out. Help people discover the weaknesses in their home security. Where you been all day?'

'Round and about.'

'Why did you come back?'

Gary shrugged his shoulders again. 'Dunno. No place else to go. It was cold.'

Foster sensed there was more to it than that.

'I think I was followed.'

'What do you mean? Did you see someone following you?'

He shook his head. 'I just felt it.'

Foster nodded. 'On foot or in a car?'

'Dunno. I can't explain it. Just like I'm being watched.'

Probably paranoia, Foster thought. Though given Gary was a lad who knew what it was like to be tailed, usually by the law, he wouldn't dismiss it.

'Do you think you've been followed here?' he asked.

He shrugged. 'Dunno. Don't think so. I bunked a ride on a train out of London. Then got off and hid and got a train coming back. Walked most of the way here. Got a couple of buses and a tube. Don't think anyone would have kept up.'

'You did the right thing. You're safe here. I promise.' He changed the subject. 'Have you eaten anything?'

His face lit up. 'Nah, starving. There's nuffink in your fridge, too.'

'Want another takeaway?'

Gary nodded eagerly.

'What sort? Indian? Pizza?'

The second suggestion met with a vigorous nod.

'What flavour?'

'Hawaiian.'

'The one with pineapple?' Foster couldn't help but wrinkle his nose up. In his world, there was no room for fruit on a pizza. In the name of hospitality he let it slide and went to the hall to phone the order through. When he returned, Gary had flicked the television on and was staring at a football match.

'You've got the sports channels,' he said with a hint of excitement.

'Yeah. God knows why. Can't stand football these days. Full of overpaid prima donnas falling over and wearing dresses. Used to be a contact sport. Who's your team?'

'Chelsea.'

'Thought an Essex boy like you would support the Hammers.'

His lip curled in disgust. 'Nah, they're shit.'

Foster shook his head. 'You see, there's something else that's changed. People supporting teams that are the best, not their local ones.'

Gary shrugged. 'Chelsea scouted me, so I like them best.'

'They scouted you? Really? When?'

'When I was eight. I used to go along to the Gateway football club every Saturday morning. Leonie took me on the bus. They had loads of pitches and stuff. Scouts used to come and watch us play. One of them spoke to me and wanted to speak to my mum. He was from Chelsea. I went to a training session. But then Mum died and Leonie went and I didn't go for a bit. Then when they heard I was in trouble they lost interest. I still went to the Gateway and played, but I haven't been for a while.'

'Why not?'

Again the shrug. 'Too much hassle, innit? Been moved around too much.'

'Do you miss it?'

'Yeah,' he said with feeling. 'I love playing football. It's the only thing I'm good at.'

'What position do you play?'

'Didn't play many games, but when we did I played centre mid.'

Foster shook his head. If only this kid could be taken off the streets and on to a football pitch then he might spend less of his time robbing. 'You should keep at it. You're obviously good. Be a shame to waste your talent.'

Gary said nothing. On screen, the commentator erupted with orgasmic delight at a piece of skill. They both turned to watch the replay. 'That was the lick,' Gary said, as in slow motion the striker drew his man towards him, performed a stepover and left the defender lunging at thin air.

'Impressive,' Foster had to agree. They sat and watched more of the game. It finished in a draw; the pizzas came. Gary wolfed his down greedily once more. Foster went in search of his indigestion tablets. Two takeaways on the trot, coupled with the hamburger he and Barnes had eaten for lunch, were proving a bit much. He still poured another glass of wine. Back in the sitting room, Gary was hopping between channels, having finally taken his coat off.

Foster sat down and sipped his wine. Gary failed to find anything worth watching. He seemed to catch Foster looking at him.

'She contacted me,' he said simply.

'Leonie?'

Gary nodded.

'When was that?'

'About a year after she disappeared.'

A flicker of caution passed through his mind. Something wasn't right. 'You were in foster care?'

'Yeah.'

'How did she contact you?'

'A letter.'

'How did she know where to send it?'

'She sent it to the Gateway football club. Probably knew it was the only place I could be found. The coach gave it me one Saturday morning.'

'What did it say?'

He reached into his coat pocket and pulled out a greying battered envelope, frayed at the edges. 'Be careful, it's falling apart,' he said.

Foster looked at the address. Gary Stamey, c/o Gateway Football Club, Barking, Essex. The stamp had long since peeled off. No postcode. He could only wonder how long it took to reach its destination. He could see the trace of a sticker in the lower bottom corner.

'Was there a sticker on this? Air mail?'

'Don't know what it said, but there was a sticker,' he said. 'It fell off. Like the stamp.'

'Can you remember what the stamp was? Did it have the Queen's head on it?'

He shook his head. 'Wasn't the Queen. It was a picture of, like, some mountains and stuff. And a sunset?'

Didn't sound familiar to Foster.

He slid the contents out slowly. The letter had been folded and refolded so many times that along the crease it was beginning to disintegrate. It was marked by grubby fingers, presumably Gary's. Yet considering it was two years old it was still in reasonable condition.

He opened the paper up. The writing was immediately recognizable as that of a teenage girl; big looping letters and fat round blobs instead of dots above the 'i's.

Gary looked uncomfortable, embarrassed even. 'Can you read it to me?' he asked.

'What, haven't you . . . ?' It took a while for him to realize. 'You can't read?'

Gary shook his head dolefully.

'You've never asked anyone to read it to you?' he asked, struggling to contain his disbelief.

'No. I knew it was a secret. I can read some of it. I knew it was from her because of the name and the writing. I know a few of the words. But I've never been able to read it all.'

The kid had kept it on his person for two years. By the

look of it, he'd taken it out of the envelope and looked at it many times. Yet he'd not been able to understand the message his sister had sent to him.

'OK.' He scanned it quickly. He would need to mentally correct much of the syntax to render it readable.

Dear Gary

I hope this letter gets to you OK and you are all right. I sent it to the football club because I know that's the one place you love. I hope you still go there.

Just wanted you to know I am OK. Sorry I left like that but I had to. The time was right. I know you must be really angry with me for leaving you but don't be. It is fine to be cross but I had to leave. I am with good people. They look after me. Bit boring sometimes but no drugs and everyone is happy. no one even drinks beer or nothing. I have learned to do lots of stuff like sewing and we have animals like cows and pigs and the country-side is beautiful to look at. Much nicer than Essex. I don't miss home at all. just you.

Don't tell anyone about this letter or else! The end days are on their way and we will be together again in the celestial kingdom as a family with our mum. too. God says so. Try and stay out of trouble even though that is impossible for you!

God loves you and so do I.

Leonie x

P.S. I'm married!

Foster looked up to see Gary's big brown eyes moistening. He was desperately trying to fight back tears but losing the battle.

'Married,' Foster said. 'This was a year after she left? So she was only fifteen?'

Gary said nothing. Just looked down at his hands and sniffed copiously. Foster read through the letter once more, silently this time. It appeared that Leonie had not only got religion, but some extreme form. The people she had fallen in with were teetotal, it appeared, which made him think it was some kind of cult. And just exactly what were the 'end days'. He asked Gary, but the boy didn't know. Once again, he seemed small and alone.

'She's still alive, sunshine,' Foster said softly. 'And she said you'd be back together one day. Now that you've shown me her letter, that's even more likely. It was the right thing for you to do. And brave with it.'

'Really?' Gary said, brightening. 'You think you can find her?'

'I know we can find her.' He rubbed the hair on top of his head. 'Let me get you another glass of Coke and we'll find a film you can watch.'

Once he'd settled Gary in front of the television, he went to the kitchen and fired up his laptop. Then he went on to the Internet and typed in the phrase 'end days'. The result was a hodge-podge of the banal and the barmy. Sites discussing the impending obsolescence of computer systems mingled with other sites predicting the end of the world – Judgement Day and the Apocalypse. Prophecies were coming true, billions were about to die and Jesus Christ was set to return to earth. Foster took a wild guess

Leonie Stamey was referring to the latter. He then typed in 'celestial kingdom'.

It led him straight to Wikipedia. The celestial kingdom was the highest of the three tiers of Heaven envisaged by the Church of Latter-day Saints.

The Mormons, he thought.

He pored over the entries. The Church's origin, Joseph Smith's visions – was he the Joe in the book Gary had spoken of? The gold plates he found, upon which the Book of Mormon was based, his treasure, the persecution of its early followers, their flight to the safe haven of Salt Lake City and its evolution to the present and its place as the world's fastest growing religion. He learned the religion's basic beliefs, shuddered at its followers' abstinence, paying particular interest to how the Church sent its youngest recruits across the world to perform missionary work door to door. Had one been working in Leonie and Gary's area?

He needed to know more.

17

Foster was stiff from another night on guard on the sofa, sleeping there to prevent Gary from leaving and anyone from coming in. He made Gary and himself a bacon sandwich each; then, while he drank some tea and came round, the kid stared slackjawed at more television. While he was enthralled by some junkie cartoon, Foster slipped out into the back garden and placed some Sellotape on the join of the kitchen window and its frame, then did the same with the back door and the battered old French windows at the back of the sitting room. Before leaving for Kensington and the Mormon Temple, after getting Gary into his car, he pretended to have left something behind, and when he returned to the house he stuck another band of translucent tape across the frame at the foot of the front door.

Sunday wasn't a bad day to be hunting Mormons. Outside the chapel in South Kensington, scores of them milled around in their Sunday best waiting for their services to start. Foster did not know what to expect – all he knew about Mormonism was that the Osmonds were members, and that it practised questionable marital practices, or used to. He was pleasantly surprised to see so many normal-looking people and not chanting weirdos in robes.

He told Gary to keep quiet and behave, and the pair

followed the congregation into the chapel. He sat at the back, trying not to look too conspicuous even if all the men, and some of the boys, were in suits, and he was in a pair of chinos and a battered jumper riddled with bobbles. Gary, in scruffy jeans and puffer jacket, looked even more incongruous, drawing more than a few concerned looks.

The ceremony lasted a long time but to Foster it felt like an eternity. Hymns, invocations, a bewildering litany of assignments and callings, blessings, namings and confirmations.

Finally, it ended. Foster told Gary, bored to catatonia, to stay seated while he headed to the front, to the rotund, rather self-important man who had opened the service. He stood to one side as he shared a few words with the congregation, before closing in during a lull. He introduced himself as quietly as he could. The man did not respond, merely frowned and pursed his lips. 'You could have chosen a better time to barge in here than a Sunday,' he said crossly.

Barge in, Foster thought indignantly. I've just spent well over an hour of my life listening to the platitudinous bilge of you and your congregation – time I'll never get back – but he resisted the urge.

'It's very urgent that I speak to you, Mr, er . . . ?'

'Brewster. Roger D. Brewster. I'm the Branch President.'

I'm inquiring about a loan, Foster was tempted to say in response. 'Mr Brewster, I can't divulge why. I just need some information that may help us regarding an ongoing murder investigation.'

His ears pricked up at the word 'murder'. He appeared

instantly less hostile. 'Goodness me,' he murmured. 'Let me just see these good people off, then we can talk.'

He went back to smiling, shaking hands and nodding earnestly for a few minutes until the hall emptied and the two of them, plus Gary, were the only ones remaining.

'How can I help?'

'I'm looking for some background information that might be able to help us,' Foster explained.

'Well, you've got the right man,' Brewster added. 'I also happen to be the Director of Public Affairs for the Church in this country.'

'You're the PR man?'

He smiled. 'I prefer my job title but, yes, more or less. What is it you want to know?'

Foster wondered whether it was wise to let anything slip to a man that dealt with the press. 'Anything I tell you is in the strictest confidence, you understand that?'

'Of course.'

'Am I right in believing that it's usual for young Mormon men to spend time on missions?'

'That's right. And not just men. Many young women are assigned to missions, too. Usually aged between nineteen and twenty-five.'

'How long do they do it for?'

'Two years. Eighteen months for the women.'

That doesn't fit, Foster thought. There was a three-year gap between Leonie Stamey going missing and Naomi Buckingham. 'Do they occasionally last longer than two years?'

'Rarely. We have some retired couples who perform missionary work and they can last anything between three months and three years, depending on their circumstances and their means.'

'What happens on these missions?'

Brewster laughed mirthlessly. 'Many things happen. Typically the missionaries are assigned to places far away from their own homes. They'll be sent to a missionary training centre. In this country that's in Preston. If they're going to a country that speaks their native language, they'll spend three weeks being briefed about their mission, taught how to conduct themselves, study the scriptures. If they need to learn a foreign language then they'll spend much longer, up to three months.'

'So a missionary working in this country wouldn't necessarily be English?'

'No, it's almost certain they wouldn't. It's more likely they would come from abroad, primarily the United States.'

'And what sort of work would they do? House-to-house calls?'

'Well, to describe it as work is slightly inaccurate, although they could be said to be doing God's work. The missionaries pay to do it – or their families do, at least. But to answer your question, yes, the missionary companionship does undertake some door-to-door proselytizing. Preaching the Gospel can also involve speaking to people on the streets, or taking part in community activities.'

'Missionary companionship? They don't do it on their own?'

'Never. Let me explain. Most missions are divided into geographical areas that we call zones, and those zones are divided into districts. There are between four and eight missionaries in each district. These are split into companionships of two, sometimes three, missionaries who go out together. Each is instructed never to let the other out of their sight unless they're using the lavatory or taking a shower. These are young people we're talking about. To abandon them to the streets of an unknown country without guidance and friendship would be a gross dereliction of duty.'

Gary only mentioned one man who had visited their flat. Foster was starting to think he was wasting his time. 'Do you have a record of missionaries that were active in certain areas?'

'Obviously I don't have access to that information personally but, yes, there is a record. But we'd need to have a good reason to divulge it. Perhaps if you were to submit a request in writing . . . ?'

'To you?'

'I could pass it on, yes.'

'I'll get something to you.' He took out a notebook from his jacket pocket. There was no need. Brewster had already produced a card from his wallet. Foster thanked him and slipped it into his pocket.

'If someone spoke about the end days, would you assume they were a Mormon?'

He shook his head. 'Not really. Almost every religion in the world has their own concept of the end times, the second coming of the Lord and the beginning of the Kingdom of God. The specific details depend upon the faith itself. Each has its own signs, traditions and beliefs about the last days. Some believe that a series of natural disasters will herald the Second Coming. Others that it will steal upon us like a thief in the night. We believe the last days are already upon us, hence the name Latter-day Saints, though that doesn't necessarily mean the end is nigh. Just that we're nearer the end of the book than the start, if you like. But we're always prepared.'

Foster wondered how someone might prepare for the end of the world. 'How about if the same person also mentioned the celestial kingdom?' he asked.

'Then I would say that they almost certainly were a member of the Church. What was the context?'

'Just a letter from a sister to a brother about how they would be reunited in the celestial kingdom after the end days. They're estranged.'

'The celestial kingdom is the highest tier of heaven, the residence of God the Father and Jesus Christ. We believe that those who have been righteous, and have accepted the teachings of the faith and lived according to the covenants and ordinances of our prophet in their mortal lives, will be reunited with their families in the afterlife. The brother – I assume he is a member of the Church, too?'

Foster nearly burst out laughing at the idea of Gary as a devout follower of any religion. 'Not quite,' he said.

'In that case, he wouldn't be allowed into the celestial kingdom. If he lives respectably but rejects the gospel of Jesus Christ, he would dwell in the terrestrial kingdom. Or, God forbid, if he lives less than respectably and refuses the testimony of Jesus Christ, he will end up dwelling in the telestial kingdom with the liars, adulterers, sinners and general ne'er-do-wells.'

Sounds like more fun there, thought Foster.

'Unless, of course, they were dead and able to receive the Gospel in the Spirit World,' Brewster continued.

'Come again?' Foster said.

'Well, we Latter-day Saints believe the dead can be baptized vicariously and allowed into the faith and subsequently the Kingdom of God.'

'How does that work?'

'It means someone can be baptized by proxy for their dead ancestors.'

Foster struggled to comprehend what he was being told. 'But these people are dead?'

'We believe that in the afterlife people should be able to accept the Gospel, particularly if they were not able to receive it while on earth. Whether they do or not is their choice.'

The delusion of religion had always puzzled him, but baptizing the dead was among the most bizarre things he'd ever come across. Brewster seemed to sense his disbelief.

'It's not a belief shared by other Christian denominations,' he explained. 'Though some would argue the Bible calls for it. Otherwise why did Paul say in Corinthians 15: 29, "Else what shall they do which are baptized for the dead, if the dead rise not at all? Why are they then baptized for the dead?" Regardless of that debate, it is central to our faith. Which is why we're so active in the world of genealogy. We ask all members of the Church to trace their ancestry and in temple baptize their dead by proxy.'

No matter where I turn, Foster thought, I can't escape people seeking out their past. He made a mental note to discuss this with Barnes later that day. However, something Brewster said was bothering him. 'So the brother I referred to earlier, who is no angel and certainly no

Mormon, he wouldn't be allowed into the celestial kingdom unless he converted to Mormonism?'

'That's correct.'

'But they would be able to convert him if he was
dead?'

'He could be given the option, yes.'

'Thanks. I'll be in touch,' he said and turned on his
heels, collecting Gary as he left.

They got back to Foster's house early that evening. Foster
had taken Nigel into the office, leaving him to surf the
Internet idly while he made a few calls and looked at the
faxes sent over from New Zealand. It looked like an open
and shut case of accidental death. No suggestion of arson.
The girl had jumped from the window before being overcome by smoke. The rest of her family had not been so
fortunate. He put the papers in his pocket for closer study
at home.

They parked up a fair distance from Foster's front door,
the weekend getaways having returned and occupied most
of the spaces around his house. Sunday evenings were
always the worst.

They reached the front door. Foster put his key in the
lock and remembered. Before opening the door, he looked
down. The tape was still there. He went into the hall, took
off his coat and then went into the sitting room and stuck
the TV on for Gary. He had intended to pick up some
food but time had run away. Another takeaway would do,
though at this rate the weight he'd lost would soon be
back on.

Gary slumped on the sofa, while Foster went to close

the curtains across the French windows. He checked the tape.

It was broken.

Someone had been inside his house.

He fished a handkerchief from his pocket, wrapped it around his hand and tried the door. It opened. The lock had been forced. Given its worn state, that wouldn't have taken too much effort. He left Gary in the sitting room, closing the door behind him. He went to the hatstand in the hall and picked up an old golf club, about the only potential weapon he had.

He walked upstairs. The bathroom was empty. His bedroom and the spare room, too. He checked cupboards, under every bed and inside the wardrobe on the landing. Nothing. He breathed out.

In the kitchen he checked the unlocked window, the same one Gary had entered by. The tape was intact. Yet on the back door it was broken. Whoever it was had come in through the back garden, forced open the French windows and then exited via the back door.

His house wasn't safe any more.

18

Sunday night and the pursuit of Naomi was getting colder. Nigel sat waiting, his stomach performing cartwheels. Foster had called to tell him the exhumation was on that night and he would pick him up at nine. When he called from his car to let him know he was outside, Nigel walked out like a condemned man, unsure what to expect. He certainly didn't expect a young boy to be in the back.

'Nigel, this is Gary,' Foster said. 'Gary Stamey,' he added simply.

The kid didn't even blink, just stared out of the window sullenly.

'I'm dropping him off at Heather's while we take care of business.'

Nigel knew instantly who the kid was. Why he was in Foster's car was a different matter. Nigel thought it best to save the questions for another day.

They arrived at Heather's. Nigel stayed in the car as Foster and the kid trudged up the path to Heather's terraced house. He was back within the minute. 'Heather says "hi",' he muttered as he climbed into the driver's seat.

'Did she?' Nigel asked as casually as he could muster.

There was the ghost of a smile on Foster's face. 'To the graveyard,' the detective said, turning the engine over.

It was an hour's drive across London, a city spattered with rain, the soaked pavements reflecting the blurred orange light from the streetlamps. As the windscreen wipers swept hypnotically back and forth, Nigel watched bedraggled people come and go, in and out of pubs and shops and houses, wrapped up against the elements, sitting stony-faced on buses on the road to God knew where. Occasionally he would glimpse young lovers laughing or some kids messing around, a bolt of illumination and happiness on a dank night. There was something about Sundays he could never shake off, a feeling of melancholy and regret he had experienced every week since being a kid. All the bad thoughts, past mistakes and anxieties seemed to come back to haunt him on that night of the week, even though he didn't have to get up and slog into an office the next day like nearly everyone else. The Sunday night blues remained.

Foster broke the silence somewhere near King's Cross.

'What do you know about Mormons?' he asked.

Nigel knew more than most. 'Without them, there'd be very few records for genealogists to search. They're probably the single biggest influence, particularly when it comes to collecting and compiling records and putting them on the web.'

Foster told him about his research trip to the Mormon chapel that morning. Baptism for the dead. 'Bloody weird, if you ask me,' he added. 'Like some sort of spiritual kidnapping.'

Nigel could see his point but knew it was not as black and white as that. 'To be fair to them, the Mormons do say that the dead are free agents – like us, they're able to choose to reject religion,' he said.

Foster snorted with derision, murmured an expletive at

a driver in front. 'How does this work for people who did something terrible? Murderers, rapists – can these people receive the Gospel after they're dead?'

Nigel nodded. As far as he knew, they could. 'It's caused a kerfuffle, not least with Jews who were very angry that their dead could be claimed in such a way. The Mormons have said they've stopped proxy baptisms for dead Jews who aren't direct ancestors of living Mormons.'

'Jesus,' Foster said, shaking his head. 'You see, the dead are dead. They're gone, let them rest. Bury them, don't keep them. It's all just so much hocus-pocus. Don't get me wrong; I think that about all religions. But at least traditional Christianity is based on centuries of moral knowledge and its values are the ones we've built our societies upon. Mormonism just sounds to me like a bloke made it up as he went along and hoodwinked a bunch of gullible knuckle-draggers into following him.'

Nigel was no expert on Mormonism. 'Maybe so. It has its quirks, I grant you. Speaking purely selfishly, I'm delighted they believe what they do. I don't care why they've collected all these records. We're just glad they have, and they've opened them up to us all. What do you think this has got to do with Mormonism, anyway?'

'Whoever brainwashed Leonie Stamey had something to do with the Mormon faith. That seems to be clear. Gary Stamey, the kid I just dropped off, remembers his sister having a kids' book about a boy named Joe finding buried treasure. The Mormon church was founded by some conman called Joseph Smith who was guided to a place by an angel where he dug up some gold tablets with writing on. Turns out, rather handily, that he also found some special glasses that allowed him to decipher and transcribe these tablets. Barking mad, if you ask me. But then what religion stands up to scientific scrutiny?

'But if we work on the basis that the man who visited Leonie Stamey was in some way responsible for her disappearance, which is linked to the kidnap of Naomi Buckingham and the murder of her mother, then there's every chance that the same person is responsible and he has something to do with the Mormon faith. I've just submitted a written request to the Church to see if they have any record of a missionary plying his trade in or around the area where Leonie lived, and the same for those that are working near to Kensal Rise.'

He stopped to swear at another driver, this time beeping his horn in disgust. He returned to the subject. 'We think he – or they, or whoever – will try to get Gary next. I think they've already tried to get him. Leonie said she would meet up with him in the celestial kingdom. That can only happen if he's dead, unless she comes back to convert him in this life. Yesterday my house was broken into. There's a team there dusting for fingerprints, though I doubt they'll find anything. I'll lay any money it was the killer.'

A thought, an inkling that had been lodged in the back of Nigel's mind since staring at the parish picture of Sarah Rowley and reading the vicar's funeral address, was floating free. It took some time for it to settle, but eventually it did. Then the recognition jolted him like a needle in his side.

Cultists from across the ocean.

'Listen,' he said. 'Sarah Rowley fled some sort of cult,

presumably from the United States.' What other English-speaking land lay across an ocean? It tallied with Margaret Howell's reminiscences. 'Traditional Christians believed, and many still believe, that the Latter-day Saints were no better than a cult. They could well be Mormons. I could check it out for you tomorrow.'

They were pulling up at East Ham cemetery.

'Let's leave that until the morning,' Foster said, as Nigel felt his heart flutter at what lay behind the black cemetery gates. 'First let's see if there's anything buried with her that helps us out.'

The night was mild yet Nigel found himself shivering despite being layered up in a shirt, a woollen jumper, fleece, scarf and a battered crombie overcoat whose best days were long gone. The rain had relented but the smell of damp sodden earth lingered. He and Foster marched their way across the graveyard to the lot where burial records told him Sarah Rowley was interred. The grave was overgrown with lichen and weed, marked by a simple headstone that tilted upwards at an angle, as if the ground beneath was slowly trying to eject it. Or Sarah Rowley is coming out before we dig her out, he thought ghoulishly. In his churning stomach he felt a mixture of excitement and trepidation, the latter not helped by the grim determination with which Foster was conducting himself. He could not bear to bring himself to think about what the detective's reaction might be if they discovered the coffin was empty.

A lone arc light lit the scene. A compact excavator was parked at the graveside waiting for midnight to pass and

Monday to arrive. The operator looked bored and pissed off, exhaling frequently and disdainfully on a cigarette. Beside him was another equally bored, unshaven young man whose role was unclear.

'I expected there to be more of us,' Nigel said, trying to roll a cigarette despite his shaking hands.

Foster watched him fix his cigarette.

Nigel gestured, as if to ask whether he wanted one rolling, and was met with an emphatic shake of the head.

'Not if you paid me,' Foster said. He looked at the meagre exhumation party. 'There would be more, if we'd been doing this officially. But we're not. These two guys are from a company that does this sort of thing for us and I'm paying them out of my own pocket as it stands. Keep that to yourself, though.' He glanced at his watch and strolled off to speak to the excavator operator.

Nigel took a deep drag on his cigarette and shook his head. Maybe some secrets are best left dead, he thought. But then he thought of Naomi Buckingham cowering somewhere, alone and petrified, or lying dead in some unmarked ditch, and he told himself to stop being so precious. Yet the revelation that Foster was doing this on the sly did little to quell the bubbling in his guts. More than he would like was riding on them finding a lead in the grave. He shivered again. Foster returned.

'I tell you what, we're lucky she's buried in consecrated ground. Over there with the non-believers they're sometimes buried one on top of each other, which would have made it interesting if she was on the bottom.' He sniffed, and clapped his hands together. 'This is how it's going to play out. Mickey in the digger is going to scoop out the soil to the required depth. Then you're going to jump in with a spade.'

'What?'

Foster smiled. 'Lighten up, eh? If some of these lot rose from the dead, they'd be less stiff than you. Seriously. Once we've exposed the coffin, young Jim there will check we have the right one, hopefully by reading the inscription plate. He'll open the lid and we have to be ready. Keep clear because it could smell a bit. A lot, actually. There's ninety years or so of decomposition in there and the gases to match, so be prepared. Once the lid's opened and whatever foul gasses need to escape have escaped, then we'll have a look and see what we can find. I've got a jemmy to open the tin if we find it.'

Nigel drew the last from his cigarette before it burned his fingers. 'Will there be anything left of her?' he asked, flicking the stub away.

Foster raised his broad shoulders and let them fall. 'Depends. If the undertaker did a good job, then there might be a fair bit of her left. We'll soon find out, won't we?'

Nigel sensed he was enjoying his discomfort. Foster checked his watch once more. Nigel looked at his. It was midnight. They waited for a few more seconds to elapse, before Foster whirled his hand above his head and the excavator's engine roared into life. Foster gestured for Nigel to stand beside him at the side of the grave.

The wet soil yielded easily, the jaw of the machine tearing it in chunks. The operator worked swiftly, clawing lumps of soil, depositing them to one side, before slicing out another layer. Each bite at the earth caused Nigel's chest to tighten and his breath grow shorter. The hole grew deeper and wider, less of the excavator's arm visible above the ground until the unshaven man at the side of the grave leaned over to see, and then held his arm up. He made a few gestures to the unsighted operator, who responded by wielding the jaws with almost surgical care, a scratch of earth here, and a small handful there. Five minutes later, the unshaven assistant held up his hand to stop and the engine died, the silence afterwards profound and ominous to Nigel's ears.

The assistant looked at Foster, nodded downwards, grabbed a spade and jumped in. The pair of them walked to the edge of the pit and looked in. There was a simple mahogany coffin, muddied and worn, but otherwise in good condition, the lid closed. The excavator had cleared a shelf to the side of the coffin on which the man stood, looking up at them. Foster walked round and lowered himself in. Nigel's heart hammering against his ribcage, mouth dry as a bone and the taste of fear in his throat, he climbed in, too, almost slipping as he turned. Eventually his feet found the shelf. He didn't care about the layer of mud that was now caked on his front. He turned, trying to keep his footing on the slippery mud. The only scent was the heady smell of wet soil.

There was a brass plate on the coffin lid. The assistant crouched down and with a gloved finger carefully wiped away the grime. Foster and then Nigel crouched, too. They were so close that Nigel caught a whiff of damp that came from Foster's sodden raincoat. The assistant finished cleaning the plate. The inscription was clear:

Nigel tried to wet his mouth but there was no moisture, just a dry, clacking sound. Foster's previous jocularity appeared to have evaporated, too.

'We know it's the right one,' he said softly. 'Go on, Jimbo – do your worst.'

He stood up and with his arm ushered Nigel back from the edge of the shelf. He put a gloved hand over his nose and Nigel did likewise.

'I should really have brought masks,' he said, voice muffled.

Nigel felt the first leapings in his stomach that indicated he might be sick. He took away the glove and sucked in a deep lungful of the moist night air while it was still clean.

With a crowbar, Jim eased away the lid at various points along its side, a faint cracking sound audible each time he lessened its grip. He worked quickly and respectfully for a minute, Nigel unsure whether to watch or look up at the sky. At one point Jim stopped and looked away; a second later Nigel knew why. A choking, acrid smell invaded the air around them. He closed his eyes, tried not to vomit. Nigh on a century of decomposition had just escaped into the atmosphere, he knew. He felt light-headed, whether from the stench or the fear and apprehension he was unsure.

Jim nodded to Foster again.

'The lid's about to come off,' he said to Nigel. 'Don't look at her, look around her and see if there's anything there. Then we'll get it out.'

Nigel nodded, incapable of unsticking his tongue from the roof of his mouth to speak. Foster nodded to Jim to open the coffin.

Nigel felt himself calm. His focus was on what was beside the body, not the body itself, and there was work to do. If only he had some water to moisten his lips. Jim knelt down and slowly opened the lid, pushing it away from him. Then he moved aside.

There she was. All that was left of her earthly remains was a skeleton. Her eyeless sockets gazed skywards, jaw set in that mirthless grin common to all skulls, hands still crossed in front of her like they would have been after being placed in the box. The skeleton appeared small, no bigger than that of a teenage girl. A few threads clung to the bones, their colour impossible to tell. Nigel found himself gazing at her for several seconds, lost in thought, no longer in fear.

Foster's voice shook him out of it. 'Look,' he said simply.

Nigel followed the direction of his finger. By the bones of her right foot lay a silver container no bigger than a shoebox. Metal. It was padlocked. A rusting Yale 'cartridge' lock, state of the art in its day, Nigel noted. She really had gone to great lengths to seal this secret from the prying eyes of the world, and here they were foiling her.

Foster leaned down and gathered it up. 'It feels empty,' he said, weighing it in his hand. He put it on the surface and hoisted himself up. Nigel followed suit. He went back to the side of the excavator and laid it down on the footplate. He pulled hard at the lock but it was not so corroded as to give way that easily.

'Hold that,' he said to Nigel, eyes burning with intent.

It felt cold and damp. Nigel could feel his heart beating fast once more. It was all he could do to stop his hands shaking. Foster produced a set of bolt cutters. Nigel hoped his hands weren't shaking as much as his own, or he might lose his fingers.

'Hold it tight,' Foster urged. Nigel applied as much downward pressure as he could. Foster placed the jaw of the cutters around the lock and snapped. The lock broke. Foster placed it in his pocket.

'You can let go now,' he said to Nigel, who was still grabbing the tin with all his might.

'Oh,' he said.

'Go on then,' Foster added impatiently. 'You're the expert in handling old stuff. Open it up.'

Nigel produced a pair of pristine white cotton gloves from his pocket. He had a stock of these back home for handling old objects and aged documents, but the truth was he always forgot to take them with him and ended up borrowing those belonging to whichever archives he was working at. He slipped them on.

'Open the lid, please,' he said in a hoarse whisper, excitement once again drying out all the moisture in his mouth.

Foster lifted the lid.

The box was empty.

At least, it appeared to be at first glance. The bottom was lined with yellowing paper. Nigel picked it up carefully, feeling it crinkle slightly between his fingers. There was nothing on it. But then he looked beneath it, on the floor of the box.

A photographic print, though it was impossible to make out what it showed in the graveyard gloaming. It was black and white, he could see that. Behind him Foster switched on a torch, careful not to shine the beam directly on to the picture, but illuminating the print. The image came into focus and it chilled Nigel to his core.

A row of hideously charred bodies, more than a dozen, some tiny, obviously children, were laid out on the ground in a row, in front of a burned-out building.

While Nigel continued to stare, Foster shut the box, took it back to the grave to put it back where it had been found. In the background Nigel heard him make a phone call to the vicar, telling him he could come in now and perform the burial rites as requested by the diocese before Mickey and Jim filled in the pit.

Nigel continued to stare at the gruesome picture. Rictus grins on each of the burned bodies, some frozen in contorted agony, the rigor mortis hands of others held rigid out in front as if in supplication. Who were these people? he thought.

The secret had been unearthed. Now it had to be deciphered.

19

The image of those blackened bodies haunted the few snatched minutes of sleep Nigel had that night. He gave up on the prospect of any rest shortly after six, less than three hours after going to bed, and fixed himself a pot of tea, as he re-scanned the photo over and over in his mind. Twelve bodies in total, at least five children, all laid out in a line in readiness for burial, he presumed. At one end was the mournful face of a man, leathered and worn, holding a spade. Sarah Rowley had not wanted anyone to see this picture, to even know of its existence.

He stayed there for an hour, perhaps more. Outside the wind howled. On the radio, Naomi's disappearance had been relegated to second item on the news list. Instead, news reporters intoned dramatically from storm-tossed coastal towns, delivering, with lip-smacking glee, dire predictions of floods and mayhem, while others spoke gravely of disrupted travel for Monday morning commuters. It was only when he sat down that he saw he'd missed a call.

The ringing phone brought him back to the present. Chris Westerberg. He had the results of the biogeographical ancestry test on Katie Drake's DNA.

'Bloody awful day outside, is it not?' the Irishman said after they had greeted each other. Nigel agreed it was. 'I managed to rush through the results of this test for you.'

'Really?'

'Yeah, six per cent of her genes are Native American. Given her age, and using the thirty-year rule for each generation, I think we can say with certainty that a maternal Native American ancestor entered the bloodline circa 1850–1860ish. You're looking at her marrying a white Anglo-Saxon man around that time. Hope that helps.'

Nigel dressed hurriedly, throwing on the mud-spattered trousers he'd worn the previous night, and ran to the street outside, ignoring the elements. He called Foster from his phone on the way. The detective was arriving at work. He explained what Westerberg had told him: that Sarah Rowley's mother was a Native American who married a white man around the mid-nineteenth century. While it would be almost impossible to trace every single marriage between a Native American and a settler in that time, if the man she married was a Mormon, and she became a Mormon – and this at a time when the religion was still in a fledgling stage – then there was a chance he might be able to pinpoint enough likely candidates, see how many children they bore, and whether any had a girl around the same time Sarah was born.

'But you said they would almost certainly have changed their name?' Foster replied.

'True. Their surname definitely. Their given name? Maybe not. It's a long shot, but it may mean that I can pick up the paper trail and find out what it was that happened in the States back in 1890, why they fled.' He paused. 'And I think the reason they fled has something to do with the burned corpses on that photograph.'

'Do it,' Foster replied.

*

Nigel had often wondered how many people had lived and died since the first man stood upright thousands and thousands of years ago. He'd seen a few estimates: the most learned and reasoned ones putting the figure between around 70 and 120 billion. Creationists – who think the human race began in the Garden of Eden with Adam and Eve six thousand years ago, and believe that an Almighty flood wiped out what there was of mankind apart from Noah and his next of kin a few thousand years before Christ was born – are more conservative and pitch their estimates around the 50 billion mark. Of those dead billions, very few left any trace of their existence. Only those born since around 1500 or 1600 are even likely to have been recorded as they passed across the earth, which means tens of billions of people are, in the eyes of the Mormon Church, 'lost souls', unable to receive the Gospel because we can never know their names and therefore never baptize them by proxy.

Yet, as Nigel knew, that still left billions of men and women and children whose brief time on the planet did go recorded. It was the task of saving those souls that the ample resources of the Mormon Church were concentrated upon. Missionaries and representatives of the Church had fanned out across the globe, filming and copying the estimated six or seven billion names stored in archives and repositories in countries worldwide. More than one and a half billion of these names had been captured on roll after roll of microfilm and stored in climate-controlled conditions in a secure granite mountain lair near Salt Lake City: a catalogue of the dead.

These names were searchable on an online database. Yet

Nigel knew that was no use. It could be searched by name only and he had no names. His only option was to visit the Hyde Park family history centre, the unassuming modern building alongside the chapel Foster had visited the day before. To be able to target his search, he needed more information, and he guessed the family history centre, run by Latter-day Saints, would be the best and quickest way.

It was Monday and the centre was sparsely populated. He found a free computer and called up the 1860 US Federal Census, the first to contain the biographical information he was seeking. A quick scan of Mormon history told him that Mormons had made their great trek west to Salt Lake City by that time, escaping persecution from other sectors of American society who believed them to be a weird cult. So he narrowed his search to Utah. He knew that the enumerators had noted down whether the person was white, black or mulatto. He knew they entered other ethnicities, too. In the keyword field, he typed 'Indian' and hit search.

112 results.

He scanned down the list. Most of the names were children, few of them older than eighteen and rarely more than one per household. They had taken on the surname of the head of the house, all of which suggested to Nigel that they were domestic servants, or farm labourers if they were males. However, there were a handful of Indian women who were married to white men, several of them based in Green River, which another Internet search revealed to be a trading post and river crossing through which the Mormons passed on their great western hike to their haven in the desert.

Nigel jotted down all the female names, their husbands and children if they were married. Then he called up the 1870 census. Made a note of the new additions, both to the families he was aware of and any new female names of interest. Numbers had swelled, mainly because of the inclusion of an Indian settlement at Corn Creek, led by a Chief named Kanosh who lived in Teepee Number One and whose wife, under the column outlining her relationship to the head, was described as 'Squaw 1'.

He moved to the 1880 census. Again, the number had grown. The first name on the list caught his eye immediately. Temperance, Utah. Annaleah Walker. He clicked the link and there was a screenshot of the original census page. Annaleah was twenty-four. Her occupation was listed as 'Keeping house'. Despite her age, she already had three children: John aged seven, Nathaniel aged five, Sarah aged four. The last name made his heart beat a little faster. Could it be? It would mean she was fifteen when she married, and had lied about her age. A possibility. He ploughed on.

Annaleah's relationship to the head of the household was described as 'wife'. Yet there was no mention of a husband anywhere on the page. There was another family listed below with the same surname: Clara Walker, aged twenty, a wife, also keeping house, who had one child and a domestic servant. Sisters? Widows? But the census would say that, surely? Next door was another family, with a head this time and his wife and numerous children. Nigel clicked a link to the previous page.

All became clear. There was one man, Orson Walker, aged fifty-two. He had seven wives, of which Annaleah was the sixth, and twenty-five children, with the promise of more to come seeing as four of his wives were under thirty. His mouth gaping, Nigel continued to scroll through the pages. The same seemed to be the case throughout the town of Temperance. A man aged between forty and seventy living in a house with several wives and a whole brood of children. Temperance? Nigel could see there was one activity from which they did not abstain.

He went through the whole town. There must have been around 500 people. Many women, lots of children, a number of middle-aged men but few aged between twenty and forty. He scrolled though all the pages for the town. There were some conventionally married couples but they were in the minority. In the last house in Temperance, yet another farm, he saw another name. Horton Taylor. He was six. He had three sisters and a brother, and his father, John, had just one wife, Nancy. He scrolled back to look at Sarah's entry. Surely no coincidence? Perhaps Horton had lied about his age, too?

He checked the 1890 census. As he suspected, no Sarah, no Horton. It was all piecing together. By mid-June they were in London. The Walker clan, like the rest of Temperance, seemed diminished and fractured. Orson Walker was there, though he lived in a new address with only one wife. Two of the other wives, including Annaleah, lived at separate addresses with a handful of children between them. The others had gone. He knew why: the Mormons officially renounced polygamy in 1890. The hierarchy had claimed God had spoken, though the US government had also done so, threatening to outlaw the Church if it didn't abolish the practice outright. It appeared to have had a quick effect, Nigel noted dryly; the Walker clan was not the only one to have become more diffuse. Meanwhile, the Taylor clan had gone and Nigel was unable to trace them to another town.

He went outside, rolled himself a cigarette. He smoked thoughtfully, trying to work out where to go next. He had found them, he was sure. An Indian mother. The same first names, neither appearing on the 1890 census in any state, never mind Utah Territory. The ages did not tally, but they might have lied about those. He shook his head, marvelling at the ability of two teenagers to undertake such an epic journey.

He returned to the centre and continued working through the census. After 1890 there was no sign of Annaleah or any of her family, old or young, in Temperance, the whole of Utah or anywhere else in the United States. The same applied to 1910 and the two censuses thereafter – the family had been erased from the records. He entered both Sarah and Horton's names into the Family Search engine. As he expected, only their births were recorded.

He asked at the information counter if there were any other records. There was a database of Mormon pioneers, those who made the trek across the badlands to Utah between 1846 and 1868, or sailed from European shores to join this new faith. In the search field he entered the name of Orson Walker. There he was, born in Hartford, Washington, New York, in 1828. He clicked the name and was immediately presented with a page of biographical information. The son of Jared Walker and Charity Wheeler – who died shortly after Orson's birth and was only baptized in 1963, 135 years after her death – Orson became a Mormon at the same time as his father, in 1839, and was endowed – a sort of initiation ceremony – six years later in Nauvoo. The date of his death was left blank.

Nigel scrolled down the page. Each of Orson's seven wives were listed, the date of their marriage, together with the date they were 'sealed', united with each other and their children for eternity; unsealed marriages were dissolved at death.

Annaleah was there. She eventually had seven children. Her date of birth was 1856. Her parents' names were listed as unknown, likewise her date of death. Sarah's date of birth was given and nothing else: 1876. There was more autobiographical information on her siblings, not least their date of death.

All but John, the eldest, were said to have died on the same day: 22 September 1890.

At first Nigel thought it might be a data input error, the wrong button pressed and the same date repeated. He scoured the details of the other 6 wives and 31 children of Orson Walker, the last of whom was born in 1889. Of the 42 members of the family, 18 of them were listed as dying on that autumn day. He asked but was assured the database was usually very accurate. What had happened? He needed newspaper reports.

Every single issue of the *Logan Leader* (which became the *Utah Journal*, then the *Logan Journal* and finally just *The Journal* in 1892) between 1879 and 1898 had been photographed and put online. Once again the energy and manpower the Latter-day Saints expended on making so much of history accessible staggered him. The nation's memory bank was being preserved and made available to all. What-ever their motives, Nigel could only applaud the results.

He went straight to 22 September 1890. By that time the newspaper was being published bi-weekly rather than weekly. He found the page and scrolled down through July and August. There was an edition on September 17th. Another on the 20th.

The issue for Wednesday 24th was missing. The next edition also. He brought it to the attention of the staff. Two or three gathered around and looked. Faces were pulled, heads scratched, an air of general bewilderment. No one could come up with a reason. Nigel went outside, into the early winter gloaming, and called Donna Faugenot in Salt Lake City, a genealogist he'd never met but had often worked with, helping him out with snippets of research in the US and vice versa. He asked if she knew of any databases the *Logan Leader* might be on. She didn't. Any chance she could pull the originals? Donna was a lone gun like himself but had a vast network of contacts and researchers she could call on across the USA. Leave it with me, she told him. Nigel went back in, scoured a few other indexes and databases without success. As he smoked another cigarette, by now plunged into darkness, he received a call from America.

Donna had a smoky voice and an unadorned turn of phrase he found highly appealing. From it, and the French surname, he had conjured an exotic image of her as a chain-smoking, straight-talking yet nonchalant blonde. One day he might even find out.

'Jesus, Nigel,' she said, a whistle in her voice. 'What is in those damn newspaper reports?'

He laughed hesitantly. 'I have no idea. Why?'

'Why? They're only locked away in probably the most secret, inaccessible place outside of Lincoln's tomb, that's why.'

'Really?'

'You bet. From what you told me, I figured this was a Mormon thing. So I called the library in Salt Lake City. They checked and got straight back to me. No, I can't see them. Then I phoned an inside contact at the library. He tells me the originals of those newspapers aren't in the usual place. They're in a vault where the Church keeps a lot of things that it doesn't want the outside world to see.'

Nigel was flummoxed. 'Is there anything I can do from here?'

Donna fell silent. 'I can send a guy up to Logan County to scout around. Ask some questions, I suppose. But as for getting those newspapers, unless you got some kind of official request you can present, and it better be pretty damn official, then you've as much chance of seeing those newspapers as I have of playing the Grand Ole Opry.'

'Well, I am working for the London Metropolitan Police and the newspapers could help save a fourteen-year-old girl's life and catch a killer.'

There was a pause. 'You're kidding, right?'

'No, actually, I'm being deadly serious.'

'Then you better get your sweet little Limey ass to Salt Lake City.' Another pause. 'And I better start practising the fiddle.'

20

Susie Danson sipped her coffee and looked through the papers spread out in front of her on Foster's desk. She had taken a few hours to look over the crime-scene photos and post mortem reports that Dave Alvin had forwarded on, while Foster had filled her in about the Mormon link.

'It appears I was wrong to believe this was all about sexual interest in Naomi,' she said, as she picked up the photos of the executed bodies of Martin Stamey and his son. 'There seems to be far more at play here.'

'It was the right call given the information we had then,' Foster replied.

She shrugged. 'I suppose.' She took another sip of her coffee. 'I think we can say, if these two cases are related and that is by no means certain, that the positioning of the bodies is significant. Three of the bodies – Katie, Martin and his son – have been dragged from the house into the garden, no mean feat, and with many inherent risks. The killer would only do this sort of thing if it was necessary. If it fitted into some sort of plan.' Susie leaned forward, warming to her theme. Foster could listen to her voice all day – clear, soft, each word beautifully pronounced. Put it over an advert and he'd buy the product, regardless. The grain of her voice made what she said even more compelling.

'All three victims taken outside were face down. This could mean the killer didn't like to see what he'd done, the look of death in their faces. Maybe he's ashamed. Or . . .' she paused.

'Or what?'

'Maybe they need to be laid face down as part of what he's doing. In Katie Drake's case he slit her throat after he killed her, when he had dragged her into the garden. In the case of the Stameys, he shot them in their beds, took them outside, where it appears he shot them again. He must have known father and son were already dead when he took them outside. But he chose to injure them some more. It wasn't frenzy or anger; it was deliberate. It's not enough for these people to be merely dead. There has to be an extra act of retribution.' She looked at him. 'The mother, Carol, is left in the house. She isn't a direct maternal descendant of the couple you mention, the ones who turned up in 1891?'

'No. She married into the line.'

Susie nodded. 'That's significant. But then Leonie's mother, Gillian, died of a heroin overdose, didn't she?'

Foster nodded his head. 'I think there's every chance the killer either gave her the dose or the heroin. It was too good for her to obtain. I think he knew that the amount she usually hit up on with this stuff, that kind of purity, was going to kill her.'

'That doesn't fit with these wounds, this sort of ritual-istic aspect.'

'This was three years ago. Perhaps he's become more ambitious since then.'

'There is a hierarchy at work here. It's not enough for the direct descendants to simply die. There is another punishment for them.'

'Do you think he expected the daughter to be there?'

'You see, that's where it gets interesting. Gut feeling, I think he knew she wouldn't be. He didn't *want* her to be. She's eleven?'

'Yes.'

'Naomi is fourteen. The other missing girl you told me about, Leonie, she was fourteen, too. They went missing on their birthday. That age has great significance for him. This girl isn't of age yet. If you don't catch him, he'll be back for her. The girls serve some purpose. Purity, virginity perhaps. The women, they have to die. The men, too. That eleven-year-old boy in your care, he's a target for certain. But the killer needs the girls. He can use them.' She brushed some imaginary dust from her lap. 'I'd hate to think what for. One other thing: he has a plan he's working to.'

'A family tree, I suppose.'

'Yes, obviously. He has a list of victims. But there's more to it than that.'

Foster nodded. He produced the print found in Sarah Rowley's grave. He told Susie about its origin.

She pulled a face but said nothing.

'Do you think this has any relevance?' he asked.

'Maybe. The bodies are laid out, but for burial. There could be something in that. This could be his motivation. What is it?'

'That's it; we don't know.' He placed it on the table. 'What do you think about our killer now; personal characteristics, that sort of thing?'

'If all this is linked, then he's stronger than I thought. Fitter. He's determined. I stick to what I said earlier about him being charming, able to mix. Even more so if he managed to lure Leonie away. He has charisma, a compelling and persuasive nature. I take away what I said about him having previous with young girls. This is about much more than having his wicked way with the girl of his choosing.'

It confirmed all Foster suspected.

'I would say one other thing.'

'What?'

'I don't think he's working alone.'

'He has a sidekick?'

'I didn't say that. Given how prolific he is, how he's working, I think he's receiving support in some way.'

'Who?'

'That's for you lot to find out.'

'Will you come with me and say all this to Harris?' he asked plaintively.

She checked her watch. ' I'm supposed to be somewhere twenty minutes ago. Can't you make your own case? I'll submit a report.'

'We don't have time. It might have greater power if you came with me.'

'Why?' She didn't wait for his answer, but saw a brief flash of amusement spread across his face. 'Because we're seeing each other?'

Until she said that last sentence in the present and not past tense, part of him had hoped Friday had been their one and only date and it had been an absolute disaster.

'Yes,' he replied. 'I'm not flavour of the month.'

'I heard. You need to look after yourself. You went through a hell of an ordeal and you need to take things slowly, anathema though that might be.'

'Harris pillow-talking, is he?'

'Grow up, Grant,' she snapped back.

He held his hand up. 'Sorry. That was uncalled for. The fact still stands that I need you to help persuade him that there is more to this case than he thinks. That Naomi may well still be alive but that unspeakable things could be happening to her right now. That another young girl might have been kidnapped and abused. That another is under police protection and could be in danger. That an eleven-year-old boy is in very real danger of being killed.'

She looked at him, brow furrowed, for a few seconds then sighed. 'OK,' she said. 'Take me to him.'

'Thanks.'

'Don't mention it.' She started to collect the papers, then looked at him with a wide grin, blue eyes dancing. 'So. You're jealous?'

As Foster was leaving his office with Susie his phone rang. Barnes. Despite the background sound of traffic and the wind that distorted the call, Foster listened as Nigel told him about the missing newspapers, the vault and its restricted access. He knew that even if the answer wasn't in those reports, it remained their best hope. He told Barnes to go home and stand by the phone. He ended the call and made his way to Harris, Susie at his side, with even greater purpose.

DS Harris oozed frustration. Even the presence of Susie failed to act as any sort of balm. He kept taking deep breaths and rubbing his hand across the back of his neck, kinking it back as if seeking relief. Foster could see the lack of sleep, as well as the lack of progress in finding Naomi, was taking tangible toll. Blokes like Harris were expected to get results – and they had nothing.

'Tell me you have a breakthrough, Grant,' he sighed. 'God knows we need one.'

I've got him at exactly the right time, Foster thought. He told him about the Mormon link. Through his weariness, Harris still managed to contort his features into a look of incredulity.

'Let me get this straight,' he said slowly. 'Katie Drake, together with some family in Essex, are being killed because they – or, more likely, one of their ancestors – broke some Mormon covenant?'

'Pretty much so, yes,' Foster replied.

'And you think that this might have something to do with the fact that if these people are dead then they can be turned into Mormons?'

He nodded. 'Baptized by proxy.'

Harris ran his hands down his face, stretching the skin. 'And an eleven-year-old boy who has been sleeping at your house might be the next victim?'

Foster nodded his agreement.

'But what about Naomi? If the killer is exacting some sort of ecclesiastical revenge, then why wasn't she killed, too? Don't they want to convert her? Why kidnap her and not just kill her there and then? The same goes for this other girl you say's missing. If she's been writing letters to her brother then that would indicate she hasn't been killed.'

Susie offered her theory of the girls serving a purpose. It might just have been Foster's jaundiced eye, but he appeared to take what she said more seriously. Harris listened intently. When she finished, Foster spoke again.

'We know that the victims shared two ancestors who turned up from the States in 1890, who seemed to have run away from something in America. Some kind of atrocity. We found a picture that belonged to Sarah Rowley showing a row of charred bodies, killed in a fire. We don't know what it means but it might be linked to the fact that eighteen of Sarah Rowley's ancestors died on the same day in 1890. We need to find out more. Maybe those two people who fled had something to do with that and their descendants are being made to pay.' He paused. 'And the answer to it could be lying in the vault of the main family history library in Salt Lake City.'

Harris's face creased. 'Fat lot of good it is to us there.' He caught the intensity of Foster's stare and knew immediately what he was thinking. 'You're proposing I send you out there?'

Foster shook his head. 'No, not me. Nigel Barnes. We send him with an official request from ourselves to access this information. It may lead to more research. He's better placed to do that than I am.'

'I don't feel happy sending a civilian out on his own, Grant.'

'Send a copper who can go with him.'

Harris took another deep gasp of air. He remained silent for a minute, scratching at the back his neck, staring at the wall. He looked back at Foster. 'OK,' he said, nodding. 'We send them tonight. I need something, anything, to kick-start this, to help us find her. Dare I say it, even if she's dead then we'll have a body for evidence and a starting point. Who do you propose we send to accompany Barnes?'

'I have someone in mind.' He turned to leave.

'Grant?'

'What?'

Another deep breath. 'Forget the return to work plan. Work as late and as long as it takes.'

Gary was brought back to Foster's office by a young male detective who wore a look of boredom and distaste. The pair had spent the previous couple of hours in the canteen, or in front of a television, and it was clear it had not been a bonding experience for either. The young cop almost bundled Gary into the office in his eagerness to get away and return to proper work, but not before Foster asked him to wait outside for them. He'd be needed in a second. Gary appeared sullen. But then he mostly did.

'What a muppet he was,' he said.

Foster ignored him. 'Look, I'm going to be really busy. I've sorted out some temporary accommodation for you where you'll be well looked after. More importantly, you'll be safe. You'll have a policeman living with you 24/7. You won't be able to get out much, which is a shame, but you'll have satellite TV, computers, game consoles, so there'll be ample compensation. It won't be for long.'

'I ain't going,' he said, his jaw sticking out perceptibly.

Foster sighed. 'Why?'

Gary said nothing.

'Look, you have my word. It's safe. Safer than anywhere else you could be. Safer than my place. Safer than the streets. I wouldn't suggest you go there unless it was absolutely cast-iron certain you won't come to any harm.'

Gary was looking out of the window, at the trees that were bowing obsequiously to the gusting wind. Foster thought he might cry.

'Look, there's an Xbox, a Wii, there's a desktop computer hooked up to the Internet, there's a DVD library with every film you can think of, takeaways on tap. In fact the more I think about it, the more I'd like to be there.'

The boy turned his large, mournful brown eyes on him. 'So why ain't you gonna be there?'

It was only then that Foster understood the kid's reluctance. For a few seconds, he was lost for words; no pithy comeback or retort. Nothing. A new experience. Instead he stroked his chin.

'I'm not going to be there, Gary, because I need to find the man who kidnapped your sister, kidnapped the girl who went missing last week, the killer of your aunt, your uncle and your cousin, the man who has been following you,' he replied eventually. 'And to do that while having you around is not that easy.' The kid's face grew more mournful. 'Not because I don't want you around, but because of having to ferry you around. Plus it's not safe for you to be with me. Trust me.'

Gary continued to stare at him, barely blinking, but his resistance appeared to be waning.

'In fact, if I know you're not in danger then that will make my job of trying to catch this psycho much easier. You understand?'

Gary nodded, even tried to force a smile

'Easy, now. You don't want your face to crack.' He went over and ruffled his hair. Gary let him.

Less than a week ago he'd have sunk his teeth into my hand, Foster thought. He smiled. Then he picked up the phone and told Barnes to pack his toothbrush.

21

The main floor was crowded with people – men and women of various shapes and sizes, backgrounds and ages – but Nigel immediately recognized the kind. Amateur family historians. There was something about their quiet, unfussy air, the atmosphere of eager expectation as they chatted among themselves, hushed yet excited. Many of them had crossed states, travelled many thousands of miles to be here, either waiting to be collected by a guide or tour organizer or having made their own, independent pilgrimage to the Church of Latter-day Saints' vast central library in downtown Salt Lake City. All of them were seeking insights into their pasts and origins. He envied them in a way. The American experience was an essentially immigrant one. Many would find stories of ancestors who had crossed oceans and risked life and limb in search of a new life, fleeing persecution or hardship, starting afresh in the new world, stories that were less common in the UK.

He stood to one side, watching, detached in more ways than one. He had never travelled further than mainland Europe, so the ravages of jetlag were new to him. He was running on adrenaline, the sense of being close to discovering something of import his only spur after a night of sleep had evaded him entirely. They had left Heathrow the night before, arriving in Chicago at midnight. The only seats were in economy, and at O'Hare airport they had a six-hour wait until catching a dawn flight over the Rocky Mountains to the Mormon capital, swooping in over snow-capped peaks that glistened in the eye-popping winter sun.

His dehydrated skin was stretched taut like a drum and his head felt as if it was half-filled with water. He felt dislocated, as if an actor had taken over his part and he was watching from afar. Little more than sixteen hours before he'd been sitting on a tube rattling across rush-hour London. Now here he was six time zones west, breakfast-time in America, in a city about which he knew nothing, other than its importance as the centre of the Mormon Church.

Heather emerged from the crisp, cold air where she'd been making a call back to the UK. Her hair was still wet from the shower she'd grabbed at the unspectacular business hotel where they'd dropped their bags.

'I need more of that fresh air,' she said. 'It's a balm to the lungs compared to London. It's like breathing for the first time.' She checked her watch. 'The fax has been sent. What time are we meeting your girlfriend?'

Nigel had suggested Donna Faugenot meet them. She was well connected and knew the source material better than he did. She might come in handy. He ignored the teasing.

'Ten. In the snack area.' He pulled a map from his pocket. 'It's on this floor. Somewhere.'

Five floors, almost 2,000 visitors daily, more than 600 million names on its database, and 2.5 million rolls of microfilm – Nigel had to admit the LDS library dwarfed the National Archives in Kew. It was Tuesday – it took both of them a while to remember that through the fog of travel – and so the library was open until nine in the evening, but even that early in the morning it was crammed full. They headed through the throng to the snack area, a small airless cubby hole that made the old canteen at the Family Records Centre look like the dining room of the Dorchester.

There was only one person there, sipping bottled water, reading a newspaper. A blonde woman in jeans, trainers and a black zip-up jacket, heavily made up, boldly attractive.

'Donna?' Nigel asked tentatively.

The woman looked up, then flashed a broad smile of perfect white teeth. She stood up. She was tall, maybe the same height as him. 'Nigel!' she exclaimed. 'Nigel Barnes!' He smiled and was about to hold out his hand when she embraced him, planting a kiss on his right cheek. 'It's good to meet you.' She looked him up and down. 'I love the jacket. Very professorial,' she added, nodding.

'Thanks,' Nigel said. 'Pleasure to meet you, too.'

'It's great to put a face to the voice.' She flashed her full-beam grin. 'You're as cute as your accent. How was the flight?'

'Er, long.' He turned to Heather, who was standing a few feet behind him, the curious smile back on her lips. 'This is Detective Inspector Heather Jenkins.'

They shook hands, agreeing it was good to meet each other.

'Thanks for helping,' Nigel added. 'You really didn't need to . . .'

'What the hell,' she said, waving away his protest. She

leaned forward conspiratorially. 'Always glad to be a guide through the evil empire,' she whispered.

Nigel smiled. The Mormon Church's tentacles extended into every nook and cranny of genealogy – libraries, websites, publications. No other group was anywhere near as powerful. But no other group made the pursuit of family history a cornerstone of their religion.

'Keep that one quiet, honey. The walls have ears,' she said and winked. 'Anyway, what's your plan?'

'We're going to check if they've got the request and see if they'll hand the material over. Shall we meet you back here later?' Heather said.

Donna shrugged. 'Sounds good. If I'm not here, I'll be on this floor. Just holler – quietly, of course.'

They turned to go.

'Fascinating woman,' Heather said, as they made their way to the special collections desk. 'Wonder how early she has to get up in the morning to put that lot on her face?'

They reached the second floor, much less crowded than the one they'd left. The special collections desk was in the far corner of the room. It was manned by a nervous, balding man in his mid-forties, wearing a pair of thick dark glasses. 'Edward,' his name badge said. Heather performed the introductions. 'A fax has been sent ahead of us about our request for information?' she added.

The man look nonplussed. 'Hold with me just a second,' he said, and disappeared behind a door. A minute or so later he returned, brandishing a piece of paper. 'I have the request here.'

'Excellent,' Heather said.

He furrowed his brow. 'There's just one problem.

Actually, make that two problems. You can't access the information as it stands.'

Nigel sensed Heather bristle.

'As what stands?'

'To enter the special collections to access this information, you need a valid LDS temple recommend.'

'How do we get one of those?'

'Are either of you a member of the LDS Church?'

'No,' Heather said, trying to suppress a snort of laughter.

'Then, broadly speaking, you won't be able to get a temple recommend and enter the special collections.'

'Can't you just bring it out here?' Nigel could see Heather's patience, frayed by missing a night's sleep, was about to break.

Edward shook his head slowly. 'No. You need to enter the special collections.'

Heather leaned forward against the desk. 'Can I just clear something up? The material we want to see could be of great help in an ongoing murder investigation. We have flown all the way from the United Kingdom because we were told the material would be handed to us on special request. We have made that request. Now you're telling us, after we've flown all this way, that the material we need, that could help us find a killer, is actually unavailable because we're not members of the LDS Church?'

'I see your predicament, ma'am, and I sympathize. It is not my decision but –'

'Let me guess,' Heather snapped. 'You're just following orders?'

'Well, yes . . .'

'Look, I appreciate all that. Can I speak to someone in a position of authority? I've flown all the way from England and I'm not going anywhere until I get to see that material.'

Edward nodded. 'I'll go and see if anyone's available. Hold right there.' He disappeared behind his door.

Heather turned round, seething. 'Can you fucking believe this?' she said, shaking her head. Nigel didn't know what to say. Already his mind was listing other ways they might be able to get hold of those newspapers. He came up blank.

'Blousey Brown downstairs, can she help?'

'Who?'

'Who do you think? Avon calling. Your friend, Donna.'

'I don't know,' he said. 'I very much doubt it.'

'Go and metaphorically holler for her, see if she's a member. See if she knows anyone who is and has one of these recommend things.'

Nigel trudged back downstairs to the main floor, and immediately ran into Donna speaking to someone next to a vast bank of microfilm readers. She saw him approaching, patted her fellow conversationalist on the shoulder and switched her smile to full dazzle. She radiated health. Next to her, crumpled after a day of travel, still wearing the same clothes he had left London in, Nigel felt grotty and unkempt.

'Couldn't keep away, huh?'

'No, we actually need your help right now. They won't give us access without something called a temple recommend.'

'Special collections? It's in there, is it? I didn't know

that. I thought they'd bring it to the front desk for collection.' The smile disappeared. 'You sure?'

'The guy up there has told my colleague she needs a temple recommend to see the material.'

She let out a low whistle and creased her brow. 'That's strange. It shouldn't be in there.'

'Why not?'

'Special collections is for Mormon eyes only. Church members use it to look up their dead ancestors who were LDS and check out ceremonies carried out in temple, baptism for the dead, sealing ceremonies, that kind of stuff. Not newspaper reports. I smell a lot of a rat.'

'Do you know anyone who has a temple recommend?'

'Sure. I do.'

Nigel almost performed a double take. For a few seconds, words failed him.

Donna sensed his incredulity. 'I take it you didn't have me down as a Mormon?'

No, he thought. You've done nothing but flirt with me since I arrived. You wear make-up. You're attractive. I thought all these things were antithetical to Mormonism. 'I hadn't presumed . . .' he stuttered.

She put her hand up. 'It's OK. We have an image problem. But be assured, not all Mormon women are dull kewpie-doll housewives. I think some Mormon men would like us to be, but there's still room for individualism.' She put her hands on her hips. 'Not much, though. Especially if you're a working single parent, and a divorcee. But enough of that crap. Take me to where your friend is.'

They made their way to the second floor where Heather

was deep in conversation with a different gentleman, this one in a suit, exuding more authority than the last. His face bore the simpering look of someone trying to be sympathetic while remaining obstinate. He glanced out of the corner of his eye at Nigel and Donna approaching, and a mote of panic crept across his bland features. Nigel could hear Heather's diatribe.

'You're obstructing a police investigation. One that may well lead to the death of more people. Does the Mormon Church really want blood on its hands?' she said.

'Hell, no,' Donna said. 'We have quite enough of that already.'

Heather furrowed her brow; gave Donna a quizzical look. The 'we' and its revelation that she was a Mormon obviously came as a big surprise, as it had to Nigel.

Donna ignored her, concentrated on the man in the suit. 'Todd.'

'Donna.' The look of panic spread.

'These people are our guests here. They've come a long way. They're working on important business, like the lady told you. Cut them a break, huh?'

He shrugged. 'Donna, I don't make the rules. They need a temple recommend.'

'I have one,' she said. 'I'm working for these guys. Ain't that right?'

'It sure is,' Heather said, nodding.

'So move along and get this information ready for these good people to take a look at.'

'OK,' he said and trudged away.

'Thanks for that,' Heather said, and Nigel could tell she truly meant it.

'Not a problem. I have a fifteen-year-old daughter. I wouldn't want any petty religious bureaucracy getting in the way of anyone finding her. Plus, I'm intrigued. Just what the hell has all this to do with the Mormon Church?'

Heather leaned against a table. 'When you said back then that the Mormon Church had enough blood on its hands, what did you mean?'

Donna smiled. 'My Church was established in frontierland America. It was a bloody, lawless place and the founders did what they could to survive and prosper. Not all of it good. Not that the current Church leaders would care to admit it. I'm different. I'm a genealogist like Nigel here. I embrace the past and all its imperfections rather than seeking to airbrush it. My guess is that the newspaper reports you're seeking don't paint the Church in a particularly flattering light, so someone is making it as difficult as possible for anyone to find them.'

Todd returned, not without trepidation. He had a moustache that even appeared to droop apologetically. He clapped his hands together softly and took a deep breath. 'There's a problem.'

'Why doesn't that surprise me?' drawled Donna.

'What is it?' Heather asked, attempting to cloak her impatience, unsuccessfully.

'The material you require isn't held at the library.'

There was a pause as they digested this information.

Heather spoke. 'Where is it then?'

'It exists only as an original copy.'

'It's never been microfilmed?' Donna asked.

Todd shook his head.

'So it's not even at the granite mountain vault?'

Again Todd shook his head.

'But we were told the LDS Church had the material,' Heather said, nonplussed. 'That's why we're here.'

'I believe the Church does have copies,' Todd said.

'Where are they then?'

'I'm afraid that information is classified.'

Nigel could contain his anger no longer. 'A newspaper is a matter of public record,' he spat out. 'You can't confiscate it, change history, not unless you're a bloody Stalinist.'

Todd looked at him impassively, soaking it up like a human sponge.

It merely served to further enrage Nigel. 'This is censorship, pure and unadorned. I thought this was supposed to be the Land of the Free? Or does that not apply to the Mormon Church?'

Todd looked at Nigel, waiting for him to finish. There was an awkward silence. He drew himself up taller. 'I'm sorry, but any complaints you have must be taken up with the Church authorities.'

He turned on his heels and scurried away to his office hideout.

They sat in silence at a café two blocks from the library. All of a sudden Nigel was feeling the effects of missing a night's sleep, as if he was wearing a hat of lead. He hoped the coffee would help. He could see Heather was seething. A girl was missing, and they had flown halfway across the world to obtain a lead that might help find her, yet they had been thwarted by the clandestine practices of the

Church of Latter-day Saints. Donna appeared to sense their resentment.

'My Church has got a lousy sense of what constitutes good PR,' she drawled, ruby-red lips blowing gently on her decaff latte, creating a rippling effect across its foamy top. 'It's an endless source of frustration to those of us who believe in openness and honesty. But the hierarchy has a somewhat paranoiac view of our Church's past.'

'Why?' Nigel asked. He couldn't see what could be served by squirrelling away documents that were part of the public record.

'We're a modern religion. The Mormon Church was founded at the start of the era of civil registration, which means there's a host of documents that people can look at, some of which can be used to question Church ortho-dox history. Then you have newspapers that print incon-venient things. I don't recall Jesus or Mohammed having to deal with the press. Things you didn't know about can turn up and cause people to dispute the accepted view of events. And, rather than saying, "Shit, do your worst – we believe it, we think this is a religion worth following and so do ten million new folks every year across the globe," the culture is to hush things up, get your mitts on anything remotely critical of the Church, or which presents an unkind view, and hide it away from prying eyes. It's self-defeating, because most of these documents and records appear in one form or another. Nigel and I know you can't sit on the past. It has a way of leaking out, like blood through sand.'

'Amen to that,' Nigel said. 'The past cannot be denied.'

'In which case,' Heather said, perking up, 'there must

be somewhere where these newspaper reports still exist.'

'I'm sure they do,' Donna said. 'But y'all don't have the time. Unless.'

'Unless what?'

'I think there's only one possible thing we can do, given the urgency of your mission.'

'What?' Heather asked.

'We take a road trip.'

The noise that woke her was the smack of a stone on her window. The rest of the night unravelled like a dream and then a nightmare . . .

It being the night before the wedding, she was granted the privilege of sleeping in a bed on her own rather than with her sisters. Not that she did anything other than stare at the ceiling. She would have preferred the tangle of limbs and snuffling breath of others to the sound of her own sobs. Yet she had dozed off momentarily when the small crack woke her.

She knew instantly it was him. Her heartbeat, pounding from fear, now began to beat with excitement.

She went to the window. A gibbous moon sweated in the sky. She cursed the night for being so clear. There was no sign of him on the ground. As always, he must be hidden behind the barn. She climbed into a dress, grabbed a bag she had packed in anticipation of his coming, with a family portrait of herself, her mother and siblings and a few items she thought she may need, and laced her boots. She opened the window and cast an eye around the room, trying not to think of the times she had shared here with the girls, before slipping out and shimmying down the front of the house as she always did.

He was there behind the barn, his jaw set and determined, eyes burning into her.

'Thank the Lord you came,' he said.

'Did you ever think I wouldn't?'

He shrugged. 'I did not know. I wasn't sure you could ever face leaving your people behind.'

'There was never any doubt,' she replied. He grabbed her and wrapped her up tightly. They held each other close for an age.

'Where are we going?' she whispered when they came apart.

'Somewhere far away from here. I have a horse tethered by the wood. We will ride as far as we can. To the east, to the coast. Then we will leave this benighted place because I swear your father and your brothers will come and they will try to find us.'

'Leave? For where?'

'England. There is money to be made there for those willing to work hard. Come on.' He grabbed his bag from the floor, shouldered it, and then took her hand.

England? she thought. *It was half a world away. All the people she had ever met from there were those that left after hearing the Gospel. They barely had a good word to say about the place, though she suspected they ran it down in such a way to justify their decision to leave. Still, if it be his will . . .*

'Stop right there.' The voice came from behind them. A voice she knew. Alfred, her eldest stepbrother. Mean, dumb and aggressive. He was the last person she wished to find them.

Horton turned slowly to face him, tightening his grip on her hand. She could see the cold flash of hatred in those eyes. She tried to smile at Alfred, even though her heart was sinking and breaking. His face carried the same vicious sneer it always did, though the dull eyes twinkled with triumph. He looked at her. In his hands was a rifle, pointing straight at them.

'I knew you'd try and make a run for it. Father said you would. Sorry, Sarah, but you have no chance. I've been patrolling this wing of the house. Orson junior is patrolling yonder and out front is

248

guarded by Robert.' He looked at Horton. 'You picked the wrong family to mess with, little boy.'

Horton's grip on her hand tightened so hard Sarah felt she might scream. What would he do? She did not want him harmed.

'Alfred, I will come back into the house. You can take me to Father. Do what you wish. But I beg you, let Horton go. This was my idea, he —'

'Be quiet, Sarah,' Horton barked sternly.

Alfred narrowed his eyes, then a smile appeared at the corner of his mouth. 'Want to be the hero, do we, little man?' He looked back at Sarah. 'Sorry, but it's not for me to decide what happens to this piece of dirt. It will be decided by Father and the elders. If it was up to me, I'd have him strung up on the nearest tree for his insolence, the filthy godless pi—'

Horton had slowly released his grip on her hand. His went into a pocket and pulled out a pistol. A shot echoed through the night. Alfred dropped his gun, bovine face frozen in surprise. No words came, just a gurgle in his throat. The bullet had gone straight through his heart. He fell down dead at their feet.

'Run!' Horton urged, and she followed, head spinning. She turned back, half-expecting it all to be a joke, for Alfred to jump up and administer a beating like the bully he always was. But no. His body lay slumped against the side of the barn. 'Just run,' Horton exhorted her again, the pistol still in his hand. But as she turned, her toe stubbed a rock and she fell face down.

She felt his arms wrap round her to pick her up, just as there was a loud crack and something whistled over their heads. Someone was shooting. She heard Horton mumble something. From the house she could hear voices being raised. On her feet again, she looked back and saw Orson junior and Robert. Another loud crack. Closer this time. Now Horton cursed louder. My own family is trying to kill me, she thought.

He led her by the hand, building up speed, veering away from the centre of the field, where they were an easy target, towards the hedgerow to one side. He turned round and fired a shot over his shoulder, without looking, almost a reminder that he had firepower, too. It met with another whistling reply, one that furrowed the soil ahead. Thank goodness they were such wayward shots.

The sky seemed to glow brighter, her senses sharpened by the fear and the excitement. She was barely a hundred yards from her bedroom but it felt like she had crossed deserts and mountains. There could never be any going back. With him she dived head first into the hedgerow, brambles tugging at their clothing like tiny grasping fists.

They emerged the other side. The horse was there. He leapt up and hauled her behind him, dug in his heels and called for the animal to respond. It did and soon they were away into the night.

She did not look back once.

22

As they sped away from the city, Nigel watched in a mixture of wonder and bewilderment as they passed strip mall after strip mall, wide characterless boulevards littered with sign after sign selling fast food and God. It was miles before they hit any kind of open road, through monotonous wilderness, few distinguishing features in any direction, a stark reminder of the brutal, vast place Utah had once been until the Mormons had conquered and tamed it.

They were on their way to Llewellyn, capital of Cache County, the nearest town to Temperance. Nigel wondered who Llewellyn might have been – a Mormon Welshman, he presumed, who left the rolling valleys for a life on God's chosen plain. Temperance itself was no more than a tiny hamlet, with a population of around a hundred inhabitants. Llewellyn lay seventy-five miles southwest, and boasted a library, a hotel and a few other signs of life, so they figured they might have more luck there.

Donna was at the wheel, intermittently shaking her head at having discovered back in Salt Lake City that Nigel didn't possess a driving licence when she'd deferred to his masculinity and asked if he wanted to drive. 'You wouldn't last five minutes in the States,' she said, eyes still wide with disbelief. 'Public transport is for the poor and we just don't do walking.'

He smiled, let his head rest on the window, gazing out at the scenery, its size and homogeneity giving it a hypnotic beauty. Religiously, culturally and geographically, he felt like he'd stepped into a different world. His body longed for sleep and rest but his mind was awake, hungry to know more and to soak up as much as he could. Not least from Donna.

He turned to her. 'Forgive me for asking, and feel free to say it's none of my business, but how come you're still a member of the Church when you doubt its approach, the way it covers up its history, and the fact you're . . .'

'A divorcee and a single mom?'

'Well, yes,' he added, a little taken aback by her directness but grateful for her sparing him having to use a polite, strained euphemism. 'It is, after all, based on family and the sanctity of family, isn't it?'

'Amongst other things, yeah.' She shrugged. 'It's my Church. I grew up with it. I have a few problems with some of the doctrines and covenants, but then show me any Christian who agrees with everything that's said in the Bible. And there's a heck of a lot of Christians who have a problem with some of their Church's attitudes. The fact is, I got married to the wrong man and it didn't work. The way I look at it, if I'm going to be sealed to a man for eternity, which is a mighty long time, then the least I can do is make sure he's not an asshole. I ain't gonna burn in hell for that. I'll just be a damn sight more careful the next time. But the basic tenets of my Church I fully believe in. We have our jerks and our fools, just like any other Church – hell, just like any other religion – but I'm not gonna let that get in the way of me following my faith. And I still have it. Long as I do, I'll be a Latter-day Saint. Soon as it goes, I'll be downing bourbon and sleeping with any man that looks cute in jeans, like the rest of you godless heathens. Ain't that right, Heather?'

There was silence. She checked the rear-view mirror. Heather was in a deep sleep.

'Maybe not then,' she added. 'Though perhaps Heather ain't the Lee Cooper jeans kind of girl.' She gave Nigel a look from the side of her eye he could only describe as sly. 'Maybe she likes her buttoned-up English guys in, I dunno, tweed or something?'

Nigel said nothing, even resisted the temptation to check his herringbone jacket.

Donna laughed softly yet wickedly. She leaned in towards him. 'I've seen the way you look at her,' she whispered. 'Is it an unrequited thing you got going on there, Nigel? Or do I sense a bit of history?'

Nigel cleared his throat. 'I'd rather not discuss it, actually,' he said.

She nodded. 'OK, I see. I'm guessing there's a clue right there in what you said, but I know Englishmen don't like to talk about these things. She's sure pretty, though.'

'Yes,' Nigel said. 'Yes, she is.'

Again the softer, wicked laugh. 'You told her how you feel?'

Nigel glanced in the wing mirror; he could still see Heather sleeping. 'It's complicated,' he muttered.

'As far as I see it, it ain't that complicated. You tell her how you feel and you all know where you stand.'

'Maybe I did once and maybe I didn't like what happened

next. You know the phrase "once bitten, twice shy"? Well, there's something to be said for that.'

Donna gave him a kind look. 'Sometimes it's worth hanging in there, honey. I don't know much, but people appreciate someone who loves them without question. My ex-husband only loved himself. Me, I'm looking for someone who loves me happy or sad, fat or thin, with make-up or without, the whole nine yards. Generally someone who thinks the sun rises and falls at the back of my ass. Do that with Heather and she might come to her senses. I mean, I look at you and I think she's mad. If you knew your doctrine and covenants and got yourself a temple recommend, I'd be looking to get sealed with you for all eternity.' She squeezed his thigh to emphasize her point.

Maybe the Mormon Church wasn't so bad, he thought.

They entered the city limits for Llewellyn as the afternoon light left. In the rapidly descending twilight it was hard to see much of the town, though Nigel suspected he might not be missing a great deal in terms of scenery. He was wrong: as they drove into town, Donna pointed out the dark shadow of the LDS Temple on a hill overlooking the town, backlit by a dramatic blood-red sky. They rode downtown, past the historic district and along the main drag, past shops and the occasional office block until they reached the library. As the car stopped, Heather woke from her slumber with a start.

'Have I been asleep all the time?' she mumbled apologetically.

'Sparko,' Donna said.

The library formed part of the county office building, a grand old department store comprising several buildings connected and remodelled over several decades. The library occupied the ground floors and seemed cramped in such a tight space, though there were few people using it at that hour. Donna wasted no time approaching the desk and asking for copies of the *Logan Leader*. They were pointed towards the library's collection of microfilmed newspapers.

The *Logan Leader* was there but its origins were the same as that in Salt Lake City – the missing editions were still absent. Nigel went back to the desk and to the demure young woman manning it.

'Do you have the originals?' he asked.

She shook her head sadly. 'We donated most of our materials to the Church,' she said. 'That includes the newspapers.'

He cursed. 'Do you have anything at all about the history of the area?'

She showed a few local histories, but they mostly told the story of the pioneers and their heroic struggles against nature, disease and apostates. He went back to the desk.

'Do you have anything, anything at all, about a place called Temperance?'

She looked shocked. 'Temperance? Why, no, I don't think so. Is it a genealogical inquiry because we have family search . . .'

'No,' Nigel said. 'Not really.' He decided to be honest. 'I'm trying to find details of an incident that took place in Temperance in 1890, maybe a disaster of some kind, where quite a lot of people died . . .'

His question tailed away as he saw the blank look on the woman's face. It was clear she did not know what he was talking about.

'Sorry, sir,' she said. 'Have you checked the newspaper reports for the area? We have them all on microfilm.'

Not all, he thought, but he couldn't be bothered explaining about the missing copies. 'Thanks,' he said and went in search of Donna. She was ploughing through another section of local histories and memoirs with an equal lack of success.

'This is pointless,' Nigel said wearily.

Donna's resigned look suggested agreement.

'You people want to know about Temperance?'

The voice came from behind them. They both turned. A woman in her forties with jam-jar spectacles and a friendly face was smiling at them.

'We sure do,' Donna said. 'Why, can you help?'

She looked over her shoulder. 'Might get myself in some trouble over this, but I know someone who can. What do you two think of frequenting bars?'

Nigel looked at her as if she was mad. What did she mean?

Donna laughed. 'These guys are English. I don't think they'll mind. Which bar?'

'Oh, we only have one in Llewellyn. Called Hooky's, just off Main. You're looking for a guy named Pettibone. Josiah Pettibone.'

'Thanks,' Donna said.

'Just one other thing,' the woman added. 'I didn't send you.'

*

Half an hour later they had found Hooky's, a subterranean dive tucked away apologetically down a side street to nowhere. The last building on the left, just before the pavement ran out. Nigel could sense Donna's reluctance and he hesitated at the top of the stairs. 'Looks like a nice joint,' he said sardonically.

Heather brushed past. 'A bar's a bar,' she said brusquely. 'I should know, I've done my time in the pubs of the north.'

She headed down the stairs and through the door. Donna and Nigel followed.

Inside, while by no means salubrious, the bar was at least clean and bright. A radio or jukebox played some muffled country music, while the only patrons were a couple of men drinking alone, who raised their heads as one to see the new customers. So this is where the local apostates celebrated the freedom to trash their liver, thought Nigel. The barman watched them approach. Heather took a seat at the bar, ordered a beer; Nigel did likewise, while Donna went for a Diet Coke. Heather paid and remembered to tip, a custom Nigel couldn't fathom.

They drank in silence for a few seconds.

'Josiah Pettibone been in?' Heather asked.

The barman narrowed his eyes. 'Not yet. But he will be presently.' He paused. 'You from Australia?'

'England,' she replied.

'Long way to come to find a man like Josiah.'

'I'm hoping he can help us.'

The barman flashed a toothy smile. 'I'd hate to know what your problem is if Josiah is your answer.'

Heather smiled and shrugged. The barman disappeared

to the other side of the bar. Heather turned to Donna. 'Donna, you get back to Salt Lake City, no need for us to detain you. We'll wait for this guy, book a hotel, and then hire a car to drive back in the morning. I'll drive.'

'It's OK,' she said. 'I'll stick around.'

'You sure? What about your kids?'

'They're with my sister and her husband.'

'She's OK to have them?'

'Yeah. Hell, she's got nine of her own. What difference's another two gonna make? We better find a hotel, though.'

'Well, if you're sure.'

Donna asked the barman about a place to stay and then went outside to make a phone call. Heather turned to Nigel, who took the liberty of ordering another beer. 'I spoke to Foster while you and Donna were in the library. They've turned up nothing new. A bit like us,' she added.

'I hear you're looking for me.'

The interloper was a tall man in jeans and a battered suede cowboy jacket, with a drooping moustache and straggling long hair, all of which suggested he was a casualty of the 1960s, except it seemed more likely that was the decade in which he'd been born.

Heather spoke. 'Yes, we are, sir,' she said politely. 'Can I get you a drink?'

'That depends on what you want me for. I can hear you're not from around here.'

'We're not.' Heather got her badge out. 'London Metropolitan Police. I can assure you that you're not in any kind of trouble, but we're hoping you might be able to help us with someone who is.'

'Now you got me intrigued.' He gestured to the

barman. 'The usual please, Jim.' The barman grabbed a beer and filled a small glass with Scotch. He placed them on the counter. Pettibone picked up and downed the Scotch and took a sip of beer, then gasped his pleasure. 'Never had a drink on the English police before. Tastes good. How can I possibly help you? I ain't never travelled further than Ohio.'

'We're after some information about Temperance.'

'Pretty ironic, huh, given you're in a bar.' He took another hit of his beer. His eyes wore the sad, haunted look of a heavy drinker.

Heather smiled. 'Are you from there?'

He shook his head, swallowed his beer. 'No.'

'Oh,' Heather said and frowned at Nigel.

Donna returned; Heather introduced her.

'You're not English.'

'No, I'm not,' she said.

'You Church?'

She nodded. 'Is that a problem? I can leave.'

A look of anger flashed across his lived-in face. He continued to stare at her. 'No,' he said finally, and the anger evaporated. 'I like the look of you, which is more than I can say for most of your bastard Latter-day Saint cohorts.'

'Why, thank you,' she said, bowing sarcastically.

Pettibone took another swig of his beer.

'Sorry,' Heather said. 'We were led to believe you could help us with some information about Temperance and its past.'

'What do you want to know? I'm not from there, never been there, but I sure as shit know all about its past.'

'Something happened there,' Nigel said. 'In 1890, people died. The newspaper reports are missing and we can't find an account of what happened in any other source. Do you know?'

Pettibone wore a look of private amusement. 'Do I know?' he said slowly and rhetorically. He finished the bottle and looked at it.

'Another round please,' Heather said to the barman.

'Another round what?'

'Another round of drinks, please,' she clarified. 'Same again.'

Pettibone killed the shot of Scotch and winced slightly. Colour had returned to his cheeks. Nigel guessed there was a direct relation between his pallor and his alcoholic intake. He breathed deeply. 'What the fuck is going on here? Two English cops, a Mormon researcher, someone in trouble. I'd like to know a bit more, please.'

Nigel caught Heather's eye. She nodded. He reached for his satchel and picked out a copy of the picture they had found in the tin beside the body of Sarah Rowley. He put it down on the bar in front of Pettibone. He squinted and focused, then recoiled in horror.

'Where the fuck did you find that?' he said, eyes wide.

'Do you know what it is?'

'Do I know what it is?' He leaned forward. 'That old man there' – his finger stabbed towards a bewhiskered gentleman in his late sixties holding a spade and wearing an expression of mourning – 'is my great-great-great-grandfather.' He looked again, shook his head. 'I've never seen this before.'

'If you've never seen that photograph before, how do

you know it's your great-great-great-grandfather?' Heather asked.

'I seen other pictures. He was a pretty distinctive-looking fellow.' He leaned forward, rested his head on his hands and stared intently, then let out a low whistle. 'Well, I'll be . . . He must have died a few days after this was taken, because I was always told he went within a week of the fire. His heart just gave out.'

'Do you know what it is?' Heather repeated.

Pettibone sniffed. 'There was a fire,' he said. 'A pretty big fire. The ranch belonged to a man named Orson P. Walker. His daughter was sworn to be married to my ancestor, Hesker. Greedy old bastard already had seven wives but, you know, he figured he could do with one more. Thing was, she didn't much like the idea of it – and who could blame her? He was sixty-seven. She had eyes for a younger boy. So, things came to a head. One night, this boy he comes for her and they try to elope. Shots are fired. The barn goes up, the building next to it, the one next to that. Women and children are sleeping. Orson had plural wives and a heap of kids. Many of them burned in their beds. There wasn't time. That's their bodies you see lined up there; my ancestor was one of those set to bury them.' He looked back at the picture and shook his head. 'It was true. I kind of figured it might be a myth. But obviously not.'

'How many died?' Heather asked.

'Around twenty or so. They sent out a search party to find the girl and the boy. But they never found them. Lucky for them. They'd have tore them limb from limb.'

It all tallied with what Nigel had found on the census.

'That picture was found in the grave of Sarah Rowley, née Walker,' Nigel told him.

Pettibone stared at him as if it was some kind of practical joke. 'You been digging up the grave of Sarah Walker?' he said with disbelief.

'They fled to England. Changed their names and set up a whole new life,' Nigel said.

'But now someone's coming back to get their descendants. We think they're seeking revenge for what happened in 1890. For the fire,' Heather added.

'So they finally found them,' Pettibone said. 'And they're finally getting what they wanted after all this time.' He sipped his beer.

'What's that?' Nigel asked.

'Blood atonement.'

23

Over more drinks, his face lit up by barlight and beer, Pettibone explained. Blood atonement was an old Mormon belief the Church had backed away from in its search for mainstream acceptance. It decreed that some sins were so awful, so unforgivable, that the atonement of Christ was not enough to provide salvation, and that the sinner could only atone by the act of spilling blood on to the soil in death. Murder was one such sin.

Heather expressed surprise about the Church's violent beginnings. Pettibone merely raised a sardonic eyebrow. 'Blood is woven into the warp and weft of Mormon history,' he said dryly.

'But the Church no longer believes it?' Heather asked.

'No longer believes it,' Donna said with incredulity. 'They claim it has never been practised by the Church at any time.'

'Bullshit, of course,' Pettibone said, wiping his mouth. 'And where I come from, it still goes on.'

'Where *do* you come from?' Heather asked.

He smiled. 'A little place a few hundred miles due northwest of here, named Liberty City. Don't let the name fool you.'

Donna almost gasped. 'You're a member of the TCF?'

'Was a member,' Pettibone corrected. 'Ain't been

anywhere near for twenty-three years or more, and I ain't planning on ever going back.'

'Just who exactly are the TCF?' Heather asked.

Pettibone looked at Donna. 'You go first, sweet cheeks,' he said. 'I wanna hear this.'

Donna smiled a half-smile. 'The True Church of Freedom. It's a Mormon fundamentalist group. One of many that has split away from the Church because of a disagreement over core beliefs. Not one of the bigger ones. But one of the most secretive. That's about all I know. Over to you.'

Pettibone cleared his throat. 'It was founded in 1891 by Orson Walker junior. He claimed Orson to be the prophet, and legitimacy for the Church, on the basis that Orson senior – who died shortly after the fire, too – had received the Gospel directly from the Lord, that the mainstream Church were apostates, and that he and his kin should form a Church according to the revelations and teachings of Joseph Smith, Brigham Young, John Taylor and no one else.'

'So every Church President up until Woodruff, who brought in the manifesto banning plural marriage?' Donna said wryly.

'You got it. My folks are fond of plural marriage.' He took a hit of beer. 'Orson junior blamed the fire on God, said it was His wrath at his father's failure to break away and form his own Church. So the Walker clan, or what was left of it, the Pettibones, and a few families headed for the hills and the Utah–Idaho border, away from the prying eyes of the Church and the state, where they've lived ever since.

'They practise polygamy?' Nigel asked.

'Hell, yeah,' he said. 'It's old school up there.'

'But why haven't they been arrested or broken up?'

Pettibone shook his head. 'Little matter of Waco put paid to that kind of stuff. You go in there all guns blazing and people will do some crazy things. I think the authorities don't really care. The community up there is a thousand or so strong, pretty self-sufficient, they don't bother folks outside much. Not till now, anyway. It was the people unfortunate enough to be born and raised there who faced all the trouble.'

'You left?' Donna asked.

'You could say that,' he said with a chuckle. 'Or you could say I was asked to leave. I'm what you might call a "lost boy".'

'What do you mean?' Heather reached for her notebook and began taking down some of what Pettibone said.

'Well, you were a teenager once. Let me ask you: if you had a choice between being with someone around your own age, or being the sixth wife of a fifty-seven-year-old man, which would you choose?'

'Are you kidding me?' Heather spluttered.

'Exactly. Unfortunately, the views of fifty-seven-year-old men hold greater sway than those of fifteen-year-old boys and girls. My crime was listening to rock music.' His fingers painted quote marks in the air as he said the word 'crime'. 'But the real reason was that I took a walk with a fourteen-year-old girl who was earmarked to be the bride of someone older and more powerful than me. They don't want you getting your hands on what is rightfully theirs. I was told to pack my bags and get out of town as quickly as possible. Or else.'

'Or else what?' Nigel asked.

'I didn't stay to find out. To be honest, I couldn't get out of that fucking place soon enough. Sure I miss my family, even though some of them were crazy as hell. That's what happens when the gene pool is kinda limited. But I don't miss much else.'

'It must have been difficult to adjust to life here after being in such a close-knit community,' Nigel said.

He shrugged. 'Llewellyn is hardly New York City. There were some pretty hard times. But I found my niche. This bar, a job, a few friends, and no God of any kind. If your Mormon friend here will forgive me, I think religion ain't worth shit.'

Donna shrugged. 'Go right ahead. Don't mind me.'

'You said a fourteen-year-old girl was earmarked to be a bride,' Heather said.

'I did. That's when the menfolk of Liberty deem them ripe for picking and marrying.'

'We're looking for a girl who was kidnapped on her fourteenth birthday, and her mother murdered. She was killed inside but her body dragged out the back of the house and her throat cut.'

'Sounds like blood atonement to me. You gonna tell me they're both descendants of Sarah Walker and Horton Taylor?'

'We are.'

He went silent. 'Jesus,' he said.

'You've heard of them?' Heather asked.

'Heard of them. In Liberty, those two are just about on a par with the Devil. Their heinous sin was drummed into the hearts and minds of every living person in Liberty. The first revelation Orson junior received from God, so the story goes, was to turn the oath of vengeance from part of the temple endowment ceremony into a piece of scripture, calling for the deaths of his father and family to be avenged and for this to be passed down the generations.' He stopped, as if suppressing a belch. 'In other words, kill the fuckers that did this, amen.'

'You've got to take us there,' Heather said.

'Sorry, ma'am, but all the money in the world wouldn't get me back to Liberty.'

'A fourteen-year-old girl is missing. You are the only person we know who can go into that town and work out where we might find her.'

He shook his head. 'They'd shoot me down for the apostate I am. Mormonism, and fundamentalism in particular, are pretty Old Testament in their outlook. Dissent isn't tolerated. Dissenters even less so.' He finished another beer. 'And what do you think I'd find out anyway? I doubt very much this has anything to do with anyone in Liberty. Few of them venture more than ten kilometres from their home. How the hell do you think they got to London and did what you think they did?'

'Sarah and Horton made it.'

He nodded as if to say, touché. 'I just don't see it. I'm sorry. I'd like to help. Any other help you want that I can give, I'll do my best. But as for walking back into Liberty, that'd be signing my own death warrant.'

Heather appeared to relent. The four of them fell silent. Heather shook her head. 'Well, I'll be going up there first thing tomorrow.'

'Good luck,' Pettibone said. 'Take your sunglasses.' Nigel gave him a bewildered look. 'You'll see what I mean,' he said cryptically and laughed quietly to himself again.

If the residents rarely left their town, Nigel wondered if they had access to any material that would allow them to research genealogy, to trace the ancestral path cut by Sarah and Horton, though he wasn't sure how, given how difficult he had found it with all the tools at his disposal – though, crucially, he had not known where to start.

'Do you know whether the TCF have any access to computers, reference books, that sort of thing?' he asked.

'They didn't even allow televisions when I was there. Maybe they do now. They do have a website – I've seen it.' He shook his head sadly but with the same wry bewilderment that characterized most of his actions and words.

'They have a website?' Nigel was astonished.

Pettibone nodded, eyes dancing with amusement in reaction to Nigel's disbelief. 'I know. Fucking crazy, huh?'

'Nearly all these groups have websites,' Donna drawled in agreement. 'Go and search and you'll see. They're competing. You ban TV and everyone else having a PC because you don't want your believers to be led astray, but you need to let people know what you believe so the cult down the road doesn't snatch your recruit – if you don't grow, you can stagnate and die. The Fundamentalist Church of Jesus Christ of Latter Day Saints; the Kingston Clan; all of them bar the smallest and most backward have a website. The TCF might only have started with a few people but it's estimated to have around two thousand members now and, like Mormonism as a whole, it's growing.'

'I just thought these groups were a bit incestuous,' Nigel explained. 'That you had to be born into them.'

'No, your friend here is right,' Pettibone said. 'They want new blood. Usually female – or it's OK if you're already married and you don't mind sharing your wife. Or your daughter, for that matter. You just have to move to the ass-end of nowhere to sign up.'

'One thing I don't understand,' Heather interjected. 'The fire, yes it loomed large in the minds of the people of the TCF. It led directly to them setting up their Church. But I don't see why the mainstream Church has withdrawn all reference to it. Why airbrush history when the history doesn't reflect that badly on you.'

'That's my Church,' Donna interjected. 'Think of these splinter groups as very embarrassing, ultra-embarrassing kid brothers. You don't even want to pretend you know them when they get into trouble or do something to shame you. You like to pretend they don't even exist. The Church is trying to distance itself as much as possible, act like they never were even Mormons in the first place – get rid of the information, then you stop people following the trail. But one thing you can't do is stop living, breathing people passing it on by word of mouth.'

24

Foster was at his desk when his phone burst to life. He had been kicking his heels, as bereft of inspiration as the rest of the team. It was Heather; she was almost stumbling over her words in her eagerness to pass them on to Foster. Blood atonement, she kept repeating excitedly. Blood atonement.

Foster managed to make her slow down and explain. She told him what she had learned from Josiah Pettibone, about the splinter sect formed from the ashes of the 1890 tragedy, and their teachings.

'You've got to go there,' he said. 'Take a look around.'

She said she planned to at first light the following day, given the lateness of the hour in the States. 'They're pretty cut off from the world,' she explained.

'Well, take care. Let me speak to Harris and let's see if we can open a channel with the US authorities. We might need them.' He paused. 'Do you think Naomi's there?'

'I doubt it. I mean, how? Unless he managed to change her appearance and get her a new identity in a week. Or rowed her here himself.'

She was right. It was doubtful. It was more likely that a former member of the TCF, or someone seeking to set up an offshoot, was doing it in their name. Heather's mind appeared to be heading in the same direction.

'They may keep themselves to themselves but they do

have a website. There could be contact with the outside world. Maybe you could have a look and pass that on to the Americans – see if there's been any particular regular traffic to the site?'

Foster took a note. Heather rang off, but not before he'd wished her luck and urged caution once more. Neither of them knew what she might find when she got to Liberty City. He woke his computer from its snooze and hunted for the website of the True Church of Freedom. He found it immediately.

It was basic in design, and didn't play the theme from *Deliverance* as it loaded. The home page was rudimentary, a few pictures of the town and the rolling hills that surrounded it. There was a brief history of the Church and a set of links to one side. One was a link outlining their difference with mainstream Mormonism. The next was a list of revelations regarding the Church above and beyond those experienced by Smith, Young and Taylor. It included Orson Walker senior, Orson junior, and two successors. Most of it seemed to be justifying their position as the one true Church and condemning the main Church as apostates. Orson junior's first revelation, of June 1891, Doctrine and Covenant 143, caught his eye:

Revelation given to the fifth prophet and fourth President of the Church, Orson Walker junior, concerning the oath of vengeance, which was only part of the temple endowment ceremony, but which, after the death of his father and members of his family as a result of a grievous fire, was, according to the Lord, to become scripture.

1. I say thus: Thou shalt seek and never cease to seek to avenge the blood of our Prophets on this nation, including the blood of my servant Orson P. Walker, and you will teach this to your children and your children's children unto the fourth generation.

2. If ye believe it, then let it be, Amen.

He read the revelation again and again.

There was the motive.

Harris agreed to approach the Home Office for permission to involve the FBI, though warned the process might be lengthy, and in the meantime cautioned against Heather wading into a small, tight-knit community, and urged patience. Foster knew there was no way he could stop Heather. He kept his counsel.

When the day was over, he decided to pay a visit to Gary, still at the safe house. He wanted the kid to see a familiar face. It was past eleven at night when Foster pulled up outside a detached cottage hidden behind some trees on the outskirts of a village just off the M4, fifteen miles outside London. The lights inside the house appeared to be off. He'd expected Gary to still be up. He checked the address he'd been given; he had the right place. Maybe the boy had got bored and gone to bed.

He got out of the car, parked half on the pavement. The area was lit by a solitary streetlight. The nearest house was 200 yards away down the road, another detached cottage. A few cars went past, then nothing. It was quiet and isolated and secluded. Ideal.

He went towards the house, which seemed to be a

simple but spacious two-up two-down. All very bucolic and homely, he thought. A million miles away from what the kid was used to. Out front was a small gravel drive where a Ford Scorpio was parked. The back and front lights were flashing intermittently. The alarm must have gone off and muted itself. The wind, probably. But why hadn't they come out and shut it off?

He found the doorbell but there was no sound when he pushed the button, so he knocked softly. No answer. This time he knocked more loudly. No answer. Odd. He thought it was the deal that at least one person stayed awake. He went to the front window, but the curtains were drawn and with the light off it was impossible to make anything out. Then he glanced at the front upstairs window. The curtain hung open. He went back to the door and rapped hard. No response. A vague sense of disquiet settled in the back of his mind.

There was no point calling headquarters to see if the address had been switched – or if they had holed up somewhere else for some reason – because there would be no one there at this hour to respond. He put his hands on his hips and thought for a few seconds, then with a sigh gave up and went back to the car. He got in. Then he got out again. There was no way he could sleep until he'd discovered what was going on here.

He crunched back along the drive to the front door. He tried the handle slowly. It turned. He pushed the door. It opened a few inches, then stopped. Something was in the way. Something heavy. He couldn't get his head through the opening to see what it was so he gave the door another heavy shunt. It inched open. He squeezed his head through. Inside, the hall was dark but he could see the obstacle.

A body. The floor beneath was sticky and coated with blood.

Without thinking Foster gave the door the biggest shove he could muster, a rasp of pain coursing down his injured collarbone. He ignored it and squeezed round the door, trying not to step on the body. It was a man. Tall, thickset, balding. There was a small gunshot entry wound to his forehead. He'd been shot as he opened the door. Foster could still smell cordite in the air. It was recent.

Foster went down the hall, breathless, a rising sense of panic in his craw. He turned into the sitting room. It was empty. A game console lay in the middle of floor, wires like spindly, tangled limbs. He checked the kitchen. It was difficult to see so he flicked on the light. There was a breakfast bar obscuring much of his view, at the end of which he could see a pair of trainers peeking out. The blood on the floor told him the person wasn't hiding. He peered round and saw the body of a young woman lying face down on the floor. Obviously dead. He looked up. On the wall was a panic button. Given no one else was here the killer had managed to murder her before she had a chance to press it.

He turned round and sprinted up the stairs, which creaked after every step. At the top he checked the first room, a small bathroom with a dripping tap that was empty. Beside it was an empty bedroom, a double. The bed was made with an unopened suitcase on it. The next room was single and unoccupied. There was another set of stairs leading to a converted loft. He stood still, breathing hard. From up there he could hear the low murmur of voices, some laughter. A television. He walked up slowly, hoping against hope that Gary was lying propped up, watching TV, oblivious to the carnage below.

The door was ajar. He pushed it open, revealing a small room half-covered with sloping eaves which gave it the feel of a den. There was a bed, creased and used. Empty. To his right were a sideboard and a television; the source of the noise was a comedy sketch show. He turned it off and looked around the room, staring at the floor and the sheets on the bed. Nothing. No sign of blood. Then, like a punch to the kidneys, it hit him.

He sprinted down both flights of stairs, ignoring the cries and protests of his body and his bursting chest, past both bodies, not even giving them a second glance. The back door was unlocked. He pulled it open and ran out into the large, dark garden walled by hedgerow, where a light rain drenched his face. He went down some stone steps and headed straight for the middle of the lawn where he expected to find the body of an eleven-year-old boy. There was nothing. He bent double, chest heaving, sucking in air. He pulled himself upright. Some mistake, surely. Gary's body had to be out here, its blood seeping on to the wet ground. He went to the borders, kicked at the bushes, peered into every nook and cranny, the drizzle soaking his scalp.

He screamed out the boy's name. Then again, from the pit of his stomach.

But there was no sign of him.

Dead or alive, he was gone.

25

They left Donna and Pettibone behind in Llewellyn, hired a car and set off before the sun had risen. The air was chill and clear; Nigel wound down the window and sucked in great lungfuls until Heather, nose almost pressing against the windscreen as she got used to driving on the opposite side of the road, told him to close it before she got hypothermia. As they left the small town behind and headed into the flatlands, a watery red sun crept up from behind silhouetted mountains to reveal mile after mile of landscape unbroken by the sight of man or beast.

Three hours of seeing only the occasional car and isolated petrol station later, the road led them up a winding hill. As they descended from the summit, in the distance they could make out a small, unspectacular town, the first they had seen for more than fifty miles. Nigel checked the map; it was Liberty. It must be – there was no other town within thirty miles. He felt his stomach tighten. It wasn't every day you paid a visit to a town filled with fundamentalists who had chosen to cut themselves off from the civilized world. He didn't know what to expect and wondered whether this was such a good idea. The plan was for them to portray themselves as innocent, bewildered tourists on a road trip, perhaps seek out somewhere to stay and hope there was one person in the whole community who might be willing to speak to them without arousing suspicion.

'Is this a good idea?' he asked Heather as they made their way down the hill, shading their eyes. The sky above them was cloudless and the rising winter sun was directly in front.

Her eyes, red from tiredness and staring at a straight road, narrowed. 'It's the best one we've got. Why, are you getting cold feet?'

'No,' he lied.

'We're going to go in and ask some questions as nicely as possible. Look upon it as a piece of local history. You once told me that nothing beat a field trip, getting out there and asking questions. Consider it research.' She smiled.

He felt partly reassured, but the grip of tension in his gut remained.

The town wasn't signed. It was just there, as if dropped from the sky fully formed and without warning. One minute there was open road and wilderness; the next, a few houses that became a street and then other streets. The houses were simple one-storey structures, sometimes with a car parked out front, which surprised Nigel. All of them were painted white. Everything was white – the fences, the doors. He expected it to be rather more basic. An American flag fluttered limply from a pole outside one or two, which gave a lie to the idea of it being some separatist movement.

'We need a shop, or some kind of café,' Heather said, driving slowly. 'We need people.'

'There's one,' Nigel murmured. A woman was out the front of her house washing her doorstep. She stopped as their car passed, watching them. Nigel checked the rear-view mirror as they pulled away. The woman continued to look. He guessed the road into town, pockmarked and battered, was barely used and rarely repaired. He checked Heather's face and saw the first signs of apprehension.

The town itself was neat and well ordered, organized into an almost perfect grid. Nigel had half-expected it to be clapboard shacks with tin roofs, barefoot inbred urchins playing in open sewers, while wild prairie dogs roamed seeking scraps for food. Instead, although his experience of small-town America was strictly limited, Liberty did not seem that different from Llewellyn, only reduced in scale.

Heather drove towards the centre of the grid, through identical white streets and past identikit white houses that made reference points difficult. Eventually she turned into a small square, overlooked by a larger building that Nigel guessed to be either some kind of town hall or civic building, a small fountain in the middle. The centrepiece was a tall dazzling temple, which towered over the square. On its roof a cherub blew into a trumpet. Like all the other buildings it was white, but it seemed to gleam.

There was a small parking bay filled by a few other vehicles and Heather pulled slowly in beside them. Nigel checked his watch – 9 a.m. He looked around. There must have been some form of recent celebration. Small white flags lined one side of the square; a small marquee and a few stalls lined the other.

Nigel did not notice Heather switch a silver band from her right ring finger to her left. She scanned the square: no more than a dozen buildings. Nigel was forced to squint, as the bright winter sun glanced off the pure-white buildings to create a dazzling glare. He now understood what Pettibone had meant when he advised them enigmatically to take their sunglasses. He did not have a pair.

Heather did, and put them on before sniffing the air. 'I can smell bread,' she said. Sure enough, in one corner of the square there appeared to be a bakery. As they walked over, Heather's boot heels clip-clopping loudly, Nigel felt as if he was being watched by eyes from every window overlooking the square. He looked up but the glare hurt his eyes. They saw no one. It was like the bright morning after Armageddon.

A painted sign above the door said 'Liberty Bakers', and the smell was enticing. Loaves were stacked in the window. A woman and a man were behind the counter in white hats. The store itself was empty. Flour hung in the air. Heather walked in, bold as brass, Nigel in her slipstream, happy to give his aching corneas a rest from the fierce, reflecting light.

'Good morning.'

The man's face didn't change from its stony setting; the woman, however, smiled a rictus grin. 'Good morning,' she said. There was a period of awkward silence. 'Can I help?' the woman finally asked, grin still fixed.

'We're lost,' Heather said. 'We're hoping you could help.'

'You don't sound like you're local,' the woman said, still smiling, her eyes unblinking and wide.

'No, we're on a bit of a road trip and we needed to make a stop.'

The man dead-panned. 'Isn't much to see round here.'

'On our way to Oregon. Pinot Noir country.'

The woman kept smiling. 'I love your accent.'

'Thanks. English. My husband here is a wine connoisseur.'

Nigel nodded eagerly, wondering inside, 'What?'

'Well, you won't find any of that here,' the woman said, a hint of disapproval in her voice. 'We're a dry town.'

Heather held up her hand. 'That can wait for Oregon. We're just after a place to wash and rest for a day before heading on. Made the mistake of driving through the night, miscalculating how far we had to go and everything.'

'A major miscalculation,' the man said, not even turning to look. 'The Oregon road is eighty kilometres north. You're way off track.'

Heather turned to Nigel. 'See, I told you we'd taken a wrong turn,' she said, rather too theatrically he thought. She shook her head. 'Is there anywhere in town we can stay, maybe get some help with directions? Lord knows we need them.'

The woman's smile never wavered as she gently shook her head. 'I'm afraid not. We have very few facilities for visitors here. But there's a motel nine or ten kilometres on the way out of town, back towards the Interstate.'

Nigel had seen it on the way in. Small and downtrodden. Not quite Bates Motel material, but not too appealing.

'OK,' Heather said. 'Is there a café of some kind? We're starving.'

The woman just stared and smiled. The man said nothing. 'There's a diner,' she said eventually. 'Just follow the road to the left and you can't miss it, just off the square. I recommend the omelette.'

'Thank you,' Heather said. 'I'll take you up on that recommendation. And when we're done, we'll pop back and buy some of the bread. It smells terrific.'

The woman nodded, the painted-on smile even wider. 'Have a nice day.'

They left, blinking in the whiteness. Both Nigel and Heather shared the feeling the town wires would soon be humming with the news that lost, alcoholic English tourists had landed. They followed the directions to a simple diner called 'Orson's'. Inside there were a few beaten leather chairs and banquettes, and – a rare sight – ordinary people. They entered and made straight for a table by the window to one side, watched by those eating breakfast, the air heavy with the smell of fried food. A waitress came over and tossed two menus on the table, the dishes typed out crudely and protected from stains by clear plastic. Nigel glanced around. They were still being watched.

'Can I get a mushroom omelette and some orange juice?' Heather asked immediately.

Nigel was momentarily startled, not just by Heather's adroit adaptation of the American vernacular. He'd not even had a chance to look at the options. 'The same,' he said, handing back his menu.

The waitress turned away without a word. Nigel continued to look. The regulars' attention returned to the contents of their plates, bar a few who continued to stare.

A young, pretty blonde came over with a coffee percolator jug. Her hair was tied back to reveal a proud, handsome face spoilt only by a toothy smile. The jug's contents weren't coffee. For a start, it was green.

'Herbal tea?' she said haltingly.

'Yes, please,' Heather replied eagerly, pushing her cup forward.

The young woman was about to pour but stopped. She looked at Heather in a state of shock.

'Yes, we're not from round here,' Heather added by way of explanation. 'We're English.'

The girl continued to stare. Eventually, she poured, hand visibly shaking. Then without saying anything, or offering Nigel any of the tea, she turned on her heels and returned swiftly to the counter.

'Now I know what it might be like to be a little green man from Mars,' Heather said, taking a sip of the tea and wincing. 'Hmm. Not sure about that.'

Nigel watched the girl disappear into the kitchen. She didn't come back. Instead the older waitress who took their order came over a few minutes later with their food. She set it down. It looked and smelled good but he didn't have much of an appetite. He made a polite effort and realized he was hungrier than he thought and the food was good. Watching them eat seemed to loosen up the waitress. She came over when they'd finished.

'You people were hungry,' she said softly, smiling at last. Nigel couldn't help but be cynical. Treat us like weirdos initially, he thought, but now you want your tip.

'Seems very quiet in town,' Heather said.

The woman nodded. 'It usually is. We're a very quiet town. But today in particular. Yesterday was a public holiday here in Liberty.'

'Is there anything to see here in town?'

'What do you mean?' She looked apprehensive.

'Any sights. We've got a bit lost. But seeing as we're here, we were wondering if there was anything of any historical interest.'

The waitress looked blank. 'No, I don't think there is,' she said and laughed nervously. 'The temple, I suppose, but . . .'

A portly man appeared at her shoulder and she stopped. He was wearing an apron. Nigel assumed he was the cook.

'Can I be of assistance?' he said, looking directly at Nigel, putting hands with fingers like sausages on his hips. He was breathing heavily through his mouth.

The waitress did not resume her sentence. She gave them a tight smile and cleared the table before scurrying back to her post.

'Your waitress was just being of great assistance,' Heather replied.

Nigel could sense the irritation in her voice. The man ignored her and continued to look coldly at Nigel.

He knew it was best to speak before Heather flipped. 'We're a bit lost and looking for some recommendations what to do here in Liberty,' he said simply.

'The best thing you can do is get in your car and head out of town,' came the response. The cook rubbed his chin. 'There ain't nothing here for you people.'

'Oh,' Nigel said. 'Fair enough.'

'And quit diverting my staff,' he added. 'Now, that meal was on the house. Just be on your way.' He wiped his hands on his apron, fixed Nigel with another stare and headed back to his kitchen.

They got up and left without speaking. Nigel tried to smile at their waitress but she avoided eye contact. No one spoke. Outside in the gleaming white light, they shared a look.

'What did we expect?' Nigel said.

'There must be someone in this place who doesn't bear a pathological distrust of outsiders. The waitress mentioned the temple, before Guy the Gorilla intervened. Let's go there. Maybe there's a vicar or priest of some sort we can speak to. A man of the cloth might be less insular.'

Nigel had reservations. For a start, he wasn't sure the Mormon faith, fundamentalist or not, had people like vicars. Heather was having nothing of it; he recognized the defiant cut of her jaw as she strode across the square to the temple that loomed over it.

The portico was supported by three white pillars. At either side of the building was a pair of smooth cylindrical towers with turrets at the top, studded with arched windows. A semicircle of white stone steps swept up to double doors, one of which appeared to be slightly ajar. Without stopping to knock or call out, Heather walked through into a cool, dark vestibule.

It took a few seconds for their eyes to adjust from the bright light outside. The temple was silent. In front of them was a wall, with open arches either side. To the right and left were doors, both locked.

Heather looked at Nigel and shrugged. 'Maybe there's some kind office where we can find someone,' she suggested.

They went through one of the arches that opened into the main part of the temple. In front of them were rows and rows of pews and a carpeted floor. There were precious few religious adornments, save an inscription on the back wall that read 'THE LORD HAS SEEN OUR SACRIFICE' and a single cross. They looked around but saw no one. In the corner to their left was a door that Heather tried, and which was also locked.

'Wait here,' Heather said, and started wandering towards the front, where there were more doors.

Nigel felt a cold chill down his spine. The fact the temple was open but as deserted as the rest of the town made him uneasy. He glanced round and saw behind him, at the back wall to his right, a small table, draped in white cloth, complete with a couple of books. Above it, on the wall, was a large notice or message board, listing forthcoming events and other community arcana. Nigel perused them – they ranged from the profound, a service celebrating the anniversary of the town's founding, to the trivial, someone advertising a crochet group for ladies. There was little to distinguish it from the day-to-day activities of any small church in any religion.

He looked at the books on the table. The first, the smaller book, was the Book of Mormon. The second was a larger book, thick and bound like a ledger. He opened it up. It appeared to be a handwritten register of the Church's ceremonies. Baptisms, weddings, sealings, endowments, going back at least three or four years. He flicked through the heavy pages until he reached the last used page, only a few before the end. He looked down absent-mindedly, wondering how they archived the information for future generations. He stopped at the last entry.

He read it again to be sure. His stomach leaped three feet in the air, it seemed. 'Heather,' he called out. 'Heather!'

Somewhere a door slammed abruptly shut. She was at his shoulder in a few seconds, recognizing the urgency in his voice. 'What?'

He pointed to the entry, the date written in American style. 'Temple Ordinance. Baptism by Proxy. Catherine

Mary Pratt b. 1969 d. 2008. Baptized 11.4.2008. Endowed 11.4.2008.'

'Katie Drake,' she said. 'This was yesterday.' Nigel pointed to the names below. Martin Stamey. His son below that.

'Can I help?' The voice was soft and patient.

They turned with a start. The speaker was a small man with neat black hair, head tilted to one side. Both were rendered speechless.

'Can I see your temple recommend?'

They looked at each other.

'This temple is for Church members only. People without a recommend are forbidden from entering. There are severe punishments . . .'

'We're just leaving,' Heather said.

The man watched them go. Nigel followed Heather as she bustled through the door, into the blinding brightness and towards the car. Nigel looked behind. The man was standing at the top of the stairs watching them go. Two vehicles, one a beaten pick-up truck, entered the square at speed, the roar of the engine and the slamming of its brakes ripping the silence apart. Heather fumbled with the keys but got the door open. The small man hurried down the steps to the two vehicles, gesturing and pointing towards him and Heather.

Heather turned the engine over – to their relief it fired to life instantly – and headed straight out of the square.

A few minutes later they were hurtling out of Liberty, no one in their wake.

26

The safe house – Foster could not bring himself to do anything other than spit those words out in light of their palpable absurdity – throbbed with activity, yet all of those present steered clear of the large brooding presence on the sofa nursing a cup of tea. Outside, for the first time in days, a pale sun peered sheepishly through the steel-grey sky, though it did nothing to alleviate Foster's sense of helplessness. He'd sworn to the kid that he'd be safe and that had turned out to be a lie. Now, for all he knew, Gary was dead and the killer had achieved his mission of wiping out or kidnapping an entire bloodline.

Foster shook his head and rubbed his weary eyes.

Had the Lord's work been done?

However, all was not lost. Foster could not understand why Gary had not been killed and dragged out into the garden where his spilled blood would atone for the misdemeanours of the past. He clung to the idea that Gary might have got away.

An outline of what had happened the night before was beginning to emerge. Gary had arrived at the safe house on Monday evening with the two officers charged with protecting him for the next forty-eight hours. The officers were Adrian Sullivan and Sylvia Tweedy – he made it his business to find out their names, and personally call their next of kin to offer his sympathies, because he felt responsible. Sullivan was to take the nights, Tweedy the day, each sleeping while the other fed, entertained and kept an eye on Gary. After a couple of days they would be rotated and other officers drafted in.

The pathologist's estimate was that Sullivan was shot dead shortly after ten the night before, Tweedy around the same time. He had been lured into opening the front door and been shot as soon as he did so. She had not gone to bed and after seeing her fallen colleague had tried to reach the panic button but had been cut down with two shots, one to the back and the other to her head.

It was the last fact that offered a lacuna of hope. The killer had decided to take out both of Gary's minders, which gave the boy time to be alerted to the trouble and an opportunity to scarper, a skill at which he'd become extremely adept. But how had he got out? The window in his room was open. Foster prayed he had escaped that way rather than been dragged out by the killer.

He went over the possibilities once more. There were two options: either Gary got away or the killer got him. He hoped to God it was the former. The idea that the kid was dead, when he knew how close they were to catching the killer and saving him, would be one he couldn't bear. As he sat on the sofa while the dawn sun came up, it crossed his mind that there wasn't much more he could take of this. Yet another sorrow, just one in a long line, would be the one that pushed him out of the force for good. His future, and any hope for it, was tangled up in the fate of that brown-eyed boy.

He took a deep breath and let it out. There was no sign of forced entry. The abductor entered through the front door like a guest. There had been a chain on the door and a spyhole. Cops in places like this didn't open the door to everyone who stopped by. Foster had pieced together what happened. The killer had set the car alarm off. It was a windy night. Sullivan, hearing it go and thinking it had been set off by a sudden gust, would have gone out to see to it and been gunned down as soon as he showed himself.

But how had he found Gary?

Foster had spent the night hours pondering that question. Gary was taken down to an underground car park and then driven here. He never laid a foot outside police headquarters. Yet there was still only one convincing answer. The killer must have followed Gary there. God only knew how.

He needed a diversion. It was late in Utah, but not too late for him to call Heather and get an update. She sounded breathless, irritated almost. He apologized for calling late. She appeared to calm herself.

'Just wondered what the latest was?' he asked.

She explained their foray into Liberty City and what they had found in the temple ledger. The names of the dead, baptized and converted to the TCF by proxy. Foster was so numb it took some time for her words to sink in.

'Is everything OK, sir?' she inquired, after a long silence.

'Not really. Gary Stamey has gone missing from the safe house.'

'Oh, God.'

'Yeah, two cops shot dead. Either the killer got Gary or he managed to get away. It's not clear. I'm holding on to the hope that at least we didn't find the body in the garden –

but, who knows?' He sighed. It wasn't something he wanted to spend too long thinking about. 'So someone in Liberty knows that Drake, Stamey and his boy are dead. We have to assume they know who's doing it then. I'll get on to Harris but God knows what the Yanks are going to think about going in all guns blazing. The locals can close ranks and deny anything. Not much we can do if that's what happens.'

'There's one thing,' Heather said. 'The name of the person who was baptized on behalf of the dead was Leonie Walker.'

'You don't think . . . ?'

'Could be coincidence.'

'Could be. Where are you now?'

'At a motel, about six miles out of Liberty. Wondering what to do next. We don't think we were followed. I don't fancy going back without a posse. This is small-town America. We have to presume they're armed.'

'Don't move a muscle,' Foster urged. 'Harris didn't want you going there in the first place – when he finds out, he'll go apeshit, but at least you got something out of it. You confirmed a link. Let us think of the next step. Sit tight. Have a hot dog and some root beer or something.'

Heather laughed. 'We have a room and a TV. No amusement for miles around.'

'Sounds cosy. Amuse yourselves.'

She laughed again. When she stopped, the silence was long and profound. 'He'll be OK, sir. One thing we know about that kid is he knows how to escape and evade capture.'

'I hope you're right,' he said, and meant it.

Outside, from the fields behind the house, Foster could hear barking. Sniffer dogs. Maybe they'd find the kid in a hole, or up a tree. With a lurching stomach, he also knew they might have found his murdered corpse. He didn't speak, trying to glean from the animals' excitement whether Gary had been found.

'Got to go,' he said, lifting his weary frame, breathing deeply to retain his brave face.

He went into the garden, breath misting in the frosty air, through a back gate towards a lone oak tree, branches bare, standing sentry on a hill. A group of uniforms were already gathering and he could hear the lone yelp of a frustrated police dog. As he neared, he saw one of the cops bend down but he couldn't see what he was tending because it was beyond the brow of the small hill. He felt sick, he felt empty, and he felt forlorn. Another cop went down on his haunches.

A policewoman stationed outside the back gate called across to him. 'Look,' she said, pointing.

Foster followed her finger. On the straw-coloured grass were a few spots of blood. He said nothing. Just carried on walking towards the group on the hill. He plunged his hands deep in his voluminous pockets, so no one could see they were shaking.

He reached the crest of the hill. Foster closed his eyes and took a deep breath. He opened them.

Nothing. Just a dirt track.

The two policemen were still on their haunches. One saw Foster.

'The scent stopped around here,' one explained. 'There are some fresh tyre tracks. A car, we reckon.'

Foster followed the snaking route of the dirt track. It seemed to run eastward away from the house back towards the main road.

'There are some spots of blood back there. Get forensics out here. I want the whole field roped off and a finger-tip search started straight away.'

'Do you reckon it's the killer's car?' a cop in uniform asked.

'I do. He's got him. If he's not killed him here, then he needs him for something. Don't ask me what. But once he's got what he needs I know he'll kill him. He has to achieve atonement.' He glanced around the field, at the pale-blue sky and the denuded tree. 'We need to find him and find him today.'

27

The motel room was part of a single-storey, U-shaped complex looking out over a deserted car park. It smelled of cheap cigarettes and cheap sex. The threadbare carpet had seen the soles of a thousand shoes, and the bed linen – well, Nigel didn't want to think about what that had seen. He wondered how many residents of Liberty had sought a fleeting moment of escape in these cabins, far from the prying eyes of the town elders, before a shameful retreat to their city of virginal white.

The fact they appeared to be the only guests did nothing to assuage a feeling of creeping dread. Heather found the most inconspicuous corner of the lot and stuck the car there. She tried to grill the guy on reception about the TCF but conversation was not his forte; he said he knew nothing about them apart from the whole lot being fruitcakes. There was nothing else for them to do but hole up and wait for further instructions. Heather's room, being slightly less soiled than his, became their base.

Heather had tried to call Foster, to report what they had discovered in Liberty, but his phone was ringing out. Heather was becoming increasingly agitated, pacing back and forth across the room trying to come up with an idea of what to do next. Nigel shared her frustration, the feeling of being so close yet so far away. He got hold of a telephone directory from reception, suggesting they see who in Liberty had a phone and start cold-calling for information, but Heather dismissed it. Nigel passed the time by flicking the television on, and meandered through a mass of channels. Back home, the prospect of doing the same would appall him, but here in a different culture he found escape in local news and weather broadcasts, adverts for local businesses and a host of religious programming. Heather reclined on her bed, one eye on the set, the other on her phone, which was charging on a simple wooden table in the corner. Nigel occasionally wandered out for a cigarette, watching the light fade away, listening for cars on the road, watching with some relief their tail lights fade to black as they passed by in either direction. The sky was cloudless; the moon had already punched a hole in the night and a few stars were visible before the sun had even set. It was going to be cold.

Heather went for a shower. He offered to leave, to give her privacy, but she told him not to be silly. When she finally emerged from the steam-filled bathroom, it was dark outside. She was wearing just a towel, wet hair falling on her shoulders. Nigel, lying on one of the twin beds, tried not to stare. She went over and sat at the table, fanned her face. 'Water's hot, at least,' she said. Nigel nodded, kept his eyes on the TV set, showing a basketball game. It promised to be a frustrating night in more ways than one.

She watched the basketball for a while, then moved for a better view on the end of the bed Nigel was lying on. The game was reaching the final few seconds and the scores were level. Her phone rang, and she grabbed it quickly. It was Donna Faugenot, asking how the trip had gone. Heather filled her in with the details and ended the call. 'Don't want to be rude,' she explained. 'But if a call comes in from England I don't want to miss it.'

She looked at Nigel.

He felt uneasy.

'Think Donna had the hots for you,' she said playfully.

'You think so?' he said, trying to sound disinterested.

'I do. Heck of a woman, Donna.'

'She is, isn't she? Not your stereotypical Latter-day Saint. You know she's divorced?'

'I know,' Heather said. Her playful smile turned into a grin. 'I heard your conversation in the car.'

Nigel felt his heart almost stop. 'You did?' A knot welded tight in his stomach.

She nodded. 'Uh huh.'

He sat up. 'All of it?'

'Most of it.'

'Oh.' He didn't know what to say.

She shuffled back on the bed. He could smell her shampoo, her newly wet hair. Her smile went. She looked at him earnestly, bright-green eyes ablaze. 'Donna's right,' she said, looking right at him. 'Sometimes you've got to hang in there.' She leaned closer to him. 'Honey.' She smiled once more.

Nigel leaned forward, head swimming. Everything else melted away. He'd had enough of hanging on in there. He reached for her, and pulled her towards him. Their lips met and he felt a jolt through his entire system. His hand found the back of her head and pulled their lips tighter together. Her hands were on his shirt buttons. He heard himself groan, months of pent-up passion let go, and almost burst out laughing. In her eyes he saw a brief flicker of amusement but they soon closed again. His hand reached for the knot fixing her towel to her side.

Heather's phone started to ring.

Her eyes flashed open. 'Are you kidding me?' she said. She pulled away, ran her hand through her hair, bit her bottom lip. 'I better answer it,' she whispered.

Nigel stood up, wanting to ram his fist into the face of whoever it was on the other end of the phone. Probably the guy on reception. 'Hello, Grant,' he heard her say, a trace of irritation in her voice. Foster, he thought. That changed things. Still, the moment had gone. And it had promised to be a bloody good moment.

He went into the bathroom and splashed water on his face. When he came back, Heather was off the phone, wearing a deep frown of concern.

'What's wrong?' he asked.

'Gary Stamey has gone missing,' she replied. 'He was in the safe house. The cops protecting him were killed.'

'Jesus,' Nigel murmured.

'They fell silent. Nigel didn't know what to say.

The mood was broken by a knock on the door. Nigel glanced at Heather. She nodded. He went over to the door. There was another knock, gentler this time.

'Check before opening,' he heard Heather whisper. He looked through the spyhole.

A girl. He didn't recognize her at first. Then he realized she was out of uniform. It was the shy waitress from the diner. He unchained the door and opened it.

'Hello,' he said.

She appeared terrified, barely looked up from the floor. She didn't say a word. Heather was at his side. She glanced over the girl's shoulder at the deserted lot. 'Come in,' she said, ushering her in. 'Come on.'

The girl walked, shuffled, still looking at the floor. How had she got here? Nigel thought. There were no other cars in the lot. He didn't feel good about it but bowed to Heather's judgement. As soon as she was in the room, he closed the door, chained and bolted it.

She stood there, shivering.

'Let me get dressed,' Heather said, grabbing clothes and heading for the bathroom.

Nigel steered the girl to the chair at the table. She sat down. He stood there, uneasily, not certain what to do or say.

Heather came out, dressed, hair still wet. 'You work in the diner, yeah?' she said softly.

The girl nodded.

'How did you get here?'

'Walked,' the girl murmured. The pronunciation strange yet familiar. Six miles walking. No wonder she shivered.

'Get her something to keep her warm,' Heather told him.

He grabbed towels and his own coat, wrapped them around her. He also handed her a bottle of water, from which she took a large swig.

'Thanks,' she muttered.

'No problem,' he said.

'What's your name?' Heather asked.

The girl looked up for the first time, first at Heather, then at Nigel. 'Leonie,' she said. 'Leonie Stamey.'

Her accent was a hybrid of estuary Essex vowels and Midwest intonation. Yet its odd cadences did not lessen the impact of her words, and her fear did not dilute the honesty of her answers. Heather sat opposite her on one of the beds, while Nigel stood resting against the wall.

'How did you know who we were?' Heather asked. Leonie said nothing, just gazed at her hands. The face had seen too much sadness for someone so young.

'I seen cops all the time when my mum was alive. When I served you in the diner and then heard you was looking around the temple I knew you was looking for me.'

'So you came to find us?'

'I don't wanna cause my folks any trouble.'

'Your folks?'

'My family. In Liberty.'

Heather paused. 'I see. Who are your folks?'

She shook her head. 'Ain't gonna tell you that. I'll tell you what you want and then you go. I come out here so you wouldn't go sniffing around town again. Just don't ask me about my people in Liberty.'

'OK.'

There was a long silence.

'Can I ask you how you ended up in Liberty? What happened after you disappeared?'

'I didn't "disappear",' she said scornfully. 'I left because I chose to. My mum and the drugs and dying like that, I just wanted a fresh start. He helped me do that.'

'Who's he?'

'I ain't telling you his name.'

'OK.' Heather nodded. 'This is the man who came to your house, the man in the suit who spoke about God.'

Her brow furrowed. 'How do you know about that?'

'Gary told us.'

At the mention of his name her face froze. 'Is he all right?'

Heather paused once more. 'Leonie, you need to tell us everything, and I mean everything.'

'Have they hurt him? I said they wasn't to hurt him.'

'Who are they?'

She fell silent.

'You have to tell me who this guy is, Leonie. Is he in Liberty?'

She shook her head. 'He's not never been, apart from the time he brought me. Then he left.'

'He's English?'

'Yes. He's related to me. Not like a brother or anything. Distant family. He was put up for adoption when he was a baby.'

Anthony Chapman, Nigel thought.

Leonie continued. 'He only found out about the family link and the sins of Sarah and Horton when he was a grown-up. He got in touch with the True Church of Freedom a few years back about coming and settling over here, and they said he could do some unfinished business for them. He started with me and he told me all about it, the Church and the family and what happened way back when. He converted me. It sounded better than the life I was living. When he said come with him, I jumped at it.'

'You left of your own accord?'

'Uh huh. We spent a few weeks at his place. He treated me nice. He got me a false identity, a new passport and we came here. It was bloody strange at first but I sure got used to it. He left to do what he needed to do. I stayed. I married.'

'Married?'

'I was fourteen, which is when the Church decree you can marry. Which is why I was spared. To carry on the line. The rest had to die. Apart from Gary.'

'Why not Gary?'

'Because I said so.'

Nigel could see Heather was shocked at what Leonie was telling her, at the teenager's quiescence. Here she was, half girl half woman, half Essex half American, speaking about leaving her life in England for a life in a cult where girls were forced to marry in their early teens, as if it was the one true path. He could also see Heather struggling about whether to tell the truth about Gary's disappearance.

'Another girl has gone missing. And the people you converted by proxy at yesterday's ceremony were murdered.'

'Oh, I know that,' she said. 'They had to die.'

'What?'

Her eyes started to gleam, lit by fervency. 'Sarah and Horton Rowley sinned against this Church and its prophet. They were responsible for breaking up the family and for the deaths of eighteen innocent souls. We all, me included, bear the stain of the sin and it must be atoned. The Church has sought and now achieved that atonement.'

'Leonie,' Heather said slowly. 'Gary is missing.'

Her face changed, the belief faded, merging into incredulity. 'I said he wasn't to be touched. That he would join us one day.' Now there was anger. She started to shake her head. 'You're lying. This is just a ploy to get me to go with you.' Her face contorted. 'You evil fucking bitch.'

The Essex girl had won out over the pious Utah child bride.

'Leonie,' Heather replied firmly. 'We didn't even come here to find you. We didn't know you were here.'

Anger gave way to bewilderment. Her eyes flicked between them. 'But why . . . ?'

'Because people are being murdered, and a fourteen-year-old girl is missing. And now, whether you want to believe it or not, your brother is missing. And you can believe any bullshit you want, Leonie, but tell me why he'd be spared when another boy about his age, your cousin, was shot like a dog and his body dragged into the garden along with your uncle. Do you honestly think they wouldn't kill Gary because "you said so"? That they would forego the chance to reunite the family in eternity and atone for 1890 on the whim of a teenage girl? You've been had, Leonie. Open your eyes.'

Her eyes filled with tears but Nigel could see Leonie remained defiant.

'No one else should die, Leonie. It has to stop and it has to stop here. You left Gary to fend for himself. Now's a chance to help us find him. What was the name of the man who helped bring you over here?'

She wept silently for a few seconds, then she sniffed. 'Dominic. I thought I was doing Gary a favour. He'd get a nice foster family. A mum and a dad who'd love him. Maybe had some money. Give him a chance. I was going to go back for him one day. Honest.' She wiped her eyes.

'Who's Dominic?' Heather asked again.

'I don't know. He was just Dominic.'

'You didn't know his surname?'

'He never told me.'

Heather asked for a description. Leonie gave it: early

forties, dark-haired, handsome, posh voice, shy but persuasive, blue eyes. Nigel made a note of it all, pointless though it was without a surname.

'Where did he live?'

'He had a flat in Plaistow but he said it was just temporary. He didn't like it there. He said he was going to get a house in Bethnal Green one day. That was where the family was from, though he'd only lived there a bit. He told me he grew up out of town near Buckinghamshire.'

'In Buckinghamshire?' Heather corrected.

'Yeah.' She gave the name of the road in Plaistow.

Heather asked if she knew anything personal about Dominic, other than his adoption. Did she know the name of the family who took him in?

She shook her head. 'He hated them, though he said the sister was all right. He did say they had money. The dad had a brewery or something like that. That's all he said. Sorry.' For a brief second it was all too clear that she was still only a seventeen-year-old girl.

Nigel made a note of all she said, doing a brief genealogical sketch of Dominic. Adopted by a wealthy East End brewer. Tracking him might be possible. Yet there was little he could do from the barren wilderness of Utah.

'Take me home,' Leonie said abruptly.

'England?' Heather asked.

'No. Back to Liberty. That's my home. You can drop me on the outskirts of town.'

'Don't you want to know what happens to Gary? Go back there and we won't be able to let you know any news.'

She shrugged. 'I will ask the Lord. He will let me know. I must go back.'

Heather's look was one of disbelief. 'But why? Come home, Leonie. There is nothing for you in Liberty. Those people sanction murder. Why stay with them?'

'Because my son is back there and nothing could make me leave him.'

28

Foster made the connection before Heather called him. As he drove to the places where he thought Gary might be, the words he'd read on the TCF website played and replayed in his mind:

> Thou shalt seek and never cease to seek to avenge the blood of our Prophets on this nation, including the blood of my servant Orson P. Walker, and you will teach this to your children and your children's children unto the fourth generation.

The fourth generation. He went back in his mind over what he knew of Sarah and Horton Rowley's descendants. The guy who was missing – the kid who'd been adopted because his mother lived in fear of them coming to avenge their ancestors' sins – wasn't he fourth generation? He dialled Heather and got her breathless voice.

She told him about Leonie.

'Have you got her?'

No, came the reply, and the reasons why. Foster punched the dashboard, not so much in anger – he knew there was no lawful reason for them to keep her. It was frustration, lack of sleep. It was the dilemma over what he would tell Gary when the boy asked about his sister. If Gary was still alive.

Heather told Foster about Dominic, and Nigel's theory

about him being Anthony Chapman. In turn, Foster mentioned the full text of the revelation on the Church's website.

'What shall we do now?' she asked.

'Sit tight. Not sure there is much more you can do on your own. Let me speak to Harris. First of all, though, put me on to Nigel.'

She handed the phone to Barnes. The two men exchanged greetings.

'Listen, mate, there's not much you can do from there. But I can be your researcher here. We need to track down this Dominic from what we know. You pull the levers, I'll be the puppet.'

Nigel paused. 'Well, we have half a name, no address, no occupation and the major building block we do have, his birth certificate, is irrelevant because he was adopted without a paper trail.'

Foster smiled for the first time in what seemed an age. 'And the good news?'

'We know his adoptive father was a brewer. There won't have been many in that parish.'

'Certainly not in the past fifty years or so. Small, independent brewers have been decimated. I've had someone get hold of a list of the current congregation of St Matthew's from the present vicar – some of them might have been involved for a long time and they'll be worth talking to. We know the adoptive parents were wealthy. Round here, they would have stuck out like a wine merchant in a working men's club. Even if they weren't regular churchgoers, people might of known of them. Where should I start the paper trail?'

'You sure you want to get lost in the world of genealogy?'

'I'm up for it. I've had a good teacher.'

Foster's first stop was the London Metropolitan Archives where the parish registers for most of the London churches were held. On Nigel's advice, he went through every single marriage held at St Matthew's since the end of the Second World War – nineteen years before the birth of Anthony Chapman. Two marriages struck him in particular. Henrietta Llewellyn Oakley and Kathryn Llewellyn Oakley were sisters who married three years apart, 1957 and 1960. Their father was Henry Oakley, the grooms were Samuel Heathcote Smythe and Edward St John Ashbourne.

He looked at the names and the chip on his shoulder told him there was money here. Closer inspection revealed his hunch was right. Henry Oakley was local, a brewer. One of Hardwicke, Oakley and Parsons, known universally as Hops, a small London brewery that passed away in the early 1980s after being bought by a national brewer. Henry Oakley was the last of the family to run the business; in fact, his retirement was the catalyst for it being floated on the stock market.

Foster fed the information back to Nigel, who told him to head to the National Archives to check out the Oakley children. He was getting nearer. He could sense it and he was enjoying the feeling.

Henrietta Oakley bore five children, all girls. Her elder brother was Henry junior. Childless, it appeared. He did not marry either. Foster went to the death indexes; in 1962

Henry junior died of pneumonia. He returned to the birth indexes, this time in search of the offspring of Kathryn Ashbourne, née Oakley, who married in 1960.

Her first child was born in 1969. She went on to have three, after nine years of childlessness. Anthony Chapman was adopted in 1964. Would four years have been enough time for the family to have panicked? The brewery was still in their hands. The firstborn was dead, the only male. Their elder daughter was giving birth to a string of females. The younger was in her fourth year of marriage, no child. Obviously the anxiety would be most keenly felt by Kathryn, who would want a child of her own. But wouldn't the lack of a male heir to a family business increase the pressure, persuade the family to take drastic action?

There was no reference to Kathryn Ashbourne in the death indexes. She was still alive.

Next was the National Newspaper Library at Colindale. *The Times* had run a detailed obituary of Henry Oakley. At the end it mentioned nine grandchildren. The BMD indexes confirmed eight. He cross-referenced his information with an old copy of *Who's Who*, which also said nine grandchildren.

One was unaccounted for.

Foster hurtled along the M40, on his way to Clifton Hampden and the home of Kathryn Ashbourne.

He turned up a gravel drive that led to the old vicarage, which had been the family's home for the past twenty-five years. The electoral register told him the Ashbournes lived there alone, the children long gone. As he got out of the car, Foster noticed the silence. A dog barked way in the distance, but apart from that nothing. It always made him feel edgy. He was a city boy – he needed the background thrum of the city, and the lack of noise made him feel uneasy.

He went to the side of the house and saw a portico entrance. He rang the doorbell. No answer. He rang again. Please let them be in, thought Foster. Just as he was about to give up he heard the sound of footsteps. A latch was dropped and the wooden door swung open, revealing a tall, proud and still-handsome woman in her late sixties.

'Mrs Ashbourne?'

'Yes, I'm Mrs Ashbourne,' she said in soft yet clearly enunciated tones.

'Sorry to disturb you at home. I'm from the Metropolitan Police. May I come in?' He flashed his ID.

The woman's pale ivory skin appeared to blanche further. 'Oh, no,' she said, panicked. 'Whatever's happened?'

'Nothing to be alarmed about, madam,' Foster explained softly. 'I just need a quick chat, if you have the time?'

'Yes, yes, of course,' she replied, and ushered him in.

The house was silent, apart from the sonorous tick and tock of a large grandfather clock. They went through a reception area into a drawing room. The windows at the back looked out on to a vast and well-manicured garden. She gestured him towards a sofa while she went and made tea. After five minutes of oppressive silence, just the sound of his breathing and the solemn ticking of the clock, she returned with a tray replete with teapot, jug of milk, sugar and cups with saucers.

'Is your husband around, Mrs Ashbourne?' Foster said, accepting his tea.

She shook her head. 'No, he's retired but he spends a few days a week as a non-executive director for some companies up in town. There's a meeting today. He's due back around four.' She glanced at a wall-mounted clock. It was just gone two.

She heaped two sugars into her tea and gave it a vigorous stir. Then she sat down, perched on the edge of the chair. She seemed fit and active. Foster guessed the immaculate garden was her doing. He also wondered at her resolve. He had been in the house for some time and not once had she asked the reason for his visit.

'Are you here about Edward?' She took a sip of tea.

'Your husband?'

'Yes, my husband, Edward.'

'No.' Foster took a sip of tea. It was scalding hot. The woman must have asbestos lips. He put it back down on the table. 'It's quite a delicate situation, to be honest.'

'Oh. Really?'

'I'm sorry, there's no way for me to do this without being blunt. I apologize in advance.' He paused. 'Did you adopt a child in 1964?'

She said nothing. Just stared at him without blinking. Then she took a sip of tea before she glanced down at the floor. 'So it's about Dominic,' she said quietly.

'Yes.'

She sighed. Her face no longer appeared proud. She looked sad, almost broken, as she nodded her head. 'I suppose deep down I've been waiting for this day for a long time. What has he done?'

'We just want to speak to him in relation to a case we're working on,' he said.

'Is he in trouble?'

'We don't know. But we need to speak to him. Are you in contact with him?'

She shook her head. Her eyes were beginning to well. 'Not for a while. Quite a while, actually.'

'Why?'

She turned her head and stared sadly out of the window. The sun had just broken the clouds. It appeared to galvanize her. 'I was desperate for a child, any child. My father was desperate for a boy, an heir for the family business. It seemed the easiest option. It didn't turn out that way.' She folded her hands in her lap.

'Why not?' Foster asked.

'He was always a difficult little boy. He didn't sleep much and he seemed to have a real anger within him. I loved him, though. My husband wanted little to do with him – he was never that sold on the idea in the first place, so when this cross little child turned up and kept us awake all hours he became even less enamoured with it all. It nearly forced us to part. Fortunately, I became pregnant and we had our own son, then another, and then a girl. And Dominic? Well, Dominic just got squeezed out of our affections, I'm ashamed to say.'

'In what way?'

'We sent him to boarding school very young. Too young, in hindsight. He didn't tell us but it turned out he had a wretched time there. In the holidays he was sullen and uncommunicative. I did try but my husband could barely stand to have him around and treated him quite harshly. Dominic seemed to be so full of resentment. I don't blame him for some of that, and I accept my fair share of the blame in making him that way, but he became impossible to deal with. The only person he seemed to get on with was our daughter. She liked him. The two boys and he fought constantly. Eventually he left school and he didn't come home any more. There was the odd letter. I sent him money once. We had one or two calls from the police. Nothing serious.'

'Do you have an address or any idea where we could find him?'

'No. The last I heard, eight or nine years ago, he was up in London. He wasn't married. He changed his surname a few times, so I heard.' She turned to the garden once more. 'I do hope he hasn't hurt anyone.'

To ease your guilt? Foster thought. He felt a twinge of sympathy for the poor sod. Given away by his parents, adopted by a new family and then cast aside and rejected when they had a son of their own. Unloved and unwanted. Runt of the litter. He thought of the daughter he'd never met. The child he never wanted in the first place. He was in no position to judge.

'Do you know anyone who might know of his whereabouts, Mrs Ashbourne?' he asked.

The old woman gave it some thought. Her eyes were red and ringed now with great sadness. 'I could ring Clarissa, my daughter. I wouldn't be surprised if they were in touch. She did tell me a few years ago that he was living in Barking. Would you like me to call her?'

'If you wouldn't mind, thanks,' Foster replied.

She left the room.

It's like a textbook on how to screw up a child, he thought.

A few minutes later, Mrs Ashbourne came back into the room. 'Clarissa hasn't heard anything since the last time she told me he was in Barking.'

Where Leonie and Gary lived, he thought. 'She doesn't have any numbers, or an address?'

'No,' she replied quickly, almost snappily. She composed herself. 'Sorry,' she said. 'This sort of news hits one very hard.'

Does it? he thought. After hearing her story, his reserves of sympathy were low. 'I better be going.' He rose. 'Thanks for your time.'

He knew where he needed to go next.

She was aware only of the putrid smell of the sheets and the ticking clock in the corner. Counting the last seconds of her life. She felt alone and so far from her home. Her dreams were all about the open fields and the empty skies, the crisp winter mornings and the long, hot summers that seemed never to end. But mainly they were filled with the look of her mother, the creases at the corners of her eyes and the soft smile. Except in the dreams those laughing eyes often frowned. And those screams, those awful screams.

This city had been a place to live but it had never been home. For her two daughters and their families it was. They would never know the joy of living from the land like she had.

The doctor had been. She had fallen asleep but it was clear she was dying. The vicar was on his way to administer the last rites. At least there will be the comfort of the Lord, and the chance to be reunited with Horton. Maybe up there – and she had prayed every night since his death that their sins be forgiven and they be allowed to join Him in his eternal kingdom – they might find other ways to be redeemed. That could only happen in the arms of the Lord. Down here, there was damnation. She must find a way to warn the little girl.

Hours slipped by. It could have been days. She half-remembered the vicar sitting by her bed, his hand on hers. He was a good man. She had found a good church. They would get what little she had, unlike those two ungrateful, godless daughters of hers. Isaac was a good boy. She knew he would be up there one day, and she longed to see him. The other two could rot in the other place.

But not the little girl. She needed to be saved.

She woke with a start, gasping for air before she settled. It was almost a disappointment. Death's warm embrace seemed a better option than the cold spare room at her daughter's. It was morning. Was it? It didn't matter. The same dreams. Her mother's soft face and her anger. Those gut-wrenching screams . . .

The sheets had been changed. The window opened. Someone had been. Emma, she presumed. It was then she noticed something from the corner of her eye. On the chair, eyes wide, sat little Maggie. Her legs were swinging ever so slightly but when she caught her grandmother looking at her they stopped. 'Hello, Grandmother,' she said weakly in her sing-song voice.

She tried all she could to muster a smile. Bless her. Sarah stretched out her hand and with great effort beckoned the girl closer with a bony finger. The child got up and walked across the room. Sarah gestured for her to come even closer. She could hardly raise her voice beyond a hoarse whisper and she wanted her words to be heard.

'You're a good girl,' she wheezed and she clasped her clammy hand around the little girl's. She held it there for a few seconds, perhaps longer. Time ceased to have much meaning.

She opened her eyes. Maggie was still there, eyes wide, unblinking. Sarah felt a bolt of pain sear up from her chest. The shot the doctor had given her was wearing off. She groaned. She was so weak. The end was soon. The little girl stood back.

The pain eventually subsided. She opened her eyes and beckoned Maggie in once more.

'They will come,' she said. 'They will come for you like they came for your grandfather.' She sucked in some more air. The little girl stood transfixed. 'By my bed, there's a box. Get it.'

The girl rooted around.

'In the cupboard,' she gasped.

314

The little girl found it.

'Put it on the bed.'

She did. Sarah fumbled with the lock and the combination. It was exhausting but eventually she opened it.

'Look at it.'

Maggie peered in.

'Pick it up,' she hissed.

She held it in her hands. The photograph the police said was on Horton's broken body when it was found crushed on the road. Killed by an omnibus, they said. She knew different. They had found him and murdered him. The police gave her his belongings and the photograph was among them. She recognized the man with the spade. Even the burned-out buildings. She went home and cleared out their things and moved away immediately. They had not yet found her, but she knew they would never stop looking. Whether she was alive or dead they would come for her kin. The rest could take their chances but the little girl must be warned and she must be told.

Maggie's hands were shaking. She stared at the picture, appalled. She was terrified, poor mite. But it was the only way. She would thank her later.

'Some of them were no older than you,' she said.

She closed her eyes. Another stab of pain. She groaned again. When she reopened her eyes the little girl was still holding the picture, her face leeched of all colour. How long had she been staring at the awful picture of slaughter? Long enough, she hoped.

'Me and your grandfather were responsible for that,' she whispered, a rattle in her throat. 'May the Lord forgive us! It was an accident, I swear. But the kin of those poor souls burned alive will come for atonement and nothing will stop them. Nothing! Not even my passing. Save yourself, my sweet. Get yourself safe.' She sucked in air. 'Never, ever have children. For as sure as the sun rises and

sets they will keep looking and they will seek atonement; all those who stem from my loins will be killed and baptized into the faith. Protect yourself as if from the Devil himself! When you sleep, they will scour the earth for you. All in the Lord's name. Hide yourself! They will never relent!'

When she next came to, the girl had gone. The photo was lying on her chest, the box by her side. She placed the photo back inside and locked the box, then wrapped her arms around it and held it to her chest. She would take it with her. There was no more to be done. She had done her duty to her granddaughter.

It was now in the wounded hands of the Lord.

29

The sky was darkening. A light rain fell, the angry clouds pregnant with more. Foster stood on a grimy yet quiet backstreet in Bethnal Green, staring at the door of number 17. A phone call of his own to a telecommunications contact gave him the number Mrs Ashbourne had dialed – that of her daughter's, or so the old woman had said. It was ex-directory, but belonged to this terraced house, the stone bricks still flecked with soot from the days of coal-burning, industrial grime and pea-soup fogs.

He ambled up the path. Darkness and silence. No one there. In the distance he could hear the rattle of trains on their way into Liverpool Street and the bustle and noise of Bethnal Green Road. But on this innocuous side street there was nothing.

He turned away from number 17 and went next door. No one in. The same with number 13. At number 11, light peered out from behind the curtains and he could hear the muffled noise of a television. He knocked. The door opened almost immediately. A teenage girl, a sneer of contempt and boredom on her face, still in school uniform, stood there.'

'What?' she said.

Charming, he thought. Must be the famous East End hospitality he'd read about. 'Is your mother home?'

'Mum,' she screamed, and went upstairs leaving the door open and Foster on the threshold.

'What?' an impatient voice cried. A woman in a pair of slippers emerged from a room at the back — a kitchen, presumably, given that she was wearing lurid yellow washing-up gloves. She looked angry. 'Yeah?'

'I'm fine, thank you.'

'You what?'

'Never mind. Number 17, the lady who lives there.'

'Lady? Number 17? Not any more.'

'Really?'

'Yeah, old Edith passed on a few years back.'

'Edith?'

'You deaf or summat?'

'So who lives there?'

'Some posh bloke. Not in, is he? Nah, he never is. Think he must have another place somewhere else. He comes and goes but keeps himself to himself. It's changed a lot round here recently, people from the city moving in, prices going up. I can't complain because we moved in seventeen years ago, so I'll have done all right when the kids leave and I sell up. Why you interested?'

'Just a courtesy call,' he said.

He thanked her and she closed the door. A second later he heard her bawl at her daughter to get her bloody arse in gear, now.

He walked back down the street, mulling over what the woman had said. At the door of number 17 he stopped, looking up at the house, still in darkness. Nothing moved.

Then, inside, a phone rang. It continued to ring. Then

stopped. Too short for an answer service to kick in. He thought he might have heard a voice but wasn't sure, given the background noise. There was a doorknocker. He grabbed it then pulled it back, letting it thud heavily against the door.

There was a thump from within. A door shutting, perhaps? It was more muffled than that. He stepped back and looked at the houses on either side. No, it had definitely come from number 17. What was it, though?

He went to the front window. It was slightly ajar, perhaps ten inches or so. Curtains blocked any view into the room. From inside he swore he heard another noise. Someone was in. He went back to the door and was about to let go of the door knocker when he heard another noise. A voice this time?

He eased the window open a few more inches, bit by bit, until there was enough space to squeeze through. He climbed in, parting the heavy curtains. He stood there for a few more seconds. The house was completely silent. With the curtains shut and overlapping, the room was dark, so much so that it took a while for his eyes to adjust. There was a smell he recognized but he couldn't think from where. Then it came to him. The fusty smell of old paper. The room smelled old, airless. Not unlike his own sitting room, the one he had barely used or entered since his parents died. As his eyes grew accustomed, he could see an old battered armchair in front of a gas fire with rings, a large, bulky television, an old piano against the far wall, a table festooned with piles and piles of paper. He tiptoed over and picked one item up, an unopened envelope addressed to Edith Chapman. He went over to the mantelpiece; he could almost smell the dust it was so thick. There was a black and white picture of an old man in an armchair. Then one of a prim old lady outside a church, too self-conscious to smile. Edith Chapman, he presumed. On the floor by the fire was a copy of an old TV listings magazine. He picked it up, the corners curling and crisp. He checked the date. It was more than three years old.

The whole room was like a mausoleum, frozen in time. Again he felt a hint of recognition. He knew all about that. He hadn't even redecorated since his father died. He slowly pulled his radio from his pocket and called for back-up. Something here wasn't right.

He found another picture. In colour, free of dust. A tall man, dark hair, good looking, troubled, not making eye contact with the camera, beside him a woman perhaps a year or two younger, fresh-faced and healthy, smiling broadly in marked contrast. Was this man Anthony Chapman? If so, the picture appeared to be the only imprint he'd made on this room. Beside it was a cross, also free of dust. Maybe that belonged to him, too.

He went to the door and opened it slowly. He was in a small hallway, stairs in front of him. The house was entirely dark, but his eyes had adjusted. The narrow hall led to a kitchen, from which an odd smell wafted. To the left of that entrance was another door.

There was a sound. Footsteps, perhaps. Wouldn't surprise him if it was mice. The place was probably teeming with them – or rats. He stood still, not knowing which way to go, desperate to switch on a light, but not wanting to draw attention to himself. There was the sound again.

A light pitter-patter. It's coming from behind that door next to the kitchen, he thought, though in the impenetrable darkness it was easy to lose track of where the sounds came from.

He reached the door. He tried it as gently as he could.

Upstairs there was a heavier noise, a thud. Then a muffled scream, as if it was coming through a radio. He dragged himself up the stairs as quickly as he could, pains shooting down his injured leg, ignoring the fire in his shin. In the distance he could hear sirens but he paid them no heed. Upstairs was dark; he opened one door. A bathroom. At last, some daylight. The smell of damp was almost overpowering. He waited for another sound. In front of him was another door. He forced it open and flicked on the light.

A dark-haired man, the same as in the picture on the mantle downstairs, tall, barrel-chested, was standing there. Both of them stopped, neither said a word.

'Who the hell are you?' the voice was plummy, well spoken.

Foster froze. He wondered if back-up had arrived. He had told them to come without sound, that he would meet them and instruct. Not much chance of that now.

'Police,' he said. 'The game's up, Dominic.' He paused. 'Or should I call you Anthony?'

The man's face, puce with anger, bled of all colour when he said the name. Foster tried to think. Here he was, sweating, out of condition, his limbs screaming with pain. There was no way he could overpower this guy and he had no weapon at his disposal. He needed to buy time.

Chapman started to walk towards him. Foster backed

off, hands held up to show he was unarmed. He wished he wasn't. 'Help is on its way, Anthony. You can fight me but not the whole army.'

'Liar,' he spat out. Foster could see a knife gripped tightly in his right hand. Foster continued to back away to the top of the stairs. Chapman closed the door of the room behind him, plunging them both into absolute darkness. The blast of light from the room meant Foster initially couldn't see a thing. He could feel Chapman's presence, though, a grim spectre.

'It's over, Anthony,' he called out.

'Tell me, do you know the Lord?' a disembodied voice said, closer to him than he had thought.

'Not personally, no,' Foster replied.

There was a muffled scream behind them. From the room they had just left.

'Well, in that case, too bad.'

He sensed a figure move in the gloom, felt its sick breath. Foster knew there was no other option. He turned and threw himself down the stairs, rolling and tumbling, the wind knocked out of him, sears of pain taking his breath away. He landed in a heap at the bottom, gasping for air, but managed to scramble to his feet. He reached for the front door, hearing Chapman race down the stairs.

The door was locked. The keyhole was empty.

Instinctively Foster turned and hurled himself at the oncoming man's midriff. It surprised Chapman and knocked him off his feet. Foster felt something in his shoulder buckle but he drove his weight through and slammed his assailant into the banister pole. He deflected into the hall and they both hit the floor, dust and lint flying through the air. Chapman had grabbed Foster's shirt and was trying to wrestle him off while the detective tried to locate the other man's arm and stop him striking with the knife.

He grabbed the right arm and held it away, but in doing so lost purchase on the rest of his body. Chapman scrambled out from beneath him and forced him to one side with his left arm. Foster's back was now on the floor, both hands grasping Chapman's knife arm, trying to shake the blade free from his grasp but his grip was iron tight. The pain in his shoulder grew worse but he gritted his teeth, trying to kick up a leg and force Chapman away so he could get clear. Chapman's left hand found his throat, all his weight bearing down. Foster just didn't have the strength. He was starting to choke, his windpipe crushed, pressure immense. But he couldn't remove a hand from Chapman's arm or his knife arm would be free. Strangulation or stabbing, which end do you choose, Grant? He let go of the right arm with one hand and started to prise away the left, gurgling as he did, head feeling like it might explode. As the knife moved closer to his chest . . .

Then Chapman's body tightened and tautened, his back arched and his weight fell on Foster. He screamed out in what Foster thought was bloodlust. Foster expected to feel the top of Chapman's blade pierce his skin, but there was nothing, just the man's heaving body pinning him down, and his hot breath on his cheek. The breathing was shallow and laboured.

A light went on. Foster blinked, like an owl in daylight. Chapman was a dead weight. He'd stopped moving.

Foster pushed with all the effort he could muster, ignoring the pain in his shoulder. He lifted him enough to squeeze out from underneath. As he did, so he could see a large kitchen knife sticking out of the man's back. In the distance he could hear sirens.

A figure was standing at the foot of the stairs, scowling at Chapman with consuming hatred.

'Gary?' Foster said.

The kid didn't react. Eventually he looked up, face still set hard.

'Thanks,' Foster added wearily. He noticed for the first time that his front was stained by Chapman's scarlet blood, which was now oozing across the threadbare hall carpet.

'I didn't do it for you,' he said.

'Wait.'

Gary ignored him, and ran into the front room, making for the open window.

Foster hauled himself up, body screaming with pain. Gary could wait. He remembered the muffled screams earlier. He dragged his frame upstairs and into the room where he'd first encountered Chapman.

'Hello?' he said. 'Is anybody there?'

Nothing. He repeated his inquiry. This time there was a response.

'Help,' a plaintive voice said weakly.

He looked around the room. There was a cupboard. Foster opened it. It was shallow. Empty.

'Help.' The voice was pitiful and weak.

He pushed at the back of the cupboard. It seemed to give. He pushed harder, then he kicked. It gave way. Behind it was an extra few feet of space.

Curled up in the corner, arms wrapped around her knees, was a girl. The blonde hair was matted and tangled, but the blue eyes and face were unmistakable. They had been staring out from the newspapers every day for the past week.

'Naomi,' he said.

She stood up and launched herself at him, wrapping her arms around his neck, convulsed with sobs.

'It's OK,' he found himself saying, as she wept hot tears on his shoulder. 'You're safe now. You're safe.'

She was shaking.

So am I, he thought.

He heard the front door give way, footsteps on the stairs. 'I'm here,' he shouted, overcome. 'I've got her. She's safe.'

Officers came rushing in from every angle. He held up his hand, making them aware they should tread carefully. 'This whole place is a crime scene,' he said.

He held Naomi for a few minutes, then led her downstairs, handing her to a WPC and asking for her father to be summoned immediately.

He took a deep breath and composed himself. Where had Gary come from? He must have been in the house before him. It was Gary he had heard moving around downstairs. He returned to the room where Naomi had been held. He peered into the cupboard and the false wall at the back of it. There was a duvet lining the floor and a pillow, but it was no more than a couple of feet deep and four feet wide. Naomi would have had no room to lie down flat, and only stale air to breathe; there would have been nothing but darkness and the fear of what might happen.

It was over. He rubbed his head, a wry smile on his lips.

'What's so funny?' a uniform asked.

'Nothing,' he replied. 'Just appreciating a bit of grim irony.'

The kid that was given up for adoption to save him from being hunted down and killed as an act of blood atonement was the one who had ended up carrying out the atonement legacy.

30

Foster was dozing on the sofa. He'd returned to his house late for a few hours' sleep and rest as they tried to tie up the loose ends surrounding Anthony Chapman. Much still needed to be explained. Too tired to make it upstairs, he propped up a couple of pillows and rested his head, fully clothed, pausing only to kick off his shoes, sinking into unconsciousness immediately.

He woke up with a start. A noise? There was a figure in the corner of his eye. Small, stocky.

'Gary?' he whispered hoarsely. 'Gary,' he added, more clearly and forcefully.

The kid stepped from the dark corner of the room into the middle where the light from the moon fought its way through a crack in the curtains.

'Nice of you to drop in again,' he said, sitting up and rubbing his eyes.

The kid said nothing. Foster got up and turned on the light. 'Hungry?'

Gary nodded. Foster asked him to follow him into the kitchen. The digital readout on his underused cooker read '03:35'. He'd been asleep less than two hours. Every part of him ached, even the bits Karl Hogg hadn't smashed up.

'The takeaways are shut. I can only offer toast,' he said. He stuck a few pieces in the toaster and filled the kettle, setting it to boil. He turned round.

Gary was staring at the floor. There was anger and concern in his eyes, the open window to a complicated young soul.

'Thanks for saving my life.'

Gary's face softened. 'Don't mention it.' He paused, uncertain. 'Am I in trouble for stabbing that feller?'

Foster tried to get angry, or at least to wear a look of anger, but failed. The kid was safe and that was a relief.

'A few people are going to want to ask you a few questions,' he said. 'No, I don't think you'll be getting into too much trouble. But as for breaking into my house yet again . . .' He spread his arms out wide. Gary half-smiled once more.

The toast popped up. Foster buttered it and put on some jam. Gary devoured it in seconds so he made some more and made himself a cup of tea. Once the boy's hunger was sated, Foster sat opposite him across the kitchen table.

'It was a bloody stupid thing to do.'

Gary shrugged. 'Is he dead?'

'No. He'll live. We think. He lost a lot of blood.'

Gary nodded, a tinge of relief to his features.

'How did you find him?'

Gary explained. 'I'd gone to bed in the safe house. Except it wasn't safe, was it?'

Foster felt a twinge of guilt. 'I suppose not.'

'I went to bed. They had a DS. I'm playing with it on the bed, with the TV on, but there was nothing on, just news and stuff. The woman comes in and she says, "It's ten o'clock. Turn that off and get some." I says OK, but I carries on playing because I'm fucked if I'm going to bed when some copper tells me. Then this car alarm goes off outside. It goes off for a bit and I hear the bloke swear. Then, I dunno, I hear something but I don't know what. Like a thud.'

Chapman had used a silencer, which explained the lack of a gunshot.

Gary continued, eyes saucer-wide. 'The woman screams and she goes running downstairs. I'm like, "I gotta run." I open the window, climb out, down the drainpipe and I'm in the garden. I just ran, out of the garden, and then I'm in these fields. Nowhere to hide, just fields.'

'So where did you go?'

'I ran to this tree. There was a car and I knew it straight away. It was the same car that man had who came round and saw my sister. A blue Mondeo, battered but still the same. The engine was still a bit warm. I just got in, thought it was the safest place. I knew he'd look for me but he wouldn't look in his own car because he's a dozy twat. I broke in and hid in the footwell in the back seat.'

'Why?'

'Find out where he lived. Sure enough, he spends ten minutes huffing and puffing around the countryside before he gets in swearing his head off, effin and blindin, and I'm there sat on his back seat. Then he drives off. It was like he was never gonna stop. He did once. Don't know where. Middle of nowhere so I stayed inside. I knew we was getting back to London because of the traffic and the lights. Then he pulled up at some garage to get some petrol. Then he drove some more and parked up. He got out. I waited. Then I opened it up from the inside and got out. Luckily the car was a heap of shit and the alarm didn't go off, innit. Not sure it had an alarm. It smelled bad, really bad, too. The guy got a real problem with BO. Anyway, I knew where he lived now. I wanted to finish it. This wanker was gonna kill me.'

'Why didn't you call us, Gary? Why didn't you call me?'

'I didn't trust you lot to do it.'

'Cheers,' Foster said. 'Where did you get the knife?'

'From his kitchen. I thought about it all day. Walked round and round. Then I saw his window was one of them with the old locks what break. Just gave it a little tickle and it did nicely. Went in, had a look around. Didn't think he was home, it was that quiet. So I waited. That's when I heard you come in.'

'Why didn't you make yourself known to me? Would have saved us a lot of trouble.'

'Yeah, I suppose. But it was pitch black and I just hid.'

He nodded. 'Next time, don't try and play the hero. That's what cops are there for. Anyway, we found the girl. She's safe.'

'Good. Now can you go and find Leonie?'

Foster paused. He'd spoken to Heather and told her and Nigel to come back. The job was done. There was an open line of communication between the law enforcement agencies in the UK and the States, but there was understandable reluctance to go wading in unless names were given and good reasons were forthcoming.

He sighed. 'We've found Leonie.'

Gary's whole face transformed, brightened. 'You have?'

'She's in the States,' he said, nodding.

'Is she coming back?'

He thought he would save the truth for another day.

'We'll talk about that tomorrow. I hope so, but there are a few things we need to sort out first. I promise we'll do all we can.'

Gary looked downcast.

I better get all the bad news over with, he thought. 'You'll need to be questioned officially,' he added. 'You'll be OK. Just be polite. Difficult though you might find it.'

The boy looked knackered.

'Come on,' Foster added. 'You can have the spare room again. You've had quite a day.'

Foster spoke to Naomi the next day. She was a strong young girl, terrified by her ordeal yet not crushed. He admired her resolve enormously. He felt a pang. His daughter, in whom he'd never shown any interest. Maybe one day soon he'd remedy that.

She told them with tears in her eyes how Chapman had taken her as she entered the house from school. He'd grabbed her from behind, covered her mouth and she'd passed out. She woke up, feeling groggy, in the cupboard, unaware of how she'd got there.

'When did he tell you that your mother was dead?' Foster asked softly.

It was the only time she broke down.

'I lost track of time. A day, maybe two days. I asked where she was and he said she was with the Lord and with her kin in the celestial kingdom.'

Foster had wanted to halt it there and then, pick it up another time, but she insisted on continuing the interview. She said Chapman constantly proselytized about funda-mental Mormonism, giving her books to read, testing her at night and rewarding her with food when she demonstrated her knowledge. He spoke to her about the True Church of Freedom, about how they would go there. They would be married and escape their previously apostate and sin-soaked lives. He would preach, rhapsodize and persuade every second of the day when he was with her. Foster had seen the literature in the house – pamphlets produced by the Church, and other fundamentalist texts.

The police found letters from Church members addressed to Chapman, or his adoptive name Dominic Ashbourne, helping him with genealogical information, seeking to reassure him of his reward: the chance to live among them with several wives of his own. An exchange of information and ideas on how to reunite the family under the fundamentalist Mormon banner, killing those beyond salvation, baptizing them into the faith by proxy, atoning for the sins of 1890, and exporting those with something to offer across to the US and the bosom of the Church. His computer also yielded communication with the sect, a series of strange e-mails that appeared to be in some sort of code. The techies were working on deciphering them, but it seemed as if he was the puppet and they were pulling the strings.

'Did he hurt you?' Foster had asked.

She shook her head. 'No, he treated me well,' she replied. 'Apart from locking me in a cupboard.' She forced a brave smile. He had not touched or harmed her, not even losing his temper. When the call came through from his adoptive mother, he'd walked upstairs, spoken to her through the false wall of the cupboard, said it was not

God's will that she join them in the celestial kingdom. He would think of another path. She had cried, thinking that meant she wouldn't see her mother again.

Foster looked at her, wondering if the brainwashing had had any effect. 'Do you have any religious belief?'

Anger raged in her eyes. 'There is no God and there is no goodness,' she said with utmost conviction.

Foster thought about disagreeing, but how could he? He was no hypocrite. The girl had learned the hardest way.

He was sure that it was Chapman who'd made the initial contact with the Church. Unloved, unwanted, troubled, he'd set out in search of his real family. His adoptive mother, under relentless questioning, had let slip the name of his real mother, with whom he'd formed a secretive, belated relationship. How much contact they'd had was unknown. Perhaps she explained to him why she'd given him up and the danger he faced. She had left her house to him in her will, which is how he came to use it as a base. Along the way he'd discovered the link with the True Church of Freedom. He'd got in touch, been attracted to what it stood for and the family he craved. On their part, they could not believe their luck. Someone willing to atone for the wrongs of 1890 and able to provide them with fresh genes for their small pool in the shape of young girls like Leonie and Naomi. When he encountered Gillian Stamey he was not yet ready to spill blood in atonement – the correspondence chided him for not doing so – but a few years later, when Naomi was fourteen, he was ready. They had wanted him to wait until Rachel was fourteen but he said he would not, that he needed to perform his duty now. He would act, then come back for her later. Not wishing to deflect him from his course, they had agreed.

All their information had been passed on to the American law enforcement agencies. They weren't delighted with the news – the last thing they wanted to do was to raid a commune full of religious nuts and see all hell break loose. The issue had gone to the Home Office, who were pressing for action. The decision was now a political one, taken out of the hands of the police. Unless she was forcibly removed, it looked like Leonie would be staying.

He would need to find the words to explain that to Gary.

Epilogue

The rain came down in great waves, as if the sluice gates had been opened. Foster had given up trying to keep dry and let the rain soak his head and run into his eyes. Had there not been more than a few minutes of the match left then surely the referee would have called it off, given that the pitch was starting to resemble a First World War battlefield. Hackney Marshes was living up to its name.

That had not prevented Gary winning the game for his team on his own. They were 5–1 up with two minutes left; he'd scored a hat-trick and created the other two goals. His low centre of gravity, ball control, ability to pick a pass – even if his teammate's ability to receive it was questionable – and his pace over short distances marked him down as something special. There was an extra characteristic Foster recognized: hunger. The boy loved to have the ball at his feet, enjoyed the challenge of beating a man, and seized every opportunity to shoot whenever the goal came into his sight.

As his third goal went in and the smattering of parents and other hangers-on applauded, Foster had found himself giving Gary a thumbs up. A man in a large overcoat and brown woollen hat saw him do this and sidled up to him.

'Your lad, is he?'

'No,' Foster said.

'Is his dad here?'

'No. Why?'

'I'd be interested in having a word with him, that's all. About his lad's prospects.'

'There is no dad. Or any other guardian, at the moment. Are you a scout?'

'Something like that.'

'Who for?'

'Queen's Park Rangers.'

'Really?' Foster said. 'My team, QPR.'

'So you know the lad?'

'Yeah.'

'I could give you the details. We just want him to come and train with our academy one day.'

'When?'

'Saturday mornings?'

'Next Saturday then?'

The man smiled. 'Yeah, great. Ten a.m.'

'See you then.'

The man slipped away.

It finished 5–1. The final whistle blew, the players shook hands. His teammates all went to clasp Gary's hand or pat him on the back. Even the defeated opposition. Foster let him go to the changing rooms and get dry and dressed. He waited in the car, feeling the water drip down the back of his neck, and the cold seep into his bones.

Still, he couldn't stop himself smiling. The boy could play. Maybe he'd come and watch him even when a new foster family was found.

Gary came out a few minutes later, drinking a can of Coke, swinging his bag around. He climbed in the passenger seat. He gave Foster a big grin.

'Well, what do you think?'

'Not bad,' he said. 'Think there were a few times when you could have used the ball a bit more wisely.'

The boy's face fell.

'Usually when you passed it to one of your mates rather than keeping it yourself.' He ruffled his hair.

The kid grinned.

'No, you were different gravy today.' He started the engine. 'I've got some news for you.'

'Was it that bloke I saw you talking to second half?'

'Him? No, nothing to do with him. This is much more important. I got a call during the first half. Guess who from?'

'Chelsea?'

'You wish. No, it was from the Law Enforcement Agencies in the USA. They've made a few arrests in the small town I told you about, the one where Leonie lived.'

'Yeah?' A look of suspicion crept across his face.

'Well, they've also spoken to Leonie.'

Gary looked down at the footwell.

'And she's coming back.'

He looked up, face alight with joy. 'Really? Will I be able to live with her?'

'We'll have to see. But as long as she's OK, I don't see why not. But there's a complication.'

'Oh.'

'She has a two-year-old baby. A boy.'

He looked stunned.

'She called him Gary.'

His eyes lit up. 'I'm not sure about babies, man. Could be fun. Maybe. But can we live together?'

'There's some paperwork that needs doing, and a few other bits and pieces but she should be home in a week.'

Gary punched the air.

'That's the good news,' Foster said.

Again, Gary's face fell. He looked anxiously at Foster.

Foster couldn't contain his smile. 'The bad news is that she won't be back in time to see you have a try-out for the QPR academy.'

Nigel drank his morning tea and listened to the radio. The story of Naomi Buckingham being saved dominated the headlines. Nigel turned it off, not wanting to hear.

'Oi, I was listening to that.' Heather came out from the kitchen, wearing one of his striped shirts from Pink – nothing else – a cup of tea in her hand.

'Sorry,' he said.

'No, you're right, time to move on.'

She bent down and kissed his cheek. Three days since they'd got back from the States and she hadn't been home.

He grabbed her now and sat her on his lap.

'Mind my brew,' she said, laughing, putting the mug on the table.

They kissed. The phone rang. They both laughed.

'There's a theme developing,' he said.

She told him to answer.

It was his television producer. She was almost hyper-ventilating with excitement. They had heard of an un-consecrated old non-conformist burial ground that had once been attached to a chapel in Islington. The graveyard had been closed in 1863 when it contained around 15,000 bodies. Ever since it had lain unused, a prime piece of

London real estate. Eventually the Council had given permission for it be used for commercial purposes, yet only on condition that the bodies which lay beneath be disinterred, moved and reburied on consecrated ground. A company, the delightfully named Necropolis Ltd, had been hired to perform the task before the developers moved in, and had agreed to allow the production company to spend one day at the site filming for use in a short pilot that could be touted to the television networks.

He cursed. It meant leaving Heather. On the way back from the airport, they had intended dropping Nigel at his place first, before the cab took Heather back home. Nigel paid the driver off and asked Heather in for a coffee. She came in with him – and stayed.

'You said you'd explain,' he had got round to asking eventually, as they lay in his bed, morning or afternoon, he couldn't remember – time had ceased being relevant. 'About why you rejected me last summer.'

She had winced at his choice of verb. 'I didn't "reject" you,' she maintained. 'It was a difficult time.' She told him about her mother's death, its effect on her, and how an ex had provided a sympathetic and familiar shoulder on which to lean. She hadn't felt it was the right time to start a new relationship – she'd been weak, vulnerable. 'I didn't want to burden you with it all. At times like that, an old slipper seems more comfortable than the brand-new high heel. Not that you're a stiletto kind of bloke. More of a nice pair of trainers.'

She stroked his cheek.

He had laughed. 'Thanks. I think. But what about now?'

She had remained silent for a while, a brief few seconds in which he allowed his heart to slide as he imagined her getting up, getting dressed and walking away once more. 'Grief is a funny thing,' she had said eventually. 'You feel like life is something that's happening to you, that you're not in control, like you're watching a film of yourself. You let things happen. You cling to the familiar, what's easy and comfortable. You have to. But now I feel in charge again. You didn't pursue me, go all crazy. You gave me time and space – I might have made a few mistakes, but I needed to make them.' She had looked at him. 'I want to make a go of it. With you.'

'But what about this guy . . . ?'

'Let me handle that,' she had assured him.

He hadn't wanted that time to end, but real life had to intrude. After the producer's call, he ventured out into the open air for the second time in seventy-two hours – the first had been to buy milk, wine and bread – to meet Guy the cameraman, the producer, Lysette, a sound recordist and production assistant on a back street in Islington on a cold November morning. The group of them were all smoking furiously against the cold. Lysette wrapped in hat, gloves and scarf appraised Nigel's long winter coat.

'Didn't you bring your tweed jacket?'

'And freeze to death?'

'You could have worn a jumper underneath. I don't like this look.'

Her assistant beside her nodded vigorously.

This isn't a look, Nigel thought. It's what I bloody wear when it's cold.

'The long coat covers too much of everything up. Makes you look like a cop.'

'Sorry,' he said. 'You didn't mention anything about a look when you called.'

'It doesn't matter,' she said, in that blithe yet irritated fashion people adopt when nothing else could actually matter more to them. 'The main thing is that we get something on camera.' She brandished a wad of A4 paper. 'Here's the shooting script. We'll find a corpse and get some film of it. Nigel and the same worker will have a chat about either a tombstone inscription they've dug up or a brass plate from a coffin that identifies someone buried here and talk about that, preferably next to the skeleton. On another day we can go to the parish records and film you finding the corpse's entry, how they died, their address, and take it from there. If we're really lucky, we might be able to film them reburying the corpse in the new burial ground, perhaps even find us some ancestors to attend the burial, though the budget might not stretch. Guy'll also film lots of GVs and other footage to flesh things out with.'

'Let me get this right. We've found a corpse that's identified by an inscription of some sort?' Nigel asked.

Lysette shook her head. 'No, we'll just film a skeleton. We'll also find an inscription to give you something to go on.'

'OK. But we'll say that the corpse and whatever means of identification we have belong to different people?'

She looked at him as if he was an imbecile. 'Why? As long as we get some film of a skeleton we can say it's whoever we like. They all look the same. We'll cut it and make the viewer believe that the corpse belongs to the person you're tracing through the records.'

'Isn't that misleading, though? I mean, the viewer will think the corpse belongs to the person I'm tracing through the records, when in truth the remains are of someone completely different.'

From the corner of his eye he could see Guy raise his eyebrows and smirk.

'Nigel,' Lysette said, as if speaking to a five-year-old. 'They won't know that.'

He shrugged. 'Just seems wrong. Dishonest, even.'

'Can we just get on with it? We can discuss ethics later.'

They were allowed through the entrance to the dig, already well under way. Lysette handed him the script. Nigel went to his mark. He read through it as he walked, committing it to memory without memorizing it so well that he merely regurgitated it verbatim. His heart sank as he scanned the text: it was the same banal and empty bilge he'd read while stumbling through Kensal Green cemetery. Then, it didn't matter; he could have been reciting 'The Owl and the Pussycat'. But this was being committed to tape with a view to being shown.

'When you're ready, Nige,' Guy shouted from his spot.

Sod it, Nigel thought. I'll read it and we can discuss its merits later. He took his first steps. 'The dead are around us all the time. Sometimes closer than we think. And sometimes our worlds and their worlds collide. The living need more space and sometimes the dead have to give way. The past must give way to the present. Here in Islington, an old burial ground is being excavated so a new development can be built. Thousands of bodies must be moved. We're here to find out about the people are who are lying beneath the soil, how they died, the story of their lives, and watch as they are found a new resting place . . . I can't read this crap.'

'Cut!'

'Nigel,' Lysette said. 'What's wrong? That was going well. You were a bit stiff, but there was a nice flow and rhythm.'

'It's the script,' he said. 'It's all wrong. "The past must give way to the present"? Why? I don't believe that for a second. The present needs to have some bloody respect for the past and stop walking all over it. Because it was the past that helped build the fucking present.'

Lysette looked both hurt and angry. 'I told you I had less than twenty-four hours to do this,' she said.

Nigel felt bad. His criticism was hardly constructive. He scrabbled around for an apology, and then had another idea. 'Look, it's OK. I like it, but I just don't agree with it. How about if I give it my own imprint?'

'Be my guest,' Lysette said.

He returned to his mark deep in thought, not even noticing when the excavator engines fell silent. He turned, and seeing Lysette give him the nod, started walking.

'Dead men don't tell tales, so the saying goes. Nothing could be further from the truth. The dead speak to us in many different ways. And we ignore their voices at our peril. It is supreme arrogance to think there is nothing we can't learn from those who preceded us. We just have to learn how to listen. In this burial ground lie the bodies of fifteen thousand men, women and children who strived and lived a long time ago; fifteen thousand stories that have never been told; fifteen thousand dreams that may never have been fulfilled. Soon they will be laid to rest once more in a new burial place. Before the developers move in, it is our job to find out how they lived. Who were they? How did they die? What secrets can they tell us from the grave? In this programme we hope to find out.' He stopped walking. He placed his hands, which he had been using to punctuate his speech as he walked, behind his back. He fixed the camera with his most earnest look. 'In our modern age we are conditioned to forget – yet the past is one thing we can't ignore. The dead will not be denied.'

He finished. There was a pause.

Guy's face popped out from behind his camera. 'Good stuff, mate,' he said to Nigel, who for the first time sensed admiration rather than scorn in his voice.

Lysette was nodding happily. 'From now on, you're writing your own scripts,' she said, smiling. 'We'll need to do a little voice-over before and after, but that was great. Still a shame about the jumper.'

Nigel shrugged, felt his cheeks redden and warm. He never knew what to do with praise. He was about to mumble something humble when a loud cry went up from the pit behind them. The archaeologists in there had downed tools. One was running towards the olive-green portable cabin that doubled as an on-site office.

'What's happened?' Lysette asked one of the archaeologists who was scurrying past, face white.

'They've found a body.'

'And? There are fifteen thousand people buried here.'

'The last person buried here was in 1853. This body's barely two years old.'